CW00920057

Legends of Evorath: The Shadows of Erathal

ISBN 978-1-964869-00-1

Free Dragon Press, LLC

www.freedragonpress.com

www.evorath.com

Edited by: Tracey Govender @ traceyedits.blogspot.com

This is Book I of the Legends of Evorath series of stories. This series takes place sixty years after the Evorath trilogy and is part of the Legacy of Evorath universe of books.

Read free stories online and keep up with future releases.

www.evorath.com

Please see the end of this novel for an appendices section, which provides a reference for Evorath, a map, and presents additional information within the world.

Author's Note

If this is your first time picking up a story from the world of Evorath, I want to begin by offering a sincere "thank you." I cannot fully express my gratitude in words but know that your interest in exploring this magical world and getting to know her history and people is what motivates me to continue chronicling the world and its rich history.

Before we dive into this tale, I want to set your expectations to ensure you understand what you're getting yourself into. See, I have devoted my life to studying Evorath and have made every effort to ensure the story included in these pages is true to what really happened. But be warned. The events you're about to read took place during a turbulent time in Evorath's history.

While I make efforts to ensure this story can be shared in a family friendly fashion, there is no skirting around the dark nature of some historical events. Graphic descriptions are limited, but some scenes may be upsetting. In other words, this story is not for the faint of heart.

Concerning the research involved in preparing this novelized account, core details were constructed using the firsthand accounts of those characters described herein. Where major historical figures did not journal or otherwise make notes of these events, other historical accounts are considered as well.

In some instances, I looked at archeological records and third-party historical accounts available from the time. All of these are tied into the direct accounts I could find, and the story is presented in the 3rd person limited perspective. That is, each chapter considers one or more historical figures and communicates the events from their perspectives.

I hope you will forgive any creative liberties taken in the capturing of this story. I assure you, the integrity of Evorath's history is near and dear to my heart. In those instances when precise details were limited, I did my best to ensure the story stayed true to the period these events occurred in.

Remember as you read, that even as sophisticated as our methods may be today, these actual events occurred nearly nine centuries ago. So, I pray you'll overlook any minor historical inaccuracies and enjoy the core of the story.

While the events may include strife and conflict, this is a tale of love, loss, companionship, community, and most important, of hope. As we look back on these events, try to imagine yourself living in these more primitive times.

Sit back, grab your favorite beverage of choice, and enjoy learning about Evorath's history in this exciting novel.

Peace and Blessings,

Joseph P. Macolino

Scribe of Evorath History

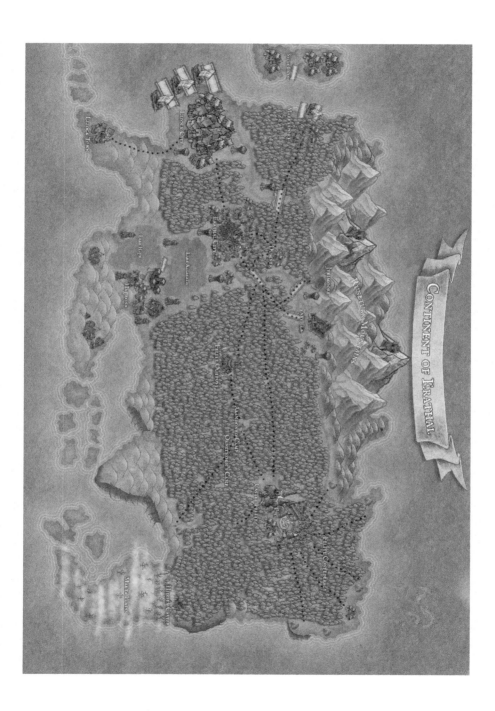

"Fear not the danger seen but be ever ready to combat those hidden adversaries."

- Ancient Elvish Proverb

PROLOGUE

The prince screamed, leaping from his bed, and tossing the silken sheets aside as he gasped for breath. He held up his hands, scaly black fingers shaking as he recounted the horrors of his dream. They always felt so vivid.

His heart felt heavy in his chest. Closing his eyes and trying to calm his breathing, he thought back to the details of the dream. So much death…and at the center of it all, a hájje.

He had always been taught that hájje were nothing more than a myth, a legend told to elvish children to scare them into obedience. If they failed to obey their parents, they might get snatched up by a hájje, a dark elf.

And yet, as he took a long exhale, he couldn't help wondering if these recent dreams were something more.

The low creak of his door drew his attention. A small flicker of candlelight illuminated the doorway as his attendant stepped inside.

"Prince Vistoro, is there something I can help you with?" Zachiro asked, his uncanny monotone providing a welcome distraction from Vistoro's nightmare.

"No, thank you Mister Zachiro," replied the lizock noble. "I just had another one of those dreams."

1

"I am sorry to hear that sir," replied Zachiro. "Would you like me to fetch you a warm cup of tea to soothe your nerves?"

"No, thank you," responded Vistoro without thinking. He stared towards his attendant for a few seconds, watching the candle flicker.

"On second thought," said Vistoro, "I could perhaps use your counsel."

"I will provide whatever counsel I can, sir. But I hardly think I am qualified to provide it."

"Nonsense," replied Vistoro, standing up from the bed and motioning towards his bedside table. "Please bring the light over here."

Zachiro walked over. He used his small lantern to light the large purple candle on Vistoro's bedside table. As he stepped back, Vistoro motioned to the upholstered chair just a meter from the bed.

"Please, have a seat."

Hesitating for a moment, Zachiro nodded and stepped over to take a seat in the chair. His attendant shifted his position, glancing around the room before looking back to Vistoro.

"Do you enjoy your work here?" Vistoro asked, taking a seat in his bed.

Zachiro's eyes darted around the room. He paused for a couple seconds before scratching behind his head and looking around the room nervously.

"I am happy to serve you, my Prince," he said sheepishly.

"Zachiro." Vistoro sighed, shaking his head.

"Please, I know that you are told I am your superior. And I recognize that as I've grown, I have treated you unkindly at times. But I ask you this now not as my servant."

Vistoro paused, reflecting on his dream.

"Neigh, I beg your forgiveness for all the injustice I have shown you over the years," blurted Vistoro. "Please, Zachiro, I am sorry. So, I ask you, not as your prince, but as a fellow lizock. Zachiro, my brother, do you enjoy your work?"

Zachiro looked around the room.

"Prince Vistoro, sir. You have no reason to beg. In all my years of service, you have been one part of my job that I have enjoyed."

Vistoro smiled, closing his eyes and nodding.

"Then it is true," he murmured under his breath.

"What was that sir?" asked Zachiro.

"I've been keeping a great secret," replied Vistoro. "In fact, I believe the secret I've kept may be greater than I could have imagined. And for once in my spoiled, miserable life, I fear this is not just my ego speaking."

Zachiro leaned in, his deep yellow eyes dilating as he gazed into Vistoro's.

"How can I help?" he asked, his eerie monotone unwavering.

"I believe I have been having visions from Evorath," replied Vistoro.

Eyes wide, Zachiro leaned back in his chair.

"Visions, sir?" he asked, eyes fluttering side to side.

"Yes, I fear I cannot avoid the truth any longer. These dreams are a part of it. But just a part. And Zachiro…"

Vistoro paused, choking on his own words.

"I don't know if I am strong enough to obey," he uttered.

Zachiro leaned in, locking eyes with Vistoro.

"Sir, would you like my true, unfiltered thoughts?" the servant asked.

To even have this conversation was a terrible breech of etiquette. But Vistoro knew it was right.

"Yes, I would. Please Zachiro. I must know."

Zachiro nodded, holding his master's gaze.

"Then I will share my thoughts, but only because I have come to trust and respect you." Said Zachiro.

"You see, Prince Vistoro. I, and many others within the castle, do not enjoy our work. And even those of us whom do enjoy it, do not accept the station we have been given in life."

Vistoro shifted uncomfortably, pulling his silk robe tighter around his body. There was a pit in his stomach, an empty void that wished to object. But even as his flesh called to object, his soul knew that Zachiro spoke the truth.

"Please, go on," he uttered unconsciously.

Zachiro looked back towards the door, again shifting in his chair before continuing.

"Well, sir. It's just that many of us have come to question whether Evorath really intended to have some of us live as servants and others, if you would beg my pardon, to live being served. Do we not all have the same struggles? Do we not all bleed the same blood? But we were born as servants, so we must serve. As you were born as royalty, so you must lead."

Vistoro took a deep breath. There was a part of him that wanted to end this conversation. That part wished to avoid any further discussion, to shift the blame, or even to go on the offensive and attack his servant.

It would be so much easier.

But no, that was not an option.

"And I understand now," said Vistoro, "that you are correct. Why should I lead, and you follow? Why should I have all the luxuries, and you bear all the burdens?"

Vistoro stood, stomping his right foot as he did. His cold blood felt warm in his chest, a heavy burden weighing on him. All the nightmares, all the visions he had experienced flooded into his consciousness.

His birthright meant nothing if he continued to use people like Zachiro.

Vistoro sighed.

"I must leave," he declared.

"Sir?" Zachiro asked.

"I must leave the kingdom. I've been avoiding this truth for weeks. But my visions have been clear. My place is no longer in the palace. No, my mission is to serve Evorath. And abusing people like you, my trusted friend, Zachiro…that is not Evorath's will."

"What can I do?" asked Zachiro.

"First," replied Vistoro. "I must know you are asking that as the individual lizock, and not just as an attendant for the prince of the Lizock Monarchy."

"I am," responded Zachiro without pause.

"Then I would ask you gather everyone who agrees with you. I understand the magnitude of my ask. If I were untrue to my word, it would be devasting to you and all your compatriots. But I pray you feel my spirit in these matters. I wish Evorath's will on you and all who think like you."

Vistoro paused, looking around his bedchambers. His room was truly massive, more than ten times the size of any individual servant's quarters. Why should he be afforded such luxury when those in his service were provided with so little?

But it seemed Zachiro was taken aback. He glanced around the room, avoiding Vistoro's gaze as he stood up from his chair.

"Prince Vistoro. It brings me great joy to hear you raise such concerns. But alas! I fear I have become a distraction for you and your mission here on Evorath."

"No!" objected Vistoro. "On the contrary. I believe you are my purpose here on Evorath. Or to be clear, not just you, but everyone who is condemned to a life of servitude."

Vistoro spun around, waving his arms out wide.

"This is what my dreams have all been about. We will establish an outpost to the north. One day, when the darkness tries to overtake Erathal, the community we build will serve as a light. We will live as Evorath intended."

Zachiro shifted, looking back as if considering whether he should sit back down. He still averted eye contact.

"I'm sorry sir, but I'll be blunt. You'd be leaving behind all your privilege. Everything of value belongs to your father, and I don't know…well, I'm not sure what you think your role would be in building this community."

Vistoro clapped his hands, keeping them clasped and smiling. He reached into his shirt and pulled out his necklace.

"Except for this," he said.

He reached around and pulled the pendant off over his head. Filling the entire palm of his hand, he regarded the pendant. The chain was made of white gold, matching the solid white gold of the item's construction. Etched into the gold was his family symbol, a terrifying dragon of old. The dragon's eyes were a pair of matching rubies and the inset in its mouth was a large diamond.

"Your family pendant," Zachiro whispered, slowly lowering himself back into his seat.

"Yes, this pendant could pay for enough materials and labor to build an entire town! And this is the one item within these castle walls that is already mine, a gift for when I came of age."

Zachiro shook his head. "But no one can ask you to part with that," he said. "It represents you and your family history."

Vistoro nodded towards the pendant, thinking for a moment before putting it back on.

"Exactly. It's a history of oppression, subjugation, coercion, and violence, among other unsavory qualities. Which is why I must part with it. I cannot sit idly by anymore and pretend my position is anything more than a glorified slave master. But no more."

Stomping his foot, Vistoro looked down at his hand, his entire body buzzing with excitement. "Will you join me Zachiro? I already know the perfect spot to start building."

Zachiro stood up and nodded. "I will follow you, but are you sure we should act so hastily? Convincing my friends to follow us may not be so easy."

"Because they won't trust me?" Vistoro asked.

"Some of them will," Zachiro said, looking down and nodding his head. "The ones who know your spirit as I do. But many will not. Perhaps a smaller group though to start."

"Yes!" exclaimed Vistoro stepping over to his bedside table. He picked up the candle with both hands and walked across the room towards his wardrobe.

"I will begin packing immediately. And I must make two requests of you Zachiro. But I want to be clear about these requests. I ask these as your friend Vistoro, not prince of the Kingdom nor as your lord or master. Can you accept that condition?"

Zachiro nodded. "I can."

"Good. Then first, I request you stop by the kitchen and secure provisions for me. Two days is all I should need, and keep to the essentials, as if you are provisioning for yourself. Second, I ask you to meet me at the northern river landing in a fortnight. Bring whomever you trust to join us."

Vistoro reached his wardrobe, placing the candle on a mahogany table to the right and glancing back at Zachiro.

"In a fortnight? But where are you going? And what am I to tell the King?"

Vistoro smiled, his tongue darting between his teeth as he turned and opened the heavy doors in his wardrobe. He'd have to leave most of his eclectic collection of clothing behind, but the first thing he needed was a bag. Reaching into the bottom drawer, he pulled out a knapsack and began thumbing through to find his most practical attire.

"Tell my father that I received correspondence from the dwarves about a trade opportunity. You know he'll never pass up a chance to grow his coffers."

Vistoro found his first outfit, a long-sleeved leather shirt, and matching pants. Made from one of his father's most prized cows, this outfit had been crafted for a recent hunting expedition and would be the perfect attire for his immediate journey.

"As for where I'm going," Vistoro continued. "I'm bound for the Koloth Mines."

"You're really going to visit the dwarves?" Zachiro asked, his stare still unwavering.

"I am. You remember the blacksmith who visited a few months back? Keldor was his name. We had some interesting discussions, some that align with these topics you and I have discussed. But more important, he told me he knows an artificer who would be keen on acquiring my pendant."

"You intend to sell it already? Are you sure that's wise?"

Vistoro nodded, pulling out a purple silk robe and folding it before tucking it into his knapsack.

"Yes, and that's why I need a fortnight. I intend to have a presentation ready for you and your friends that is so convincing you won't be able to resist leaving the Kingdom behind."

"Alright sir, I will return shortly with your provisions," replied Zachiro.

As the door creaked shut, Vistoro glanced back down at the drawer, his attention drawn to the leatherbound Xyvor. The spoken word of Evorath captured by the prophets of old, the pages now seemed to call to him. And as he picked it up, he heard a feminine voice in his head.

"Go in peace, my good and faithful servant."

CRAPTER I

The sun reached over the mountains, spring flowers soaking in the first morning light. A soft breeze passed through the city, the sweet smell of jasmine tickling the farmer's nose as he meandered towards the market square. The murmurs of merchants setting up their carts for the day was accompanied only by the faint clang of metal in the distance and the steady rotation of wagon wheels on the dirt road.

With a loose hold on his rope, Jaldor led his trusted donkey forward. This morning march might have been the most mundane part of his daily routine, but as the donkey pulled along his wagon full of dairy, he couldn't help but feel a certain level of excitement for the day. Winding towards the market stalls, he looked around the market square.

He always wondered why they called it a square. It was shaped more like a half circle; or was it a quarter circle? Regardless, Jaldor glanced around the market area. Passing by the first stall on his right, he caught sight of its owner bending over to move a crate.

"Good morning, Emma," he said with a smile and wave.

Emma looked up from her spices, returning the smile as she stood up to full height. Her long, blonde hair was pulled back in a ponytail, and she wore an unremarkable brown dress and her

11

usual blue apron. Blowing a strand of stray hair away from her face, she waved to Jaldor.

"Good morning Jaldor," she replied. She reached into her apron and walked towards the dairy farmer.

"What can I get for you today?" Jaldor asked as she approached.

"I'll take a kilo of butter and a liter of buttermilk if you have it available."

Jaldor nodded and turned around. Giving his trusted donkey a pat on the side, he walked around to the wagon and reached into one of the crates. Pulling out a liter of buttermilk, looked to the next crate and picked up a roll of butter.

"You're in luck today," Jaldor said as he offered both the bottle and the butter.

Emma took the bottle first, pulling out a small bag of salt.

"I assume you could use more of this?" she asked holding it up.

"I could," Jaldor replied with a nod. "Three copper pieces will cover the rest of it."

She handed over the salt before reaching back into her apron and pulling out a few copper coins. Freeing up her hand, she now accepted the roll of butter.

"Thank you," Jaldor said as he deposited the coins in his right pocket and stashed the salt in the crate of buttermilk.

"Thank you!" Emma replied with a smile. "Please give Samantha my best."

Jaldor nodded, walking back in front of his donkey, and grabbing hold of the rope.

"Of course! I'll see you soon."

Exchanging a final nod and smile, Jaldor continued towards the rest of the market square. Gritting his teeth as he passed the Merchant Guild office, he continued north on the road to the next stall. Different fabrics were on display here, including some featuring quite interesting and unique dyes. He had purchased a scarf for his wife last winter, but it was not a usual stop on his rounds.

Still, he offered a wave as he passed by, exchanging a quick "good morning" with the stall's owner.

Moving past this stall, he approached his primary destination. The owner of the booth, Samuel, was behind one of the tables, meticulously arranging some loaves of bread for the display. Fair skinned and lean in stature, the young merchant wore an even gaudier outfit than usual. His purple shirt and red surcoat somewhat muted when considering his gold pants. Seeing Jaldor's approach, he put down the loaves in hand and stepped around the front of the stall.

"Good morning Jaldor. I've got a whole table with your name on it," he said pointing to an empty square table on the left side of the stall. His nasally voice and slender build always reminded Jaldor of a weasel.

"Very good," Jaldor replied.

Leading his donkey to the other end of the stall, he walked back to the cart and started removing the crates.

"You don't happen to have any more of that soft cheese, do you? Like I told you last week, I can pay a little more for that than the hard cheeses."

Jaldor finished pulling out the fourth and final crate. He shook his head and looked over at Samuel.

"Not today. But Samantha has a few wheels aging now. I'll bring them by when they are ready. Should be within the next few days."

Turning his attention back to the table, he started setting out the butter, buttermilk, cheese, and whey he had brought along. He never wasted too much time trying to organize them; Samuel would rearrange them even if he did.

As he emptied the crates, he kept a bottle of buttermilk, a small wheel of cheese, and a roll of butter in the crate with the salt he had procured.

Putting all the crates back in his wagon, he glanced back at Samuel.

"That's what I have for today," he said motioning to the table.

"Let's see," Samuel said as he walked over. He let out a sigh, murmuring under his breath as he looked over the contents of the table. He used his fingers to count a couple times, then looked back to Jaldor with a wide smile.

"Not bad!" he exclaimed stepping behind the table with a pop in his step and exuberance in his voice.

Reaching into his coin purse, he pulled out a handful of assorted coins and began counting.

"Let's see, uh…" he held that last syllable for entirely too long before finally sorting it out and clutching an assortment of coins in his fist.

"Here you are," he said handing it over to Jaldor.

The dairy farmer squinted, taking the coins, and giving them a quick count. It looked like six copper coins and three pieces of silver. Less than yesterday, but it would do.

"Thank you, Samuel. Like I said, I'll bring that soft cheese as soon as I have it. Any other requests?"

"None right now," Samuel replied. "You know if you setup a stall here yourself you could make a lot more than what I give you, right?"

Jaldor shook his head and frowned.

"And I'd have to register with the Merchant's Guild. I'm happy wholesaling to you."

Samuel nodded and turned his attention to organizing the items Jaldor had brought. But just as Jaldor was about to lead his donkey away, the merchant let out a loud gasp.

"Oh, do be careful though! I don't know if you heard, but there was another missing shipment from Erathal City yesterday. And you know how Henry had half his flock vanish without a trace -makes me think something evil is at work."

Jaldor shook his head, scratching behind the back of his neck.

"I'm still not so sure about that Henry situation. But you know I'll keep my eyes open."

"Of course," Samuel replied. "Well anyways, stay safe. And hopefully I'll see you tomorrow."

With a nod, Jaldor took hold of his rope and led the donkey onward. Guiding his donkey back to the road, he continued north. The sound of the blacksmith's hammer grew louder as he made his way towards the source, and to his final stop in town.

He could already feel the heat as he approached the blacksmith's forge. Smoke billowed from the chimney, a metallic taste on his tongue as he led his donkey to the front entrance. The open-air design was undoubtedly necessary for ventilation, but the loud clang of metal made Jaldor wonder how all blacksmiths didn't go deaf.

Tying his donkey to an iron hook on the front of the shop, Jaldor stepped inside. A wave of heat washed over him as he stepped through the billowing smoke and towards the blacksmith hammering at his anvil. Hoping to overcome the deafening sound, the farmer waved his hands and yelled at the top of his lungs.

"Fredrick! I've got your butter and cheese."

Fredrick swung twice more, striking the red-hot metal with his hammer. He lifted his hammer again, pausing and looking at Jaldor.

"Just one moment," he said, his breath heavy.

Jaldor winced as Fredrick hammered a few more times, watching the sparks fly as the blacksmith molded his steel. With a final strike, Fredrick set down his hammer and lifted the rod of steel with his tongs. After looking it over, he stepped over to the forge and deposited the piece of steel.

"It could use some more heat." Fredrick shouted, pulling the thick leather glove off his left hand before wiping the sweat from his forehead.

Scrunching his face, Jaldor nodded.

"Should we step outside?" he asked.

With a glance at his forge, Fredrick turned back and smiled, his weathered tan skin glistening with sweat.

"Yes, I've got your goods next door," said Fredrick, his gravelly voice still too loud for normal conversation.

Leading Fredrick outside, Jaldor stepped over to his wagon and retrieved the buttermilk, cheese, and butter from the crate in the back.

"As promised, a fresh wheel of cheddar aged a full year, a liter of buttermilk, and a kilo of butter."

"Perfect!" Fredrick exclaimed. "If you want to bring it inside, hopefully you'd find what I have fits your needs as well."

Jaldor followed Fredrick, stepping past the entrance to the forge and heading to the storefront. It was all one building, constructed from stone and wood. But there was no way to go directly from the forge to the shop.

17

As they stepped into the shop, Jaldor looked around with eyes wide. The place was even messier than usual. A couple barrels of raw ore greeted them right as they entered, forcing them to squeeze around the mess. While the wall was filled with its share of swords, maces, and other weapons on display, the countertops were also full of various tools and implements.

Squeezing himself behind the counter, Fredrick bent over and lifted the goods he promised. In his left, he held a hay hook, and in his right, a pitchfork.

"Here we have them," Fredrick said. "I forged them both from the finest steel available and used the hickory wood you brought for the handles."

Fredrick paused, looking across his overflowing countertops with a frown.

"Go ahead and move that shield for me, will you?" he asked, motioning towards a round shield to his left.

Jaldor nodded, tucking the buttermilk under his right arm, and transferring the butter and cheese to his right hand. Using his left, he picked up the shield and set it down to lean against the counter. It was heavier than he expected.

"Perfect, just leave the goods there. I'll walk these back to your wagon," Fredrick said, holding both the pitchfork and hook overhead as he squeezed back out from behind the counter.

With a nod, Jaldor set down the goods and pivoted around. Navigating through the mess of the shop, he made his way back outside and to his wagon.

Upon arrival, he turned back to Fredrick.

"I hope these serve you well," said Fredrick offering the pitchfork and hook.

Accepting both tools, Jaldor took a moment to get a feel for them in his hands. The pitchfork was a bit lighter than his current one, just as he hoped. Holding the hook in his right hand, he took a closer look at the sharp point. The small wooden handle was the perfect size, the wood grain comfortable in his hand.

"I'm sure they will make things much easier," Jaldor said upon finishing his inspection. "I'll definitely let you know when I need anything more."

Jaldor turned and deposited both tools in his wagon before stepping back around and untying his donkey. The donkey brayed, nuzzling its owner's side, and offering a snort.

"I'll feed you when we get back home," Jaldor responded, scratching behind the animal's ears.

Fredrick chuckled, stopping just outside the entrance to his forge.

"Oh, by the way," the blacksmith spoke. "Whenever you have more of that special soft cheese, make sure I'm on your short list of customers. I'm sure I'll have something you'd be interested in trading for."

Jaldor smiled, giving the rope a slight tug and leading the donkey away from the shop.

"Just don't let Samuel know when I do get you some. Apparently, a lot of his customers have been enjoying it."

"It will be our secret!" Fredrick exclaimed with a wave. "Have a good day Jaldor."

"Good day," the farmer replied, starting back on the road south towards the town exit.

Passing the market square, he noticed the road was a bit livelier already. The sounds of town folks haggling with the merchants at the market would soon fill the air. Jaldor was delighted to be done with his business before the crowds arrived.

He walked to the town gatehouse in silence, nodding and waving to those who greeted him along the way. But his focus was inward; on thoughts of what he had to accomplish that day.

Approaching the town gatehouse, he looked up at the massive guard towers and across the stone walls. Even though he made this trip every other day, he was always awed by the sheer scope of these walls. But today, something else caught his eye.

Clothed in the standard guard uniform, an eight-point star on a blue shield stamped over his white tunic, a man was stepping away from the town bulletin board. Though not unusual by itself, the way the guard stomped away, murmuring under his breath, was too peculiar to ignore.

Jaldor slowed his march, glancing over to read the notice.

MANDATORY CURFEW

To ensure town safety, until further notice, road travel to and from Paxvilla will be restricted. Anyone seen traveling after sunset or before sunrise will be stopped and detained by the town guard. Stay safe and stay vigilant.

CHAPTER II

Sarah felt her heartbeat heavy in her chest, her throat tight with anticipation. Closing her eyes, she took a deep breath through her nose and exhaled through pursed lips. Allowing the moment to linger, she cracked open her eyes to behold the results of her spell.

As the room came into focus, she was greeted by the bright smile of her husband George. His light brown eyes seemed to glow, his teeth beaming as he nodded and motioned towards his arm. Mustering the courage to look for herself, she glanced down at his outstretched arm.

It was healed. There were no signs of the gash that was there just moments before, the skin completely stitched back together. Even the hair around the wound looked undisturbed!

"I did it!" Sarah exclaimed, jumping up from her seat at the small, square table. The chair thudded against the back wall, causing her to startle and stumble away from the table.

"I knew you could, my love." Said George, his deep, compassionate voice always a welcome sound to her ears. He spread his arms wide, as if ready to embrace her in a hug.

"Yes, well done Sarah," offered her mentor, Savannah.

Sarah turned towards Savannah and smiled. The elvish druid's emerald eyes sparkled as she returned the look of joy.

"I'm really proud of you," Savannah continued. "I know you already have a profound understanding of elemental magic. But I hope you recognize how impressive this is. You really have a gift for the healing arts!"

Sarah blushed, taking a slight bow, and holding her hands close to her heart.

"Thank you, Savannah. I couldn't have done it without your teaching and guidance."

Savannah brushed back her long, light brown hair.

"You make an excellent student," she replied. "But I knew you could do this. And I'd say your husband did too, offering himself as the subject for your exam."

George chuckled, closing his eyes scratching the back of his unkempt brown hair. He shrugged.

"If I know one thing in this world, it's that Sarah can do anything she sets her mind to. That's why I blame her whenever Henry or Elizabeth gets into trouble; I was certainly not that devious as a child!"

He finished with another chuckle; his round cheeks rosy as he stood up.

"Oh, am I devious now?" Sarah asked, placing her hands on her hips, and widening her eyes as she tilted her head to the left.

"Sounds like I should leave you two alone to discuss this," Savannah joked.

"No, but speaking of our children, we probably should head back home and relieve your husband," said George.

"Yes, it was nice of him to watch them this morning, but I'm sure he's ready for a break," Sarah agreed.

Savannah shook her head.

"Don't let Artimus fool you. He might not admit it, but he loves it. You should have seen him when Artimus Jr. was little. I don't think he's ever smiled so much as he did in those early years."

Sarah always felt a bit awkward when talking about Artimus Jr. as a child. Thinking of someone nearly twice her senior as a young child really brought into context how amazingly long elves lived for. Then again, remembering Savannah was over two centuries old when she didn't look a day over thirty was even more difficult to swallow.

"In either case," Sarah said after a moment to reflect on this, "it probably is best we give your husband a break."

She paused, glancing out the large round window nearest her and seeing the sun was at its halfway point in the sky.

"After all, George promised he'd take us all to Sissera's Tavern for lunch. Speaking of which, you are welcome to join us if you two don't have other plans!"

Savannah looked at the door, hesitating for a moment.

"I wouldn't want to intrude on your plans," she said, her voice soft.

"Nonsense!" interjected George. "I'll even let Artimus pick up the tab if he wants." He said grinning.

Savannah chuckled, shaking her head.

"I'll defer to Artimus then," she said after a moment.

"Excellent!" exclaimed George, clapping his hands together. "Now, do we feel like walking, or are we looking for the fast way home?"

"You know my preference," replied Sarah immediately.

She stepped over beside George, putting her hand behind his back. He leaned in and pulled her closer, giving her a quick kiss on the forehead.

"I won't say 'no' to skipping the stairs either. I told them when we were building this tower that we'd all grow tired of climbing so many steps!" exclaimed Savannah.

"I'm tired just thinking of all the steps!" replied George with a chuckle. "But there's a reason I practice the magic I do. Let us make for the Peterson home!"

As he spoke, he reached over and retrieved his staff leaning against the wall. It was almost as tall as he was, constructed from the gnarled branch of an Erath tree and embedded with a large chunk of quartz at the top. While the staff was carved down and enchanted, Sarah always felt it was a bit unwieldy. Still, her husband handled it with a surprising level of grace.

To focus on the spell, he let go of Sarah and took a couple of steps away. He faced the nearest wall, moving the staff in a circular motion as if drawing an invisible doorway on the wall.

"Arna barnarba!" he exclaimed, pointing the tip of the staff at his invisible drawing.

An outline appeared immediately, as if a door was forming on the wall. The light from the spell spilled inward, blue energy coalescing and filling in. Within a few moments, the area was engulfed in blue light. It looked almost as if they were peering through a door that led straight into the ocean. But through the blue glow, Sarah could just faintly see the front of their home.

"Putting us right at the front door?" Sarah asked.

"Yes, ma'am," he replied with a wide smile. "Please, ladies first," he said with his left hand outstretched towards the portal.

"Arnaba-what-now?" Savannah asked, cocking her head and raising her right eyebrow as she looked from the portal and back to George.

"Don't ask," said Sarah. "You'll just encourage him."

"Too late," said George. "I guess I'll cross that one off the list. Eventually I'll get it right. Anyways, you know I can only hold these open for so long. So…"

"Oh, right. Savannah, let's go," said Sarah, walking past the elf and approaching the portal. With a glance and a nod back to her husband, she stepped through.

It was always a bit disorienting, a wave of pure energy washing over her as she breached the gateway. Like that tingling sensation one might get in the back of their head but flowing throughout her entire body. This lasted for only a moment. And the next moment, she felt her feet hitting the wood steps outside her front door.

Stepping up to the front door, Sarah turned around and watched Savannah step through next, followed by George. As the tail of George's blue robe cleared the portal, the blue energy disappeared into the ether, leaving behind no sign that it had ever even existed.

"I don't know if I'll ever get used to traveling that way," said Savannah, inspecting her hands. She shifted around, looking behind at her legs and adjusting her flowing green dress as if making sure she came through in one piece.

Sarah had to admit, she still had some trepidation around her husband's magic. But since he mastered the spell a few years back, she had become accustomed to the convenience of travelling through the ether.

"I promise you're still in one piece," said George after a brief pause. He leaned on his staff, wearing a wide smile as he shook his head. "And I bet with your magical prowess, you could get a handle on it in less than a decade."

"But then how would we make you feel useful?" Savannah teased.

Sarah chuckled.

"Alright, alright. Let's head inside already. I need some backup if you two are going to gang up on me."

Stepping forward, George knocked his staff against the door a couple of times before twisting the handle and stepping inside. Savannah stepped to the side, motioning for Sarah to follow behind him. Sarah hesitated for a moment, brushing a few stray strands of hair from her face before stepping inside.

"MOMMY!" came the shrill shrieks of her children as she stepped through the door.

Opening her arms wide, she went to one knee and braced herself. Henry and Elizabeth sprinted across the room, their bare feet pounding on the wood floors as they jumped into their mother's arms. Embracing them both, Sarah gave them a quick squeeze and smiled ear-to-ear as she rocked them back and forth.

"Did you behave for Mr. Artimus while mommy was gone?" she asked, letting them go and standing up to full height.

Henry hopped in place, waving his arms up and down.

"Yes, I was good mommy," he said.

"And I was really good," added Elizabeth, pushing her way in front of her younger brother.

George shook his head, stepping over and placing his staff inside the holder by the door.

"I guess I'll just head back outside since no one missed me," he said in an exaggerated tone, an overblown frown on his face.

"No daddy!" objected Henry.

"Yeah, we missed you too daddy," said Elizabeth.

"Oh good," George replied with a smile. He stepped over and picked up Henry, offering his hand to Elizabeth.

"Why don't we clear away from the door so Ms. Savannah can come in and mommy can close the door?"

The children giggled. Elizabeth took her father's hand and the three of them moved into the home. Artimus, who had been seated in one of the chairs by the hearth stood up and approached the others.

"It looks like you made it back in one piece," he said approaching George. He paused as he got closer, looking down and winking at Elizabeth as he did.

"It's unfortunate they couldn't do anything about your face though."

Elizabeth and Harry both giggled while George shook his head.

"Yeah, I asked if Sarah could make a change. But we all agreed your looks were the only thing you have over me, so I couldn't in good conscious take that away from you." Quipped George.

"Oh, you're so right. Because archery, fletching, hunting, horse riding, swordplay, and all my other skills are *so* inconsequential compared to your…what do you call it, portal magic?"

"Oh, you're going to get on my magic, are you?" George asked, bending over, and letting Henry back down.

Sarah glanced back at Savannah, who was covering her face with her hand. They had talked on the subject extensively, and neither could understand why their husbands felt the need to tease one another so mercilessly.

"I'll tell you what," continued George. "Sarah, the kids, and I are going to Sissera's for lunch to celebrate. If you and Savannah can beat us there, I'll buy you both lunch. But if we make it there first, lunch is on you Mr. Handsome Archer Man."

Artimus glanced down at Henry and Elizabeth, his eyes narrowing as he did. Despite their childish banter, Sarah recognized the gears turning in the elf's head. Aside from her own husband, Artimus was one of the smartest men she knew.

"You're on portal man," he replied with an extended hand.

George accepted his handshake, and the pair smiled. Just as Artimus took his first step away, he paused and lifted his right hand.

"Oh, right," he said before squatting down and whispering something to Henry.

With a wide grin, he came back to his feet and leapt for the door.

"Hey, what did you tell him?" George asked as Artimus made his way alongside Savannah.

"Oh, you'll find out," said Artimus. "Sarah, we will see you at Sissera's. Savannah, let's win this!"

Savannah rolled her eyes, giving Sarah a look that said, 'what is wrong with these two?' before turning towards the door.

Artimus opened the door and the couple stepped outside. Sarah could hear their rushed footsteps as she turned back to her husband.

"Could you grab my staff?" George asked.

Shaking her head, Sarah stepped over and took the staff from its holder. As she picked it up, Henry tugged at his father's pants.

"Daddy, I have to go potty," he whined.

"You can wait until we get to the tavern," George replied.

Henry stomped his feet. He flailed his arms and spun around as Sarah approached with George's staff. Elizabeth just stood in place, her face painted with a mixture of amusement and confusion as she watched her brother. George merely stood watching until Henry stopped and plopped on the ground with his arms crossed.

"Whatever Mr. Artimus promised you," George said after a momentary pause, "I'll double it. And I'll throw in a day of adventure -just you and me. What do you say?"

Henry frowned, his lips quivering as the light in his eyes betrayed his excitement. His frown curled up into a smile and he nodded as Sarah reached the trio.

"Deal!" he exclaimed, grabbing George's legs, and squeezing them.

"Now that we have that settled, are we all ready to go?" Sarah asked.

"No," interjected Elizabeth. "I want a day with daddy too!"

George smiled, extending his hand and taking his staff from Sarah.

"And a day of adventures with me and Elizabeth," George said with satisfaction. "You know I can't say 'no' to that!"

"Alright. Then I am ready too," replied Elizabeth softly.

"Both of you take my hands," said Sarah, extending them out and clasping both Henry and Elizabeth's outstretched hands.

As usual, George focused on the wall in front of them, holding out his staff and drawing a circular shape in the air.

"Abracadabra!" He exclaimed, extending the staff almost perpendicular, the quartz began to glow as the blue outline formed and spread to engulf the entire wall. Through the portal, Sarah could make out the shadows of people moving past, along with the unmistakable outline of Sissera's Tavern not far behind.

"Alright, you three go first." he said, his face stern and eyes locked on the portal ahead.

Sarah shook her head as she led the kids forward. She stepped through, grasping their hands tight. The familiar tingle washed over her as they all stepped through. Her children both hopped through, shaking their hands, and wearing wide grins as they came out the other side.

A cool breeze blew in from the west, the smell of sea air washing over Sarah as she led her children towards the tavern. As expected for this time of day, she could hear music from inside the tavern, accompanied by the ambient murmur of merry conversation.

Looking back, she watched George step through, the portal staying open for only a moment before closing behind him.

"Before you ask, that's a 'no' from me on the whole 'abra kidabra' or whatever it was," said Sarah.

"Yeah, daddy, that's just silly," agreed Henry.

Elizabeth held her hands locked behind her back, swaying back and forth.

"And what do you say?" George asked, bending over, and looking her in the eyes.

"It sounded silly to me too," she said with a giggle.

"Alright!" George exclaimed, standing up. "I supposed that one was a long shot. No one will ever associate 'abracadabra' with any sort of magic."

"Like I've said," replied Sarah, unable to hold her tongue. "I think the whole idea of yelling out anything when you cast a spell is just ridiculous."

George shrugged and stepped forward. Using his staff as a walking stick, he took the lead and approached the tavern entrance.

"I'll find one that wins you over one day," he said turning back with a wink. "But for now, let's get a table!"

George approached the doors to the tavern, the large brown oak double doors towered before him. Like most common buildings in the town, doorways were made to accommodate large creatures like centaurs and trolls, which always made these trips seem that much grander. Grabbing the bronze door handle, George opened the right door and held it wide, motioning for Sarah and the kids to enter.

"Thank you dear," beamed Sarah. She placed her hands on both children's shoulders and corralled them through the tavern door.

She could feel the energy in the room as she entered, light from the runestones on the walls and chandeliers illuminated the entire tavern and created a warm and welcome atmosphere. A couple of bards were on a small stage to the far right of the tavern -Sarah could never remember their names, but they were a married couple that lived just up the street from her and George. The man played a lyre, and the woman a pan flute.

With lunch in full swing, extra tables had been pulled out and placed on the dance floor before the stage. The sounds of laughter, friendly banter, and impassioned conversations filled the air. Scanning around at the various tables, she noticed the usual diverse crowd, which included: elves, felites, lizock, barghest, and even a troll and a couple lamias.

Fortunately, she also found an empty round table to the left of the entrance. Leading her kids over to the table, she lifted Henry up first and placed him in one of the chairs facing the wall. She then did the same with Elizabeth before sitting down between the two. George stepped around the other side and sat opposite Sarah.

"What do you think," he asked as he leaned his staff against the wall and adjusted his robe. "I'm guessing Artimus is - well, never mind! That was faster than I expected."

Standing back from his seat, George waved towards the entrance, a wide grin plastered on his face. Sarah glanced back to see Artimus and Savannah approaching their table.

"I see Henry relented." Artimus said with a straight face. He extended his hand to George as he reached the table.

George shrugged, offering Artimus a handshake.

"I guess lunch is on me." Said Artimus as he shook George's hand.

Savannah skirted around the table, sitting next to Henry, and rolling her eyes at the men. Sarah curled her lips, closing her eyes and nodding to the druid.

As George and Artimus took their seats, a young elvish woman approached the table. She wore a white dress with long sleeves, the cotton fabric stopping at the middle of her shins. With a bright smile and bloodshot blue eyes, she brushed back her flowing blonde hair. Sarah hadn't seen her before, but judging by the bowl of nuts she carried, she was their server.

The elf arrived at the table and looked at everyone, her face still locked in an abnormally large smile.

"It is such a pleasure to have you here with us today," she said, her soft, ephemeral voice sounding distant.

34

As she leaned over and placed the bowl of nuts on the table, Sarah picked up the unmistakable smell of pipe weed. The eyes and smile made a bit more sense.

"I'll be serving you today," she said with a subtle curtsy. "My name is Arnona. What would everyone like to drink?"

Sarah exchanged a disapproving look with Savannah but politely smiled and looked at Arnona.

"Thank you Arnona. The kids will both have a small cup of apple juice please. And I will have a glass of lemon ginger tea if you have some."

"Oh yes," replied Arnona, looking up to the left and sighing. "Sissera makes the best teas."

She held her gaze skyward for a few more moments, her blank expression making Sarah wonder if she was still with them.

"And I'll have a lemon ginger tea as well," said Savannah after a few more moments.

Arnona blinked rapidly and looked down at Savannah, her face forming back into a smile.

"Of course. And what about you two?" she asked, her voice rising ever-so-slight in pitch as she looked to Artimus and George.

"I'll take the spring mead," said Artimus. He glanced at Savannah after saying so, raising his right eyebrow and pursing his lips. Savannah responded with a simple nod.

"And I'll have the winter cider if you still have any. Otherwise, whatever cider you have will be fine."

35

Arnona closed her eyes and nodded, her cheeks rosy and smile so wide it looked like it might split her face in half.

"Excellent choices, all around," she muttered softly. "Two small apple juices, two lemon ginger teas, a spring mead, and a winter cider. I'll be right back to take your food order, and of course to bring your drinks."

Sarah's eyes widened as Arnona walked away. She was a bit surprised Arnona had been able to keep the orders straight in her head considering her clearly impaired state of mind. This would surely be an interesting experience.

"Do you recognize who that is," Artimus asked Savannah. Savannah narrowed her eyes and glanced back at the waitress before turning back to Artimus, her mouth agape.

"No way!" she exclaimed.

"Yep, that's Zeidrich's youngest daughter. I mean, she's the right age, right eyes, and hair -it must be her." said Artimus.

"Wow," Savannah said, leaning back in her chair and shaking her head. "We might need to look out for that one. If he knows she came here, we might have some unwanted visitors from the Republic coming by."

"Yeah," said Artimus scratching behind his head. "That's a good point. After this, I'll pay Vistoro a visit and see if he knows anything."

"Zeidrich," George interjected after a moment. "He's that Erathal General, right?"

"Yes," Savannah replied. "And I think she's probably the first person to move to Marftaport who is directly related to such a prominent official. Well, aside from Vistoro, but that's different."

"Do you think we need to alert the Guild to potential aggressors?" Sarah asked.

"Maybe we should see what Sissera knows about her," offered George. "After all, she hired her to wait tables; she must have gotten to know something about her."

"Yeah, that's a good point. But" Artimus paused, looking towards the tavern entrance. "Uh, we might have another situation to deal with."

Sarah turned, an unmistakable figure standing just inside the tavern doors. With sleek black fur, deep greenish-yellow eyes, and an all-too-common scowl on her face, Luna Freya stomped towards their table. Her muscular feline build and large frame were covered only by her usual armor. The studded leather covered all her vital organs, the modest but form-fitting build leaving her arms and legs completely free, along with a strategic hole for her tail, which swung back and forth as she approached.

"Huh, what luck!" she exclaimed, the raspy tenor of her voice perfectly fitting her gruff personality.

She barred her teeth and pulled out the chair next to George, spinning it around and facing the back of the chair as she sat. Her whiskers twitched, as she sniffed the air.

"Oh, yes. Go ahead and join us," said George, a clear note of sarcasm in his voice.

Luna Freya growled, gripping the back of her chair.

"Tel' Shira had another vision." She said looking around the table. "Apparently this one is a big deal. She even wanted you old timers involved," she finished motioning towards Artimus and Savannah.

"Well, we were just sitting down for lunch," Savannah replied with a glare, her voice resolute.

"Oh, that works for me. I figure George here can zap us wherever we need to go," Luna Freya replied, clapping George on the back. "So, I'll join you. It smells like they have some freshly caught crab cooking back there."

Before anyone could object, Arnona returned with a tray of drinks.

"Oh, bless me! I didn't know anyone else was joining you," she said as she stepped around to the empty seat and placed down the tray.

"And what can I get you miss?" she asked, picking up the two juices and handing them to the kids. She proceeded to pass out the other drinks, while Luna Freya spoke.

"I'll take an ale. And I'll take a dozen oysters and crab to eat. Is everyone else ready to order?"

Sarah took a sip of her tea, closing her eyes and releasing the breath she didn't realize she was holding.

"Yes, I think the rest of us are ready," she said noticing everyone else seemed at a loss for words. "The kids and I will share the seafood platter with your harvest vegetable plate."

With her eyes closed, Arnona nodded along as Savannah spoke up next.

"For me, just let the chef know that 'Savannah wants her usual salad'. He'll know how to make it."

"And I'll have whatever the catch of the day is," added Artimus.

Arnona opened her eyes at his order, pointing to Artimus and then mouthing a count as she looked around at the rest of the table.

"Oh, and that just leaves you, right?" she said, pointing to George.

"Yes. I will also have crab, and you can garnish it with your harvest vegetables."

"Ergolicious!" Arnona exclaimed. Sarah glanced around the table to see if anyone else knew what that was supposed to mean but was met with an array of confused looks. At least she wasn't alone.

"So, two crabs, a dozen oysters, a seafood platter, harvest vegetable plate, one catch of the day, and 'Savannah wants her usual salad'. I love it when groups order so many different things. I'll give your orders to the chef and check back in a bit to make sure you are still good on drinks."

Whipping her hair to the side, Arnona hopped around and skipped off to the kitchen.

"OK, the new lady is flying high," said Luna Freya as the waitress walked off.

"Let's be mindful of the children," interjected Savannah. Sarah looked at her and smiled, offering a subtle nod of gratitude. She hated confrontation and appreciated Savannah speaking up on her behalf.

"Come on! I'm just being honest," replied Luna Freya. "These two are smart enough to see she's got a few screws loose without me pointing it out."

"The lady does seem funny," said Elizabeth.

"Exactly," said Luna Freya. She lifted her hands up by her head, holding them limping to either side and contorting her face as if she was intoxicated. With an exaggerated bob side-to-side, she let out a low growl.

Elizabeth and Henry both laughed. And George brought his right hand up over his face, clearly struggling not to laugh himself.

"Alright, let's not forget why we're here," said Artimus lifting his glass. "We're here to celebrate Sarah's magic accomplishments. So, let's hear it for Sarah!"

The others raised their glasses, including the kids, who were still giggling. Sarah smiled wide, raising her own cup and taking a sip.

It may not have been what she envisioned when they decided to celebrate by eating out, but for better or worse, this was her family. And she was grateful for them all.

Even Luna Freya.

ChAPTER III

Marftaport, Vistoro's Manor
12 Julla, 1149 MT

Luna Freya leaned back, stretching her arms above her head, and releasing a long sigh. The room was filled with all the usual suspects, but not feeling particularly social, the young felite had taken a position just inside the doorway in her favorite wooden chair. Everyone else was scattered about Vistoro's study, talking about one disinteresting subject or another.

It appeared everyone had been called in for this one, including Mojo, whom Luna hadn't even realized was back in town. The wizened old dog stood hunched over, his greying fur and scarred face a testament to a lifetime of combat. He leaned against his gnarled oak staff, wearing his usual tattered robe and an assortment of creepy jewelry, including his unsettling bone necklace.

Luna couldn't make out what he was saying, but as usual the barghest brothers, Morn and Neman, appeared enthralled by the story. Standing a good ten centimeters taller than their elder, these two were at the peak of their fitness. With lean muscular physiques, and light brown fur, the duo was practically inseparable. The lumbering oafs weren't good for much more than their strength, but they made for formidable allies on the battlefield. Of course, Luna derived an almost sadistic level of joy from the fact that she could outwrestle either one of them, despite their size advantage.

The one person she couldn't outwrestle stood just a couple meters away from the trio of barghest. The veteran troll, Oogmut may have been advanced in his years, but like all his kind he was massive. With gray, heavily blemished skin and wearing a simple bearskin tunic, the large druid was looking down at Artimus, Savannah, and Artimus Jr., undoubtedly discussing something disinteresting.

Though Luna would never openly be so affectionate, she always thought of these elves as her true family. Yes, she was widely considered a child of Marftaport. But after being orphaned in a battle against Yezurkstal sixty years prior, it was Artimus and Savannah who had first welcomed her in and showed her kindness. She felt more at home among them than she did among her own kind.

She could feel herself smiling as she looked at them. Savannah, with her stoic demeanor and outward confidence always inspired Luna to be strong. And Artimus, with his father-like advice and wisdom had been invaluable to her martial training and discipline. This left of course Artimus Jr., whom she considered a younger brother.

The young elf's dirty blonde hair was always disorderly, his bluish-green eyes emitting a youthful exuberance. He always wore unfashionable clothing, his boring leather armor and pants accompanied only by a short sword hanging from a belt about his waist. And while he was a few centimeters taller than his father, the Jr. archer had no impressive features of note.

Standing opposite the room from this group, the party was rounded out by George and Sarah Peterson. Even though they had lived in Marftaport for over a decade now, Luna had still not fully formed her opinion on these two. They were some of the only humans to call this town home, which meant they had to be smarter than most of their kind; or so Luna Freya figured. But it seemed so strange that these two were just barely thirty years old and already had two children. Humans had to be a lot more fruitful than the native peoples of Evorath.

Beyond her general caution about humans, this couple seemed reliable, however. With her blue eyes and light brown hair, Sarah always had demonstrated a good sense of style at least. She wore a beautiful blue dress with gilded accents, and around her neck she wore a silver choker with a large amethyst.

Whatever poise Sarah demonstrated George lacked. He always wore silly blue robes, claiming that "one day, all self-respecting wizards would be known for their glorious robes." Recently, he had even commissioned a matching pointy hat to go along with his blue robes, which Luna noticed was sitting on the rack by the door. But worst of all, the thirty-five-year-old human was physically about as useful as a felite toddler.

Sure, Luna had a few extra pounds, but she also carried it with a large mass of muscle and wore it all on an unusually large frame. George, on the other hand, was only half a dozen centimeters taller than his wife and his rounded figure suggested he must have weighed close to twice her weight. If not for his quick wit, general good humor, and unique magic, Luna would have dismissed him altogether.

As she continued thinking about whether George and Sarah should be considered friends or acquaintances, the old lady finally made her way in. The unmistakable sound of her creaking wheels pulled Luna's attention to the doorway.

Pushed in by Vistoro, the lizock owner of the estate and original founder of Marftaport, Tel' Shira sat in her wheelchair, eyes closed and face unrevealing. Her arms rested to either side, the chair fitted perfectly to keep them parallel as she was wheeled along. Sitting up in her chair, Luna stretched her neck as Vistoro continued towards the center of the room.

According to the stories, Tel' Shira had been a fearsome warrior in her time. Though Luna had a hard time believing someone with such a delicate frame could have ever been such a powerhouse, everyone in the village claimed she was one of the greatest, perhaps even more skilled than Luna herself. But during the battle against Yezurkstal, she had narrowly escaped with her life, leaving her forever bound to that wooden contraption.

While the stories of her physical prowess always seemed a bit overblown, Luna still felt a bit intimidated by her elder. Perhaps it was the way she peered into the soul with her bright, hazel eyes, a sharp contrast to her snow-white fur. Or perhaps her profound gift of foresight created an intangible aura of power and control. Regardless, she commanded the utmost respect, despite her physical frailty.

As Vistoro stepped back from Tel' Shira's chair and took his seat on the sofa, the chatter about the room faded away; the other party members ended their respective conversations. The group all circled around the elder felite, except for Luna. She remained in her chair, unconcerned as the barghest brothers obscured her view of Tel' Shira.

44

"Thank you all for gathering," Tel' Shira said, her voice as serene as ever.

"Another vision, I have had. This vision concerns a family essential to the very future of life on Evorath. For many months now, a great darkness has been plaguing the humans of Paxvilla. Facing this darkness, it seems, is unavoidable for this family. However, it is our duty to ensure they survive. And afterwards, to make sure they find sanctuary here in Marftaport."

The room was silent as Tel' Shira finished speaking, a few seconds passing by without anyone saying a word. Luna always hated these dramatic pauses, but Vistoro insisted this was Tel' Shira's polite way of allowing people to ask questions. It always seemed obnoxious to Luna Freya.

Tel' Shira continued after a few more seconds of silence.

"We have sent word to Irontail, who will undoubtedly want to join you on your journey. By void magic, you shall travel to Dumner. Once there, make haste for Paxvilla. But the location you seek is outside the town walls."

Tel' Shira closed her eyes and let out an audible sigh.

"You are to head north on the road to Paxvilla until you reach a fallen Erath tree. From the death of this tree, you will find new life springing up. There is a path just east of this growth which will take you to a small farm. This farm must be protected from the darkness. But this is not all."

Pausing once again, Tel' Shira looked around the room with wide eyes before proceeding.

"Many outcomes, this battle could have. Preserving the future generations of this farm is necessary to the preservation of the legacy of Evorath. And when the battle is over, you are to pay a visit to the Paxvilla castle. Let them know that a storm is on the horizon. If you fail in this task, I fear this conflict may be the spark that ignites the fires of war."

Luna Freya had to admit, this was a bit more interesting than Tel' Shira's usual visions. Sure, Luna had been tasked with rescuing the occasional person or providing protection for a convoy. But never had she been sent to prevent a war.

Sitting up straight in her chair, Luna cleared her throat.

"So, if we fail all hell breaks loose?" Luna asked. "What is this 'darkness' you are referring to? It might help to know what kind of enemy we're up against."

The barghest brothers both turned and looked at Luna, nodding in agreement. Though the young felite couldn't see the other members react, she assumed they all agreed as well.

"Yes," Mojo added, his gravelly voice a touch more hoarse than usual. "Knowing what we are up against will greatly impact our battle strategy."

There were a few whispers around the room. Luna tried to distinguish what was said, but the hushed tones were too quiet even for her ears.

"Unclear, my visions sometimes are," Tel' Shira said after a moment of silence. "And these visions have been clouded as of late, a great many enemies lurking in the shadows of Erathal. I fear for this attack, you will find yourself facing profane magic."

Luna Freya chuckled.

"Sounds like you're on the hook old man," she said with a snicker. "But don't worry; I'll make sure you don't get killed."

Mojo grumbled but didn't say a word. And since no one else spoke up, Luna Freya sprung from her seat. Stretching her neck to the right and then the left, she let out a loud sigh.

"Alrighty then. If there's nothing else to discuss, I guess I should go collect my gear. I'll be back here in an hour then?"

The barghest brothers exchanged blank stares, Artimus shook his head, Oogmut placed his palm over his face, and Artimus Jr. stifled a chuckle. Luna Freya glossed over the other reactions, returning her glance to Tel' Shira.

Her gaze was met with an unwavering stare as she locked eyes with her elder.

"Prepare for battle," Tel' Shira instructed, her gaze unwavering, "you all should. You should make haste to depart as soon as possible."

"Ah, I see," replied Luna, struggling to hold her elder's gaze. She glanced to the right, blinking a couple times before closing her eyes and pulling her shoulders back for another stretch.

Not wanting to let the moment go any longer, Luna spun around and stomped out of the study, proceeding through the doors into the main atrium. The gaudy decorations in this room were always a bit off-putting. Upholstered chairs, an oversized chandelier, and ornate sconces along the wall all felt too structured and proper. Tor Noga's paintings were the only part of the room that didn't make her uncomfortable.

Reaching the mahogany double doors, Luna pushed her way outside, taking a deep breath of fresh air. The cacophony of spring flowers breached her nostrils, an overwhelming barrage of fragrances causing her eyes to flutter. As she scrunched her face and her secondary eyelids helped shield her from the sun, she stepped forward down the path towards the gate.

She kept her eyes forward, trying her best to ignore the beautiful landscaping about the grounds and the buzzing of bees and butterflies. The gentle trickle of water from the fountain caused her gaze to wander. While she appreciated the beauty of nature just as much as anyone, she always felt this garden was overdone; a common theme for Vistoro. It seemed even though he left his birthright behind, he couldn't part with the luxuries that came along with his former position.

As Luna turned left and stepped through the topiary path, she let her mind wander. Vistoro may have been a bit too aristocratic for her preferences, but she respected and admired everything he'd done. He had given up an entire kingdom to build this town. Luna couldn't imagine ever leaving Marftaport, and all she had here was a few niceties and her family.

Before she realized it, she had reached the end of the path, forcing her to turn right and continue out past the bushes. She gave an unconscious glance to the cherry blossom tree overhead, watching a stray leaf drift away in the wind. With a nod to the shrine at the left, she instead proceeded down the winding path on the right.

Though she spent much of her young years living in Vistoro's manor, she felt much more comfortable in her own humble abode.

Reaching the end of the path, she considered her home for a moment before proceeding inside. Over the decades, the tree had consumed more and more of the structure, but that only made it that much more charming. The small shack was built right alongside a mature oak, the solid tree stretching up high above and offering abundant shade.

A branch had begun growing out along the eastern wall and the western side of the home was practically part of the trunk by now. The thatched roof and crooked window had both been level at some point in their life, but now sat warped and malformed. Twisting the brass handle, Luna stepped through the round door, breathing a sigh of relief as she took in the familiar scent of preserved meat mixed with tree moss.

Her small home consisted of only a single room. And though she would insist it was well-organized, it was never tidy. A simple chandelier hung from the ceiling; four glow stones placed around the iron circle to illuminate the dwelling. The uneven wooden floor was riddled with books, scraps of parchment, and an assortment of throwing knives.

A pile of clothes sat to the right of the room; her entire wardrobe encapsulated in just a few articles. A large book was placed on the rickety side table to the left, Vistoro's latest book on comparative political systems. Though he had given it to her two weeks prior, she still hadn't opened the cover.

Luna hesitated for a moment, glancing at her bed. The green silk sheet looked so inviting, the comfort of her straw bed calling for her to lay down for a nap. For a moment, she held onto the temptation and closed her eyes, but shaking her head she focused on the mission at hand.

She dropped to her knees, grabbing for each of the scattered throwing knives and placing them in their various compartments along her armor. This custom-designed armor was really starting to grow on her, the convenience of having such a wide array of weapons at the ready was something she could never do without again. Of course, her favorite weapon was even more unique.

Securing the last throwing knife along her waist, she turned back to the side table and opened the drawer. Pulling out her gauntlets, she thought back to her sixtieth birthday when she had received these from Keldor. They were made to exact specifications to fit her hands, the mythril chain-link of the sleeve running about halfway down her forearm as she slid them on.

The back of the hand was made of solid mythril, with the fingers fully wrapped, each piece fitted so perfectly that she maintained virtually complete range of motion in her fingers. As she placed the second gauntlet on her left, she opened and closed her fists a couple times, making sure everything was fitting snugly in place. The palm also included chainmail covering, woven perfectly in with the solid pieces of metal.

Of course, the material itself was strong enough and the design kept her hands safe in combat. But what Luna Freya appreciated the most was the extra touches Savannah had placed

50

on them. They were magically bound to Luna, and as she closed her fist one final time, she heard the almost silent click, confirmation they were locked in place.

Opening both hands, she looked down at her palms and extended her claws. The gauntlets responded in kind, mythril claws extending from each of the fingertips. Things had been so peaceful these past few years that she had hardly gotten to used them, but as she examined the blue glint of the claws, she couldn't help but crack a smile.

With a wide grin still on her face, she shook her head and retracted her claws, the gauntlets returning to their non-lethal configuration. Again, fighting the urge to lie in her bed, she regarded her humble little home one last time before turning about and exiting through the door. Without a look, she kicked the door closed and proceeded back towards the main path through the hedges.

It seemed no one else was out and about here, so Luna proceeded through the path and back to the main courtyard. Sniffling as she again smelled the flowers from the courtyard garden, she took a brisk walk to the front doors and pulled the doors open.

Artimus Jr. stood just inside the foyer, leaning against the left wall with his arms crossed. He smirked and stood up straight as Luna stepped inside. It looked like he had retrieved the rest of his own equipment, a quiver loaded with arrows on his back and a short bow slung over his shoulder.

"You sure you don't want to take some extra time to prepare?" Artimus Jr. asked, glancing back towards the study.

"How much did you bet?" Luna replied.

"Just a night of town watch." The elf replied frowning. He glanced down at his boots, bobbing his head back and forth.

"Well, doesn't sound like I gain anything from delaying then," said Luna with a shrug.

She continued forward, stepping past Artimus Jr. and into the study. George was waiting there alone, facing the entrance, and leaning on his staff. He lit up as Luna stepped inside -not the response she was used to.

"I told you she wouldn't imp about." George exclaimed confidently.

"No need to rub it in. I've got your next watch," replied Artimus Jr.

"Alright then, I'm sure some of the others will be surprised we're so close behind." George said lifting his staff.

As he finished drawing the outline of a portal, he extended his staff out towards the wall and shouted "Umaguma!"

With a sigh and shake of her head, Luna stepped forward, her whiskers twitching as she breeched the blue barrier of the portal. As she passed through the ether, she was pleasantly surprised to find the usual wave of nausea missing.

Perhaps George was getting better at this magic after all.

CHAPTER IV

Paxvilla, Jaldor's Farm
13 Julla, 1149 MT

Jaldor tightened the straps on his boots, standing up from his chair and wiping his hands on his shirt. Bringing his left hand up to his face, he rubbed his eyes and shook his head. This better not have been another false alarm.

Both his dogs, Samson and Deliliah, had been barking for at least the past five minutes straight. The deep bellow of their barks echoed throughout the farm, rousing him and his wife from their sleep. But since it was still dark outside, likely an early hour of the morning, that meant it was Jaldor's job to take a torch and ensure the cattle were safe.

Grabbing a flint, he stepped over to the torch by the front door. With just a few strikes, the oil-soaked cloth lit up, the whoosh of flame quickly overtaking the top of the torch. He removed the torch from its iron sconce, pushing the door open and stepping outside.

The brisk night air swept over him, the warmth of the torch helping him avoid a shiver. Shutting the door as he stepped outside, he glanced to his right and shifted the torch to his left hand. Picking up the spade left outside just for these situations, he started south towards the cow enclosure.

He could only see a few meters before him, the torchlight illuminating the dusty path towards the cow pen. Besides the loud raucous of his dogs, the only other thing he could hear was the steady hum of the crickets' songs. Obscured by clouds, the full moon offered little additional light to work with beyond his torch.

As he made his way south towards the cows, he could tell the dogs were further off in the distance, a hopeful indication. He allowed himself to relax a bit more as he drew closer, hearing a couple of low moos from the cows, their voices gentle and clear of any signs of distress.

Reaching the fence line, he walked east along the fence, making sure there were no breeches or gaps. He was still a bit groggy from being awoken mid-dream, but it occurred to him that a cow could have broken out. After all, the fence wasn't in the best condition, various patch jobs over the years just barely keeping the fence in working order.

Making his way all the way to the eastern end, he continued south, making more observations along the exterior. He could see a few of the cows standing about inside, probably enjoying the night air. It took him a few minutes to make his way to the southern end of the fence. At this point, he started west, pausing for a moment as he reached the southern gate and ensuring it was securely shut. Still no sign of disturbance, he arrived at the southwest corner of the fence line.

The barking stopped.

After a momentary pause, Samson started back up again, but his barks sounded even more aggressive than before.

"This better not have just been a deer or something," murmured Jaldor.

Jaldor let out a sigh and continued south towards Samson. He tightened his grip on the spade, choking up on the handle so he could easily swing it with one hand if necessary.

Stomping through the wildflower field, he called out for his dogs.

"Samson, Deliliah! Come here!"

He pivoted right and left, taking slow and deliberate steps towards the southwest.

"Samson, come on boy! Deliliah, here girl!"

Silence.

As he crept forward, he could feel his heart beating faster in his chest. Growing increasingly concerned there might be an actual threat, he slowed his pace even further, keeping his eyes wide and torch held as far out in front as he could.

But then came the first sound of relief.

The soft chime of a dog collar and a low growl. A few seconds later, he caught sight of Samson, the 68-kilo dog running his way. Stopping his advance, Jaldor waited for his dog to arrive, keeping a close eye on his movements.

There was something out there, and it wasn't a deer. The white fluffy dog ran right up to Jaldor, turning about as he arrived and leaning his rear end into the farmer. Samson's muscles were tense, and as he lowered his stance, he barred his teeth and released a low growl.

The torchlight revealed nothing ahead but the empty night air. Jaldor kept his eyes trained ahead.

Samson resumed barking, his deep tone echoing throughout the fields. As if in response, Deliliah barked off to the west, her shrill howl causing Jaldor's hair to stand on end.

And then the night erupted.

With a high-pitched whine, Deliliah went silent. The cloud passed from over the moon, allowing the full light to shine down from the night sky. Jaldor dropped his torch, his mouth hanging open in terror as forms emerged from the distance. Seconds seemed like minutes. Samson shivered and cried out with a feral howl.

The massive dog took off in a dash, bounding towards the shadowy figures in the west. Jaldor didn't hesitate for a moment, leaving his torch to roll on the ground and sprinting after his trusted companion.

He grabbed hold of the spade with both hands as he ran, Samson cutting ahead at an unbelievable speed.

The shadows came into clearer view as he grew closer, the pale of their skin reflecting the moonlight -there were dozens of them.

It was an entire hájje army.

Jaldor wasn't sure what kept him charging forward, but in that moment, he felt no fear. No hesitation.

Samson leapt towards the nearest dark elf. The enemy's black eyes constricted as the massive dog tackled him to the ground. Jaldor continued his charge, not more than ten meters behind.

His blood boiled as he drew nearer, Deliliah just entering his line of sight. Her broken, bloodied body lay a few meters to the right of Samson and the hájje he had pinned.

Releasing a primal yell, Jaldor raised his spade overhead and charged the nearest enemy. In the moment as he closed the distance, he saw Samson biting into the first hájje's flesh, growling as he tore away.

Swinging his spade towards the next hájje, he cursed as his foe brought up a sword and parried his strike. The defense caused him to reel back, stumbling before regaining his balance. Two other hájje closed in, swords drawn.

It felt as though time slowed to a stop, and seeing the mass of foes encircling him, his thoughts drifted back to his home. His wife Samantha, his daughter Mary, and his elderly parents, who would surely not survive without him. He needed to fend off this attack, but what could one man do against dozens of enemies?

As the realization of his demise filled his body with dread, he shook in fear, his heart pounding in his chest.

He was helpless.

But he couldn't give up. He couldn't let these monsters hurt his family. And just as the closest elf came within striking distance, it felt as if his entire body went ablaze.

"NO!" he screamed, diving under his foe's sword strike and taking out the hájje's legs. His spade fell to the floor as he plowed through this first enemy, reacting only with instinct and fear. His mind went blank, and he prayed for a miracle.

57

He wrestled with his immediate foe, struggling to reach for his sword arm and keep the blade at bay. Grunting as he clawed his way for the sword, his attention was pulled just a few meters to the north.

"Eat mythril, snow skins!" came a primal call.

A black shadowy figure leapt over Jaldor and his foe, taking down both the other two hájje with it. The thud of their landing was accompanied by shrill screams of pain and followed by the unsettling sound of tearing flesh.

The new figure roared, a primal war cry that sounded like it came from a large cat and not a humanoid. But Jaldor still had his own enemy to deal with.

And for a moment, he thought he would fail at even handling that. The hájje still had the upper hand, kicking away and regaining a grip on his sword. As the foe went to bring the sword back around, a more familiar ally came to his rescue.

Samson growled and joined the fray, biting down on the hájje's sword arm. The dark elf released a scream of pain as he let go of the sword. Samson was merciless, barking before jumping back in for the enemy's throat.

Not wasting the opportunity, Jaldor grabbed hold of the hájje's sword and scrambled to his feet.

"Stand aside!" came a masculine voice from the north.

Turning towards the source, Jaldor found himself in shock yet again. For charging towards him was what he could only hope was the answer to his prayers.

A massive centaur was at the head of the charge, his colossal form causing Jaldor's heart to skip a beat. The beast held an oversized sledgehammer in his hands, the blue glint of the head glowing in the moonlight. Trailing just behind this warrior, two brown-furred barghest charged, followed by a troll, another barghest, and a few elves.

And as Jaldor took a couple steps back, he recognized there were two more in the party of unexpected rescuers -they appeared human.

"Hang back!" yelled the first shadowy figure that had arrived.

Jaldor turned back and beheld -she was a felite, her black fur and slightly less black leather armor making her form hard to distinguish in the moonlight. But the blue sparkle of her claws helped bring her form into focus.

The army of hájje were all closing in on the felite. But she stood perfectly still, as if unfettered by the impending assault. Before Jaldor could even register her movement, she sprung back into action.

Darting left, she slashed one hájje's throat. She spun around without delay, slashing at another's face, clawing a third's chest, and catching the sword of a fourth. With a low growl, she yanked the sword out of this one's grasp, flinging it into one of the nearby enemies before proceeding to claw across the now disarmed one's chest.

She moved so gracefully. Five enemies slain in a matter of seconds, and yet she remained stoic.

The centaur joined the fray next, passing within a meter of the black felite and trampling through the front line of hájje. He was like a scythe to a field of wheat, mowing down all who stood in his path. The aggressing soldiers began to scatter, a cacophony of shouts and muddled screams echoing through the ranks. It was all so difficult to keep track of.

Samson, perhaps sensing his owner's energy, darted to Jaldor's side, and took a defensive posture, barking towards the melee. Jaldor was shaking, unable to keep his hands steady as he watched the carnage.

Leaping after her apparent ally, the black felite continued her assault. The troll and barghest all ran past to join the fray next, but the trio of elves approached Jaldor. Samson, still on high alert, moved between his owner and the three strangers, barring his teeth, and growling between barks.

"Calm yourself," said the female elf, her voice soft and tender.

Jaldor was uncertain how to respond at first, but he realized after a moment that the elf wasn't talking to him -she was talking to Samson.

"Yes, we are here to help." she whispered, stepping closer. Samson relaxed his stance, continuing to bark but with less aggression than before.

His barks continued to lessen in intensity, waiting a few seconds between each one. Jaldor had no idea what to do. The sounds of clashing metal, shouts of pain, and general chaos of the melee were something altogether foreign to him.

"What is your name?" the woman asked. It took Jaldor a few seconds to realize she was addressing him now.

"J-Ja-Jaldor." He stammered.

"I am sorry we are not meeting under better circumstances Jaldor. But I promise you, we are here to assist. We've been sent to keep your family safe from this attack."

"Though it seems the threat might have been exaggerated," interjected one of the male elves. He appeared the youngest of the trio.

"Don't count on it," said the other elf, his gaze looking past Jaldor. He pulled out an arrow as he said this, bringing up his bow and taking aim.

Jaldor twisted around, squinting in the distance. Amidst all the noise of the nearby skirmish, he hadn't heard it before. But now looking back, he could hear the steady march of footsteps. And see the faint outline of more shadowy figures in the distance.

"There's more coming from the south," shouted the elf as he let the first arrow fly. It soared over Jaldor's shoulder, the yelp that followed seconds later indicating it had hit its mark.

"Jaldor," said the elf woman. "My name is Savannah. This is my son Artimus Jr." she motioned towards the younger elf. "He'll lead you and your Jyrimoore Mastiff back to your home and ensure you are safe. Allow the rest of us to dispense with these uninvited guests."

Jaldor couldn't keep everything straight. The sounds of bloodshed and clashing of metal around him was overwhelming.

The arrival of these protectors seemed almost too convenient. But for the moment, he was still alive. And if they could ensure he and his family remained that way, he wasn't going to ask questions.

Artimus Jr. nodded back towards the farmhouse, waving for Jaldor to follow. The farmer hesitated for a moment, looking back to the bloodied body of Deliliah, and taking a step towards her.

Savannah frowned and shook her head.

"She's already gone," she uttered, her voice laced with sadness.

Jaldor could feel his eyes swelling, but he nodded in response, looking down to Samson.

"Come home Samson," he instructed, his voice cracking as he fought against the barrage of emotions.

Samson barked. He turned back towards the melee and released a low growl.

"No!" shouted Jaldor. "Follow me."

Though he could tell the dog was having an internal struggle, it seemed Samson's obedience won out the battle. Following after Jaldor, the pair walked towards Artimus Jr. Joining the elf, they started at a brisk jog back towards the farmhouse.

As they ran through the fields, Jaldor's mind raced. He thought about his wife and child waiting for him and said another prayer that they would make it through the night.

Luna Freya ducked, her left ear twitching as the sword passed just a centimeter above. Without a thought, she sprang back up, landing an uppercut square on the hájje's chin. She continued her own momentum, throwing a left hook with claws spread wide. As the blood-stained foe fell to the dirt, she glanced to her left, where two other enemies were approaching.

Her heart pounded in her chest, the adrenaline fueling her every move. These dark elves might have had an advantage against the rest of her party, but not against her. With her felite night vision, she could see everything as clear as day. And while there were still a couple dozen troops in formation before her, she marched forward without hesitation.

The two dark elves nearest her both had swords and shields, with full steel plate armor to provide protection. Aside from their notable height difference, this meant they were difficult to tell apart. But since one was about her height and the other was a good ten centimeters shorter, she had her strategy ready to go.

"So, I'm guessing shorty over here wants to die first. It must be tough living life from so far down there. You can hear me alright, can't you shorty?"

Shorty grunted, smacking the flat of his blade against his shield as he continued forward. The taller hájje proceeded as well, stepping more slowly and flanking to the right. They were going to make this too easy.

Keeping her hands held up defensively, Luna Freya ceased her advance, allowing the enemies to take position to her left and right. As they continued to widen the distance, going for a classic pincer maneuver, Luna opened her mouth, clicking rapidly. She glanced to her right past the taller guard, confirming that Irontail was still nearby.

Just a few more steps.

"Assist!" Luna shrieked, her voice pitched right to shatter glass.

Pausing their advance, the two armored hájje hesitated just long enough for Luna to make her move. She pivoted towards the smaller guard, diving past him and spinning around with a swift kick to his rear. This shorter guard couldn't keep his balance, stumbling towards the taller one.

As the two clashed, Irontail made his move. His hammer landed with a sickening thud, the taller elf collapsing on his shorter comrade. The smaller foe squealed, flailing his arms as he struggled to get out from under the weight of his fallen ally.

"Thank you Irontail," Luna said with a curtsy.

"You're welcome," Irontail nodded, turning back towards the rest of the hájje.

Luna bent over, pulling the surviving hájje's helmet from his head.

"Please, spare me!" he objected; a look of horror plastered on his face.

Luna widened her eyes and stared at him for a few seconds. Her instinct was to deliver the killing blow, but there was something in his void-black eyes that made her hesitate.

Reaching out with her right index finger, she scratched the dark elf under his left eye. Careful to make it just deep enough to leave a scar, she stood back up to full height.

"Go back to your master with that scar, knowing it was a felite who spared your life. Or learn to live free. Either way, if I see your ugly face again on the battlefield, I'll make sure you endure the most slow and painful death imaginable. The choi-"

"Luna, look out!" boomed Irontail.

Luna adjusted her gaze, but she was too late.

An arrow landed square in her left shoulder. It penetrated her leather armor, a sharp pain running down her left arm as she stood up to full height.

"Son of a dragon!" Luna cursed, grabbing at the arrow.

With a deep breath, she clenched her jaw and growled, pushing the arrow further into her arm. Craning her neck, she watched and pushed the arrowhead out the back of her shoulder. Without delay, she snapped off the head and yanked the arrow out of her arm.

After an initial spurt of blood, the bleeding slowed, and she reassessed her immediate surroundings. Irontail had cleared away most of the nearby foes, which meant her window was closing. She could fall back and have one of the mages heal her, but that would mean she'd miss out on the fun.

Weighing her options, she knelt and dug into the ground, pulling out a clump of dirt and slathering it over both sides of the wound. The surviving hájje gasped and Luna scowled as she stood back up.

"Remember what I said," she exclaimed before running towards Irontail and the other enemies.

"You should fall back and get that closed up!" Irontail shouted, swinging his hammer, and crushing another fully armored opponent.

Luna smirked, charging towards the centaur.

"Get me to those archers!" she howled.

Irontail lowered his stance and dropped his hammer. As Luna reached him, she jumped and extended her arms. The centaur barely had time to react, clasping her outstretched arms and flinging her around. With a grunt, he threw her over the next row of enemies.

"Thanks again old man!" she quipped as she flew past rows of hájje soldiers.

She kept her eyes trained below, zeroing in on the row of archers in the back.

But it looked like she was coming up a bit short. And as she soared towards a hájje with an outstretched spear, she wondered if she had been just a bit too reckless in her thirst for battle.

CHAPTER V

George kept his eyes wide, staying the furthest from the action but keeping track of it all. His vision was enhanced with a simple spell, allowing him to see as clear as day. He watched as Artimus Jr. led Jaldor from the scene, the farmer's Jyrimoore Mastiff following right behind the pair. It always amazed George how loyal animals could be to their owners.

"Eyes on the battle!" Sarah shouted back to him.

He turned her way with a smile. She was always so beautiful in the heat of battle. Her hair was pulled back in a perfect ponytail, her blue eyes practically glowing in the moonlight. She wore a long-sleeved dress, which flowed down to her ankles. And for battles like this, she wielded her own small staff; made from oak and featuring a large aquamarine at the top along with an assortment of smaller gems around it.

She followed closely behind Artimus and Savannah, who were focusing on a second contingent of hájje. Of course, it was George's job to keep an eye on everything from the rear, which was fortunate. Glancing over to Luna Freya, he noticed the felite was in trouble.

Irontail had just thrown her over some of the first contingent of enemies. But this reckless maneuver sent her on a direct trajectory for an enemy spearman.

"Always bailing you warriors out," said George pointing his staff towards the felite warrior.

It bothered him that in the heat of battle he couldn't test out new catchphrases for his spells. But since he didn't have the burden of picturing a destination, it at least meant he could cast his spells much quicker.

Releasing the ethereal energy, he opened a portal just beneath his ally. Luna fell through, coming out the exit, which George placed a few meters further ahead. She landed directly on one of the enemy archers, whom she proceeded to dispatch. As she continued to attack the rest of the archers, George confirmed that Irontail didn't need any assistance.

The centaur was a juggernaut. Each swing of his massive sledge made enemies crumble before him. And it seemed none of the opposing hájje were a match for his physical might.

Oogmut had engaged with this grouping of enemies as well. His height and thick skin gave him a unique advantage, but George could tell that he had slowed down in recent years. Still, the wizened troll was in the thick of it, knocking down hájje by the pair with his powerful spells.

Turning his gaze towards the other enemy contingent, George watched his wife channel arcane energy. Thrusting her staff towards the enemies, Sarah unleashed a torrent of water, the concentrated force knocking down an entire row of enemies.

Meanwhile, Artimus released arrow after arrow. It was always awesome to watch the experienced archer at work, each of his shots landing true. One after another the enemy fell.

The barghest brothers were doing their part too. As usual, they were both in the thick of the melee, Morn with his dual axes and Neman with his short swords. The duo wasn't quite as adept as Luna or Irontail, but neither seemed to struggle against their foes.

Like George, Mojo and Savannah were both hanging back. Mojo would throw the occasional projectile and Savannah would cast the occasional spell, both providing magical support as needed.

Luna tore through the last of the enemy archers as Irontail and Oogmut continued to trample the infantry. Artimus continued unleashing arrows, taking out one enemy after the other. Sarah released spell after spell, keeping their foes off balance.

Morn and Neman had moved into the thick of the melee, but it seemed their eagerness had gotten them into trouble. The brothers were surrounded by over half a dozen hájje, all armed with swords and shields. Their attempts to break through the enemy defenses were met with perfect resistance, each strike being blocked or parried as the enemy closed in.

This was the perfect opportunity for George to help, but timing was crucial.

He focused on the exchange of blows, holding out his staff and readying another spell. Morn cleaved, and he cast the first spell, opening a portal, and placing the exit just behind one of the nearest foes.

It worked like a charm, Morn's blade shifting through the ether and landing in his foe's back. As he withdrew the axe,

George cast another spell, this time targeting Neman's stab. Again, he opened the portal and put the exit to the enemy's rear. Neman's blade sliced through his foe's armor and into the enemy's back.

Seeing their two allies fall in this manner, the other four hájje faltered, which gave the brothers an opening. With some swift slashes, cuts, and cleaves, they broke through the enemies, taking out all four of the remaining foes.

With a grin, George widened his gaze again, making sure no one else needed his assistance. The enemy lines were faltering, defeated hájje laying all about the battlefield. But as he watched his allies dispatch foe after foe, George couldn't help but feel like something was off.

It started as an almost imperceptible itch in between his shoulder blades. Continuing to watch the melee unfold, the sensation traveled up his back and to his neck. Then he felt a tingling sensation along the back of his neck.

The enemy was holding something back. There was dark magic about. But where?

George did another scan of the battlefield. His allies were keeping the enemy at bay.

Focusing his arcane energy, he searched for the source of the dark energy. He released the energy, an echo of almost imperceptible light blossoming out in all directions. The dark magic pulled on this energy, and George could feel it calling.

But it wasn't channeling towards either of the enemy formations. He was drawn north.

"Sarah," George shouted to his wife. "Do you sense that dark energy to the north?"

Sarah was mid-casting, her knees bent and eyes focused ahead. She held her left arm straight ahead, using it to help balance her staff, which she aimed towards the enemy formation. After a moment's pause, she released the gathered energy, a bolt focused into a green projectile and cutting through a row of approaching hájje.

Standing back at full height, she looked back towards George and narrowed her eyes.

"I hadn't noticed it. But I think you're right!" she exclaimed. Locking eyes with her husband, she turned back to Savannah.

"George and I are falling back to ensure the family is safe. It looks like you all have this in hand!"

Savannah nodded, moving her hands like a conductor directing a choir. From the looks of it, she was engaged a two-pronged defense against the hájje, featuring explosive overgrowth of the local wildflowers coupled with a concerted effort from the pollinating bees. It was quite a spectacle, but not her most impressive feat.

Confident that his wife was correct, George turned to follow Artimus Jr. and Jaldor, who had fled to the north. He chuckled internally at the notion that Artimus would have been better equipped for the task. The hunter would undoubtedly be able to track their footprints. George would have to just try his magic to lead him down the fastest path.

71

This dark magic was strong, perhaps the strongest he had ever felt. There was a voice in the back of his head that warned him not to pursue without more support. Perhaps Sarah, he, and Artimus Jr. would have insufficient strength to handle the threat.

George paused, Sarah passing a few paces ahead of him.

"Mojo, please join us. I think we might need the backup!"

Mojo threw a projectile, another lightly armored enemy falling to the ground. He then turned without hesitation and jogged towards George.

With a smile, George turned back around and started after his wife. He pumped his legs harder than before, pushing to catch up. After a few seconds, his heart racing in his chest, he came up alongside his wife.

"I feel it too," Sarah called between breaths.

George didn't have the stamina to respond, but he matched her gaze and offered a slight nod.

They passed by the cow enclosure, the unpleasant odor wafting by as they made their way to the farmhouse. It was a simple home with a thatched roof. A thick, unevenly hung door was just off-center of the two-sided structure. A small bit of light was coming from the window to the room on the right of the home.

Jaldor and Artimus Jr. were standing to either side of the front door, relaxing their stances as George stumbled up between them. Sarah came to a more graceful stop beside him, with Mojo trailing just a few seconds behind.

72

"What is it?" Artimus Jr. asked, lowering his sword.

George took a deep breath, holding up his hand as if asking for a moment.

"There's more hájje about," interjected Sarah. "And they have a powerful mage on their side."

George nodded.

"Yeah, what she said!" He gasped out between breaths.

The farmer's Jyrimoore Mastiff lowered its stance, running around the west side of the home and barking towards the northwest.

With a momentary exchange of glances, the rest of the party took off after the dog. George took up the rear, using his staff to expedite his pace.

As they gathered behind the Mastiff, George glanced over to Mojo.

"Do you see them?" he asked.

Mojo shook his head, his gaze running all along the horizon.

"I take it you don't either?" Mojo countered.

"No, but I feel them. I don't think the mage is alone," offered George.

"Neither do I." Replied Mojo. "Everyone, take a step back."

Mojo reached down into a pouch on the left side of his belt and pulled out a small sphere-shaped object with what appeared to be a small stone sticking out the top of it. Pressing down on the stone, Mojo dragged across the sphere, igniting a spark.

As the spark ignited, an unseen fuse lit and Mojo tossed the sphere to the northwest. The sphere released a thick red mist as it flew. The mist filled the night air, stretching out for meters. And with a close watch on the mist, George could see a faint, shadowy outline.

"There!" he exclaimed, pointing his staff and releasing a shockwave of arcane energy.

The mist cleared away, but in its place were a half dozen hájje soldiers, one of which stood separate from the others.

In fact, it was quite eerie to see just how different the center hájje was from the others. But this was less due to the uniqueness of the hájje. Rather, it was the uniformity of the soldiers around him that made him stand out.

Each of these soldiers was garbed in sleek, black leather armor. The contoured fit and emblem of Death stamped across their chests provided them with an ample amount of physical protection. Each of them carried an identical mythril bastard sword, their light-blue blades shining in the moonlight. On their left arms, they each had tiny, triangular black shields attached to their armor, which must have offered a unique level of dexterity in close-quarters combat.

Judging by their formation, these foot soldiers were there to protect that hájje at the center. And there was no doubt about it. This center hájje was the source of the dark magic.

Seeing they had been discovered, the formation of hájje halted their advance. The center representative removed his hood, revealing his sinister face.

Like all his kind, his skin was pale, like the lightest shade of white chalk. This made for a harsh contrast with his jet-black eyes, which were darker than the darkest cavern, like two empty voids upon his face. He had an unblemished face, his angular features and yellow teeth completing his malevolent features.

Jaldor and his Mastiff were closest to the group of hájje. Though the massive dog kept an aggressive stance and released the occasional growl, it seemed his owner had quieted down his bark.

"You offer more resistance than we expected for such a small farm," the hájje spoke, his grating voice harsher than a harpy's song, but deep and foreboding.

"Just poor timing on your part I suppose," Artimus Jr. replied. "But this farm is under our protection. Leave while you still can."

"I'm afraid you're mistaken," the hájje retorted with a scowl. "This farm is now property of the hájje. You can either leave or serve as compost for the next season of crops."

"And who are you to think you can just march in here and take someone else's land?" asked Mojo. He took a few steps forward, holding up his hands as if to shrug.

"I am Zallenstal, son of Yezurkstal, General and Necromancer of the Hájjeona army. I have divine authority to claim any land I please."

George did his best not to move, looking out the corner of his eyes to his wife, who was standing just a few meters front and to the left. She had squared off her stance, angling her right foot away and keeping her left pointed towards the enemies.

Artimus Jr. was positioned further to the right and just a couple meters in front of George. Mojo was furthest to the left, and less than a meter in front of George. It was moments like this that made George wish they could all communicate telepathically.

Zallenstal spread his arms wide, his five guardians fanning out with a leap.

Though not as quick to draw as his father might have been, Artimus Jr. reacted first, drawing his bow and notching an arrow. Within moments, he unleashed the first shot. The arrow rebounded harmlessly off the enemy's chest, like a pebble bouncing off a wooden shield. Their armor was more resilient than it appeared.

Sarah was also quick to act, raising her staff and hurling a fireball towards the enemy necromancer. George kept his eyes trained on this exchange, ready to step in.

Zallenstal held up right hand, a large talisman in his grasp. The fireball struck the talisman and dispersed, an invisible barrier providing protection from the attack.

Bringing back the talisman to his chest, he muttered something under his breath and cast a spell back at Sarah.

George was ready, throwing out a portal to intercept the spell. Refunneling the attack, George winced as the dark stream left the ether and impacted one of the hájje foot soldiers. His scream was tortured, shriller than any the young void mage had heard before. He watched the soldier writhe on the ground before going limp.

It seemed Zallenstal had not expected resistance like this. The necromancer looked dumbfounded, his mouth agape and eyes wide as the other four soldiers continued their charge. Mojo took a step towards the one nearest him, pulling a handful of Zerrum dust from a pouch on his right. With a quick blow, he sprayed the dusk over his assailant, who fell unconscious.

Artimus Jr. had drawn his sword and was engaging with another enemy, matching blade strikes and holding his own. As they exchanged blows, Sarah cast another bolt of green energy, this one striking the soldier nearest her. The bolt itself might not have been lethal, but the concussive force threw the soldier back at least three meters, leaving him sprawled in the dirt.

It looked like Artimus Jr. had gotten the advantage too, a quick parry and riposte leaving his enemy to stagger back and clutch at the wound. That left just one more foot soldier. And it was clear the coordinated display by George's allies was making Zallenstal question his mission. The necromancer was stunned, stammering as he watched each of his soldiers fall.

With just one swordsman remaining, it looked like it was George's turn to act. Jaldor, still wielding the sword he had wrestled from a hájje, was squaring up against this final enemy. His Mastiff looked eager for the fight, baring his teeth, and barking as the enemy approached. In a flash, the dog leapt upon the hájje, grabbing and tackling him to the ground.

George remained focused, timing his next spell precisely. For as the hájje fell, he thrust his blade towards the dog's ribs. Throwing out a portal, George narrowly intercepted the attack, redirecting it to land in the attacker's back. The mastiff continued its assault, ensuring the hájje's demise.

With all his allies incapacitated, Zallenstal finally made a move.

"I will have what is due to me," he exclaimed, throwing his hood back over his head. The talisman in his hand pulsed, a wave of dark energy causing George's vision to blur. As the world around him came back into focus, Zallenstal was gone.

"Well, that was fun!" exclaimed George with a nervous chuckle.

"And we have a couple alive we can question." Added Mojo. "Well done, Sarah. I'm glad I'm not the only one capable of non-lethal combat."

Sarah gave a subtle bow, smiling as she walked back towards George. But just as George thought about how it couldn't have gone any better, the panicked bellow of Irontail in the distance gave him pause.

"Regroup back at the farmhouse!"

The echo of his call rang through George's mind, and he prayed no one was hurt.

ChAPTER VI

Paxvilla, Jaldor's Farm
13 Julla, 1149 MT

Jaldor's hands shook. He was paralyzed with fear, watching as these extraordinary heroes dispatched each of the enemies with such ease. But as he heard the centaur's deafening call from the southern field, he gasped and dropped his sword.

"Samson!" he shouted, clapping his hands together.

"That's enough!"

Without delay, Samson disengaged from the slain hájje and returned to Jaldor's side. The loyal Jyrimoore Mastiff turned back to the south, leaning into Jaldor's leg and barking.

"Let's grab the one Sarah got," shouted the wizened barghest, limping over towards the further of the two surviving hájje. Everyone but Sarah followed his lead, walking towards the downed enemy. It appeared Sarah was on her way to Jaldor.

"I know we haven't been formally introduced," she started mid-stride. "My name is Sarah, and I think we should be getting you inside."

Jaldor hesitated for a moment, unsure of what to do. Gathering his wits, he nodded.

"Yes, I gathered that much. I am Jaldor, and it seems I owe you all a great debt. So, I'll take your advice. Samson, follow me!"

Not waiting for Sarah to reach him, he started back around the house. He heard Sarah following close behind. As he arrived in front and started towards the door, he paused, heavy hoof steps drawing his attention south.

The centaur ran into view, slowing to a trot and looking from Jaldor and Samson back to Sarah.

"Is everything handled here?" asked the centaur.

"Yes, we are all clear it seems," replied Sarah. "You guys?"

"We are clear as well. Only one injury," answered the centaur.

"Luna?"

"Naturally," said the centaur with a nod.

Feeling uncertain about his next move, Jaldor let out a low, elongated "uh."

"Right, Mr. farmer. My name is Irontail," said the centaur extending his right hand.

"The name is Jaldor," replied Jaldor, accepting Irontail's handshake. He had a surprisingly reasonable grip, firm but not aggressively strong, which said something, considering he could have easily crushed Jaldor's hand.

Jaldor glanced past Irontail, hearing some heavy footsteps approaching. It was the felite, followed closely by the two younger barghest.

"I told you!" the felite exclaimed. "I'm like black lightning!"

The two barghest wagged their tongues, smiles stretching across both their faces.

"We'll get you one of these times," said one.

"Or at least I will!" quipped the other.

"Pfft. I won't count on it. But Irontail, what did I say? I told you those four could handle whatever other troops they brought." The felite turned towards Sarah.

"You know he didn't think you guys could handle yourself? He was so worried we had to rush over here to regroup that we ended up leaving Artimus and Savannah trailing behind."

Irontail turned towards the felite and shook his head.

"You were right Luna. Enjoy this rare treat."

Jaldor forced himself to grin, looking about at this odd menagerie of friends who had come to his rescue. Who were these strange fighters and why were they here?

As he contemplated ways to ask this question, his attention was drawn back by the squeaky hinges on his front door. Samantha stepped outside, leaving the door cracked open behind her. She held a torch in her left and a hammer in her right.

Samson darted to her side, taking a defensive posture in front of her.

"Are the animals alright?" Samantha asks, her eyes darting around at the various strangers.

Just as she asked, Savannah and the older male elf made their way back into sight, taking slow steps towards Jaldor.

"And who are all these people?" she continued, squaring up her stance.

"It's alright," Jaldor attempted to reply, holding up his hands palm out as he walked over to her. "These people just - well, I'm not quite sure where to begin. They made sure…uhm, they helped fight-"

"Look lady," interrupted Luna. "You had a hájje infestation and we cleared them out. You're safe now. You're welcome."

Samantha looked confused, her mouth hanging open and eyes slowly drifting up across the night sky. After a few moments with this bewildered expression, she batted her eyelashes a few times and shook her head.

"Wait. Where is Deliliah?"

Samson whimpered, and Jaldor closed his eyes.

"She didn't make it." Whispered Jaldor softly. He leaned in and hugged his wife.

He couldn't say for sure if it was the shock of the fight to remain strong for his wife. But as he squeezed her and held on tight for an extended embrace, he managed to hold his tears at bay. Opening his eyes back up wide, all he could think about was how grateful he was that his wife and child were safe. Samson barked, jumping to his hind legs, and joining the hug. After a moment, Jaldor broke away and turned back towards the others.

As Samantha stifled her tears, Jaldor addressed their unexpected saviors.

"I really don't know what to say. I'm not sure there would be room for you all in our home, but we are forever grateful for your help this evening. Thank you."

Jaldor's mind raced. He had the occasional thought about defending the farm from intruders. But it usually consisted of some wild beast, or at worst a band of highway robbers. To be assailed by an army was something he'd never imagined, even in his wildest dreams.

And how had these mysterious people found him. Why had they helped? Nothing about this night made any sense to Jaldor, and as he tried to assemble the pieces of the puzzle, he found it difficult to really articulate his thoughts.

"We're sorry that we didn't get here a little sooner," Savannah said, closing to just a few meters away.

"But I'm afraid you're not likely out of danger yet," came a voice from the darkness to the south.

Jaldor startled out the sound of the deep, gruff voice. But as the figure approached, he was able to relax. It was the troll.

Samantha dropped her hammer and squeezed Jaldor's left arm.

"It's alright," Jaldor muttered. "He's with them."

"I'm sorry if I startled you," the troll said holding his hands close to his heart.

"My name is Oogmut, and I am also deeply sorry for the loss of your brave Jyrimoore Mastiff. Her fighting spirit and brave defense of your land will be remembered and talked about for generations to come."

Jaldor suspected this troll had a sandy foundation.

"Um. Thank you," murmured Samantha.

"Samantha, maybe you should go back inside and make sure Mary knows everything is alright," suggested Jaldor.

"Yes. I'll. Yes." Samantha was shaking as she pulled open the door and slunk back inside.

Jaldor wished he could afford to retreat inside as well. But it would be impolite, or so he thought.

"Oogmut is right," said the male elf, his eyes still darting all around. "Where are the others?"

"Just back behind the house," answered Sarah motioning in that direction.

"I think they are looking to question the ones I incapacitated."

The elf raised his eyebrows and tilted his head back to the right.

"Interesting. I better go check on them to make sure my son and your husband don't end up causing any trouble."

Sarah laughed and shook her head.

"Alright. Go check on them Mr. 'I need to have my hands in everything'."

The elf, who Jaldor now assumed must have been Artimus Sr., raised his hand and opened his mouth as if to object. But as he stepped towards Sarah, he shook his head and proceeded around the back of the home.

Luna looked directly at Jaldor for a moment before turning to follow Artimus. The two younger barghest exchanged glances with each other, but they kept stepping around as if uncertain which was to go. Irontail, Oogmut, Sarah, and Savannah all converged towards Jaldor.

"So uh," Jaldor began, giving up on trying to make sense of things. "Do you really think they will send more soldiers? What could they want with my farm?"

"We're still gathering all the pieces of the puzzle together," replied Savannah. "But it seems your farm was not the only one they were making moves on."

She broke eye contact with Jaldor, looking off to the right as the color left her cheeks.

"I'm not sure how to tell you this, but we were coming to protect your farm. The reason we were not here sooner was because we stumbled upon some signs of offensive activity on our way here. My husband, you see, is quite a skilled investigator.

"So, when he noticed signs of foul play, we proceeded to investigate. We believe the hájje we fought off tonight raided at least two other farms before coming here. And we suspect had we not intervened, yours may not have been the last one they were going after."

Jaldor was beside himself. He found it difficult to process everything and his jumble of thoughts left him unable to move. After what felt like at least a minute, he finally grasped onto a thought he could articulate.

"Have these hájje declared war on Paxvilla?"

Sarah and Savannah exchanged nervous glances. Oogmut scratched behind his head, looking back at the two barghest. It was Irontail who stepped forward and answered.

"No one really knows much about the hájje. Sixty years ago, after Death's demise, we agreed it was best to leave them be. In many ways, they were as much victims as the rest of the forest. Recently, there have been some reports of hájje sightings all around Erathal. But it's mostly hearsay and legend at this point."

"I think perhaps I should join the others to question the surviving hájje," interjected Oogmut. "I fear our new friend here might be asking the right question. Morn, Neman, come with me!"

Oogmut waved towards the back of the house and started lumbering in that direction. Morn and Neman followed without hesitation.

"What am I supposed to tell my daughter?" Jaldor blurted. He didn't mean to say it out loud. But the thought slipped from his lips. And as he ruminated with that thought, his eyes swelled up, tears forming as he considered the implications.

"Your daughter will be safe," Savannah declared. "I promise you; I will keep her safe."

Jaldor considered the elf. She looked directly into his eyes, holding his gaze. Her green eyes glimmered in the moonlight, but she did not falter.

She would keep her word; or at least try to.

"Alright," Jaldor started, closing his eyes. "How am I supposed to deal with this? I'm just a dairy farmer. Murder, war, death...I don't understand any of this."

"I'm sorry that you have to," interjected Irontail, his deep voice full of unexpected compassion.

The large centaur trotted towards Jaldor. But as the two locked eyes, there was an unexpected understanding. It was strange, as if this massive beast somehow understood Jaldor's fear and confusion. As if he shared Jaldor's burden.

Jaldor felt his knees buckle. For a moment, he felt as if he might collapse and burst into tears.

Samson barked, interrupting his thoughts, and drawing his gaze. As he looked down at his loyal companion, the guard dog pushed his rear against his legs, his tail wagging rapidly. Tongue wagging and eyes begging for attention, Jaldor felt an unexpected vigor. There was no avoiding it.

His life had been turned upside down. But this was not the end. No, this was a new beginning.

And in that moment, gazing into the eyes of his Jyrimoore Mastiff, Jaldor knew that nothing would be the same. His life as a dairy farmer was over.

No, not over. He would not let this stop him.

Instead, this moment would move him forward. No matter what the future held, he vowed that he would do whatever it took to ensure his family was safe.

Nothing else mattered.

"No," Jaldor declared looking right into Irontail's eyes.

"You have nothing to apologize for. I may not understand the depravity that would cause such violence, but I know this: I will protect my family."

Jaldor smiled, turning away from Irontail, and looking to Sarah and Savannah. Perhaps it was his ego reasserting itself, looking for some confirmation that his claim was justified.

That wasn't it. Not at all.

Yes, it was as if his life was a puzzle, and he was just now learning to fit the pieces into place. He was a husband, a father, a dairy farmer…but he was also so much more. Whatever designs these hájje might have for his farm, for Paxvilla, or even for the entirety of Erathal forest, Jaldor would not sit idly by.

"And no matter what the cost might be, I will ensure my family can continue on," exclaimed Jaldor.

Irontail looked back at Sarah and Savannah.

"We are happy to hear," said Savannah. "Because there's something else you should know."

"What is that?" Jaldor asked.

"We were not just passing through by coincidence," replied Savannah.

"What do you mean?" Jaldor glanced at Irontail and Sarah, both avoiding his gaze.

"One of our friends had a vision of the attack on your farm. We came here because she believes your family is important to the future of Evorath. And in all likeliness, that means your family is still in grave danger."

Jaldor felt dizzy. He fell back to lean against his home, and took a deep breath. Closing his eyes, he thought how just twenty minutes earlier he was coming outside expecting to find his dogs barking at some harmless wildlife. Instead, his entire world had been turned upside down.

"I'm a farmer, not a fighter. What do you expect me to do?"

"We'll want to have your entire family come with us," said Irontail matter-of-factly.

"My whole family? We can't just pack up and leave! This land has been part of our family since we were brought to Evorath. The animals on this land rely on us to take care of them. So, if you want us to leave, sure. As long as you have somewhere all my family can stay, including the livestock."

Irontail looked at Sarah and Savannah. It was Sarah who stepped forward and answered.

"We can arrange that," she said with a nod.

Jaldor's eyes went wide, opening his mouth in surprise.

"I hadn't expected that response," he scratched behind his head, looking skyward.

"Look, I'll entertain the suggestion, but need more convincing. I never imagined I'd ever meet a hájje, much less have an army of them come attack my farm. It's all a lot to grasp onto." Jaldor nodded as he strung his sentences together.

"That's understandable," replied Savannah. "How about we do this? We'll hang back on the outskirts of the farm, making sure there are no other threats tonight. At sunrise, we'll come back and discuss while you check on your herd."

Jaldor nodded. "I'd appreciate that, yes. Except let's discuss it over breakfast. My wife and daughter should be present to discuss this."

"Alright, breakfast it is!" exclaimed Savannah.

"One other thing," Jaldor held up his right hand. "What about the hájje survivors?"

"Don't worry about it," interjected Irontail.

"Yes," added Savannah, "we will make sure they are no longer a threat to you."

Jaldor nodded, forcing a nervous smile.

"Alright. I guess I will see you again at breakfast. I hope you don't mind sitting close to each other."

Not wanting to give his visitors a chance to respond, he opened the door, stepped inside, and slammed it shut behind him.

"What am I going to tell Samantha?"

CHAPTER VII

Lizock City, Melora's Tavern
14 Julla, 1149 MT

Zelag scratched the back of his bald head, his scaly brown skin a constant irritation. His forked tongue darted between his teeth, scrunching his face, unable to find any relief. Of all the shapes he could take, this lizock form was his least favorite.

Aside from the dry, itchy skin, his hearing in this reptilian form was subpar, his color vision was limited, and the tail always seemed to get in his way. He also found nothing he ate or drank in this form ever really tasted good.

"What will it be?" the barkeep asked, her gravely but youthful voice making him ponder her age. Her black scales obscured her features in the dim tavern lighting.

"I'm here to see Melora. Tell her 'Zelag is looking for information.' Is she in the office?" Zelag motioned to the hallway behind the bar.

The barkeep turned and looked, shaking her head as she turned back to Zelag.

"She's back there, but she asked not to be disturbed. So, I'll tell her you dropped by when I see her. Until then, you can order a drink, or you can leave."

"Fair enough," replied Zelag without pause. He hated these dances. These younger girls were always trying to prove their worth, looking for ways to demonstrate their importance.

"Why don't we make it interesting. The yellows of your eyes tell me you have a story to tell. I'll have two of your favorite drinks, as long as you're drinking with me."

The barkeep batted her eyelashes, a predictable response.

"Two bog whiskies!" That explained the graveled voice.

Though he abhorred these rituals, Zelag had become quite skilled at them. He flexed the muscles in his neck, leaning back in his seat and allowing his tongue to dart out for just a moment longer than usual, all while looking directly into her eyes.

The barkeep tried to avert her gaze, but she couldn't prevent her scales from shimmering.

"You know," whispered Zelag as his mark poured the drinks. He gestured with his pointer and middle finger, motioning for her to come over.

She barely managed to finish pouring the second drink. Snatching them up in one hand, she scurried back to Zelag.

"The information I'm after would result in quite the large finder's fee," continued Zelag. "This sort of find could really make a lasting impression."

Sliding one of the glasses to Zelag, the barkeep picked up the other and held it out. "To large finder's fees," she tapped her glass on the bar top before gulping it down.

Zelag kept pace, hitting his cup down just a bit harder and washing back the entire glass in one gulp. As he looked back down and met her gaze, he again let his tongue dart out, leaving it for just a moment too long.

"Alright!" the barkeep squeaked. "I can tell you're one of the big players around here. I'll let Melora know you're here."

Placing the half-bottle of remaining bog whisky on the counter, the barkeep offered a wink before retreating down the hall to the office.

It was the middle of the morning, perhaps the least busy time of day. Aside from Zelag and one haggard old drunk down at the other end, no one else was at the bar. A young couple was sitting at a nearby table, and an adult lizock and his elderly mother were at a table well out of his immediate line of sight.

Zelag put double pours in both glasses. He lifted his own glass, keeping an eye on the young couple at the nearby table. They were speaking in hushed tones and Zelag didn't care to eavesdrop. But he did want to observe their sightlines, waiting for the opportune moment.

There it was!

Zelag leaned over the bar, pouring his glass into the waste bucket before replacing it on the bar. After glancing back around the bar, he turned his attention to the hallway.

It shouldn't take too long.

"Zelag!" Melora's jarring tone echoed down the hallway. "Send him back here! And have Belrod join us."

Belrod? She was really underestimating Zelag's abilities.

Closing his eyes, Zelag listened for the barkeep's footsteps. As she drew closer, he opened his eyes.

"You can add two more doubles to my tab. Sorry I didn't wait." He gave her a wink, nodding up towards the ceiling as he stepped around the bar and proceeded down the hallway.

Reaching into his satchel as he walked, he pulled out a handful of coins. Though his instinct called him to keep wide eyes, he narrowed his focus to the office door. He strode right inside, keeping his eyes fixed on Melora, who was seated just a few meters away.

She wore a shimmering pink dress, silk fabric adorned with extra intricate lacework and accented with pearls. Her pruned purple scales had lightened in recent years and the heavy reliance on perfume strained Zelag's breathing.

She was seated in a custom-carved Erath chair. Zelag had heard the entire story at one point, but suffice it to say, it was a custom piece with great artistic detail. Before her was a small, matching table with two matching scrolls rolled up upon it.

"Melora, you look as charming as the day I first met you," lied Zelag.

"Flattery will get you nowhere. Six months ago, you promised me the royal pendant. If you don't have it by now, I hope you have your affairs in order."

"Relax," rejoined Zelag, tossing the coins onto the table. "You know I ran into some unexpected complications. But I've got a solid lead on it. I just need your help."

"And you think this sad pittance of an offering is going to buy my help?" she asked, glancing at one of the coins before tossing it back onto the table.

Zelag took a step closer, motioning towards the coin.

"Look at them more closely," he suggested.

Melora squinted, sitting up in her chair and grabbing the coin. She brought it up close to her eye and examined it for a few seconds.

"I can't believe anyone else could have spotted this. How did you even know to look for it?" Melora asked.

Zelag shrugged.

"I don't know what I'm looking at," he said. "I could just tell the money was enchanted. I'm hoping you can tell me who might have done that to the coins."

The tavern owner kept the coin close to her eyes a moment longer, smiling as she pulled it away.

"It's quite ingenious of them really. While these appear to be Erathal Republic gold ulagrets, these are just bronze ulagrets. This enchantment would likely even go unnoticed by the most skilled merchants and tax collectors. And I only know one lizock who could pull off this convincing of a forgery."

"What about non-lizock?" asked Zelag.

"Maybe a handful more," replied Melora.

"Good. Any not on this list?" Zelag reached into his back pocket, pulling out a scrap piece of parchment and placing it on Melora's table.

She glanced down at the parchment, glaring up at Zelag as she finished reading.

"Just the lizock," she uttered.

"You give me that lizock's name and location," said Zelag, "and I'll get you that medallion within a fortnight. Guaranteed, or I'll turn myself in so you can collect the bounty from the highest bidder."

Melora smiled, a slimy, unsettling gesture.

"Alright," she said opening one of the scrolls on her table. It was a map, and as she rolled it out, she pulled a small knife from a hidden pocket in her dress, stabbing it into the forest just west of Marftaport.

"His name is Shadiro, and you'll find him here."

Zelag sighed, taking a deep breath and nodding.

"But if you're not back here within a fortnight, surrendering for a bounty will be the least of your concerns. I collect my debts in scales."

With a smirk, Zelag reached town and collected the coins he'd deposited on the table.

"No, leave them. Consider it a down payment."

Zelag showed his teeth, offering a slight bow and dropping the coins.

"I will see you in a fortnight. I expect our original deal still stands?"

"As agreed."

But even as he walked from the office, Zelag feared it wouldn't be so simple.

CHAPTER VIII

Jaldor stepped through the portal, the initial wave of dizziness leaving him off balance. Blinking rapidly, he looked down at the palms of his hands.

"I know it's a bit jarring the first time," said George extending his hand. "But it sure makes traveling fast, doesn't it?"

With an unconscious nod, Jaldor looked around. He really was in a different place. From his best estimates, Jaldor figured at least a square kilometer of forest had been cleared. Some of the larger trees were left behind, the branches of an old oak to the east looking like an intricate tangle. To the south, there was a solid row of various natural trees. And to the north, he could see more heavy forest and the hills beyond.

All around, there were piles of lumber spaced out, raw logs with all their branches removed. Each pile was spread out at seemingly random intervals. By the looks of it, Jaldor guessed they were planning to stake these out as the various parcels of farmland.

"So, we're on the west coast now?" Jaldor glanced to the west. Aside from a few stray trees left in the clearing, all he could see was more dense forest coverage off in the horizon. He could smell a mixture of soil, ash, and the remnants of a recent burning of brush. Judging by the various piles spread about the field, he assumed they had the larger trunks prepared for construction and burned all the smaller leaves and branches.

Artimus Jr. took a few steps to the west.

"Technically, the coast is through all those trees. About 50-60 kilometers from here."

"And you plan to turn this entire area into farmland? You must really expect the city to expand."

Jaldor was still struggling to take everything in. Part of him was excited by the prospect of moving to this new land and starting over. Instead of inheriting a farm from his parents, he'd have the opportunity to rebuild it to better fit his vision. But then he thought about leaving Paxvilla, and some of the relationships he and his wife had formed there. Would he ask others to join them? Could he even extend that invite?

"In truth," replied George, "the city is already expanding. You'd be doing us a favor in some ways -we're actively looking for farmers who want to have liberty to grow their operation. Some of the earlier settlers here have committed to expanding their own farms. So, some of these parcels are already claimed. Over the course of the next year, many of the original, smaller farms in town will be moving out here and expanding."

"And then we'll work on repurposing those old farm parcels in town to offer additional housing for other new arrivals," added Artimus Jr. "But not quite all of this will be farmland. You see over there?"

Artimus Jr. pointed to the north, towards the hills.

"One of our town members is going to be rebuilding his home at the base of the hills up there. The remaining forest you see there will be converted to serve as a perennial lumber operation. And then we have the construction to the east."

He turned that direction, pointing to some tighter groupings of lumber.

"We're building out some more residential housing that way, complete with a new tavern. And with the growth in our felite population, there are designs to build a new Capabolo course over there as well."

"But you should see the harbor district," interjected George. "There's a bunch of new homes being built there, and a large amphitheater. Maybe after we're done here, we can stop over there."

Scratching behind his head, Jaldor shifted his gaze to the sky. This was a beautiful location, but he had a lot of things to consider.

"Let's start with the parcel you had in mind for me," replied Jaldor.

"Of course!" exclaimed George. "Uh…I think it's that way?" he pointed to a pile of lumber southwest of them.

"No," Artimus Jr. disagreed with a shake of his head. "It's that one." He pointed to another spot to the southeast; it was a bit closer to their location.

"Are you sure?" asked George.

"Just follow me," breathed Artimus Jr.

The trio all walked southeast. Jaldor kept his eyes on the ground as they did, trying to get a solid lay of the land. It was mostly flat, but as they approached the pile of lumber, he noticed a few steep inclines that could make a good location for building a cheese cave.

"Are we on the parcel now?" he asked.

"Not quite," said Artimus Jr. after a short pause. "But…"

He extended the word for a few extra seconds, until he stopped in a spot just a few meters south of Jaldor.

"I believe this is about where the northern border would be." The elf motioned to the ground at his feet.

Jaldor regarded the pile of lumber, which was still a good distance to the southeast.

"Can we just walk straight to what you're figuring would be the southern end? I'm imagining a square parcel would be easiest. Is that what you were figuring?"

George laughed and Artimus Jr. chuckled.

"This entire new development is meant to be a perfect grid," replied George after a few moments. "But getting it that way was interesting, to say the least."

Jaldor scrunched his mouth, curious what could possibly be humorous about parcel development.

"But yes," added Artimus Jr. "We can just walk south. I think I can tell where the edge would be."

Not waiting for the other two, Jaldor started south, keeping his eyes on the ground. There were at least two burn piles he spotted on the way, the potash remaining from where tree branches had been burned. The soil looked healthy even without the additional nutrients, but he still noticed a few good spots where his family could grow enough vegetables to feed at least a dozen families.

They were approaching the center of the parcel, or at least what Jaldor assumed was meant to be the center. The pile of lumber was directly east, and with a glance he could see it was composed of a plethora of different trees: oak, pine, cedar, maple, and a couple others that he was not certain of. It looked like there was a slope south of this pile, but it wasn't very steep.

As they continued south, Jaldor took note of a pair of standing oaks. They were enormous trees, moss covering whole branches, which weaved through one another and locked the trees together as if they were embracing. The large canopy would provide an excellent area for his cows to find shade on sunny days. Further to the east, he noted a few more trees remaining on the property.

"Is there a pond, or other fresh water source on the parcel?" asked Jaldor, glancing back at Artimus Jr.

"There is not," replied the elf. "But we've found groundwater is not more than a dozen meters down around here, at most. We'll make sure you have a well to provide all the water you and your livestock might need."

101

Jaldor nodded, continuing to look for useful spots in the ground. If nothing else, there was plenty of pasture for his cows to graze on. But there was still more to see.

After another minute of walking in silence, he finally spotted what looked like a good location for his cave. The ground to the east of them dipped down at a sharp angle, piquing his interest. Jaldor pointed to the spot, looking back at Artimus Jr. as he did.

"Is that on the property?"

Artimus Jr. nodded.

"We're getting close to the southern border, but yes. I thought that might be an interesting feature. With just a bit of tunneling, you could make a cheese cave three times the one you have currently."

"It looks like I could," replied Jaldor, scratching behind his head and looking skyward.

"So, what do you think?" shouted George from the rear. He had fallen behind the other two.

"I still must discuss this more with my family. Can we all come back here to look around?" Jaldor shrugged, looking left and right.

Squinting, Jaldor listened intently. Hearing hoofbeats from the south, he turned back in that direction and saw an elf approaching on horseback.

"It's my father," said Artimus Jr. "I wasn't expecting him to join us."

George came up alongside Jaldor, his breathing a bit heavy. With a long sigh, he widened his stance and held both his hands at his hips.

"Good afternoon father," shouted Artimus Jr. waving towards his father. Jaldor could see the rider now, the elf's features coming into sight. He wore a wide grin and held up his hand as if returning the greeting.

Slowing his large brown destrier to a trot, he called out.

"Good to see you again Jaldor! I hope my son and the half-witted wizard here haven't bored you too much."

"Pfft. If I'm half-witted, I'd hate to think how dumb that makes you," replied George. He exchanged a look of understanding with Artimus, the two smiling.

In just over a day, Jaldor had already figured out that these two were friends. He didn't understand why that meant insulting one another every opportunity they got, but that seemed to be their strange way of affirming their affection for one another.

As Artimus slowed his horse to a halt, he jumped off the side, giving his horse a pat before stepping over to the others.

"I hate to cut this tour short, but I think your guides might be interested in the news I bring. We had an unexpected visitor show up in town. He's currently enjoying a meal at Sissera's. Either of you want to guess who it is?"

Artimus Jr. arched an eyebrow and looked at George, who shrugged in response.

103

"King Ulagret?" the younger elf asked.

Artimus brought his palm to his face, smiling and shaking his head.

"I don't know why I bother with you two. It's Zelag. He's apparently got some counterfeit coins that one of our citizens allegedly made. I could use you with me, son. George, maybe it's best if you sit this one out."

"Me and Zelag don't exactly see eye-to-eye," volunteered George as Jaldor looked his way.

"Ah," uttered Jaldor. "Perhaps I should return and chat everything over with my family while you take care of all this."

"Yes, I think that would be a good idea," agreed Artimus.

"Remember," said George. "I'll be back before nightfall. And Irontail and the others will hopefully stay out of your hair as they keep watch on the place."

"Of course," replied Jaldor. "Thank you all for everything. And good luck with this Zelag fellow."

George held up his staff, opening a portal. As the blue sea glowed before him, Jaldor could just barely make out the shadow of his home.

With a gulp of air, he closed his eyes and stepped through.

CHAPTER IX

Zelag leaned back in his seat, sipping down his drink with eyes closed. Placing the mug back on the table, he let out a satisfied sigh. The taste of everything in this human form was so much more enjoyable, the hops of his beer and the subtle hint of citrus leaving a bitter taste on his tongue.

Scratching his unkept brown beard, he looked around, realizing he recognized almost no one else in the tavern. He shifted in his chair, adjusting his studded leather armor to make sure his weapons were out of the way. Humans may not have had any physical advantages over the many species of Evorath, but he sure felt comfortable in this skin.

Seated in the back right corner, he had an exceptional line of sight, the upholstered sofa offering a comfortable place to sit as he waited. Picking up one of the small pillows, he pressed down and smiled, the feathers provided an extra luxurious feel, not something he was accustomed to in the places he frequented.

Dropping the pillow, he took another swig of his beer, continuing to survey the bar and look for any changes. He wasn't sure if it was a fault of his memory, but from his recollection it seemed this cozy little corner was the only major change. Though the lights were an interesting development. It appeared the candles had been replaced along the walls with some kind of glowing runestones -presumably the work of a Mage's Guild member.

Aside from that, the tavern was busier than he ever remembered. The whole place was full of tables now, compared to the more open and spacious walkways he recalled.

The crowds were as diverse as ever. Lizock, felite, elves, barghest, trolls, a couple of centaurs, and even a lamia, whose gaze he averted. And it seemed a pair of satyrs were the performing musicians of the day. Nodding his head to the calming melody coming from the other side of the tavern, he sat up straight and took another sip of his drink.

"Your meal will be out in just a moment," called Arnona from behind the bar, her voice oscillating to the melody of the music.

Zelag lifted his mug and offered a friendly smile. If he did end up staying the night in Marftaport, he intended to make sure he got better acquainted with this mercurial young elf.

Turning his attention back to the crowd, he kept his eyes peeled on the front door. That's when he spotted a couple of unexpected, but familiar faces.

Artimus and his son strode through the door, pausing to look around the tavern. With a quick scan, it seemed the older elf spotted him, patting his son on the shoulder and pointing back to Zelag in the corner.

The elves looked just like Zelag remembered them. Which wasn't surprising, considering how slowly they aged.

Tempering his smile, Zelag stood from his seat, leaving his mug on the table.

"Artimus! And Little A!" Zelag exclaimed extending his arms. "It is great to see you both!"

Artimus smiled, and Artimus Jr. shook his head.

"Shh!" Artimus Jr. held his index finger before his lip as he approached. "We don't need to be resurrecting that nickname," he said in a hushed tone.

Zelag cracked a smile, quickly leveling out his expression and extending his right hand.

Artimus Jr. accepted the handshake, offering a firm grip before stepping back and allowing his father in next.

Artimus grasped Zelag's hand and pulled him in for an embrace. He clasped Zelag tightly, giving him a couple pats on the back.

"It's good to see you, old friend! We wondered when you might find your way back here. You know Vistoro still has your old room open if you want to stay awhile."

Feeling the hug had lasted long enough, Zelag gave Artimus a firm squeeze before pulling out of the embrace.

"It is good to see you too Artimus. I know it's been a while since I've come through. But I've been keeping busy. And I'm not sure if I can even stay the night to share some of the adventures I've been on since I last saw you."

"Five years and you aren't sure if you can stick around for one night?" Artimus Jr. asked with his hands on his hips.

"Well, I'm following up on a time-sensitive lead," replied Zelag. "Sissera is suppo-"

"Excuse me," interrupted Arnona, her soft voice barely cutting in over Zelag's. "I have your meal."

She was holding his order, the smell of cooked turkey leg complimented with fresh herbs on the potato and plated with a side of seasonal green. The aroma was another reminder of why he enjoyed this human form so much.

"Thank you," said Zelag, reaching between Artimus and his son to grab the plate. "Do you mind?" he asked nodding towards his food.

As Arnona skipped off towards another table, Artimus turned, regarding the nearest table. There was a table just a few meters away currently occupied by an elderly lizock couple. They were both seated on the bench against the wall, sipping on drinks.

"How about we take a real table?" Artimus asked.

"If you can get them to move," replied Zelag.

Nodding, Artimus turned and stepped over to the table.

"Excuse me, Marlisa and Kirolin. Sorry to interrupt. Would you mind taking my friend's seat on the sofa and allowing my son and I to sit here with our old friend? It would mean a lot to us all."

The lizock couple exchanged a glance before looking up at Artimus and smiling.

"Of course, Artimus. We're just having a few afternoon drinks anyways. Please, take a seat."

108

The lizock couple stood up, scooting from out behind the table with cups in hand and passing by the trio as they took their place on the sofa. Zelag retrieved his mug, offering a slight bow to the elderly couple before walking over to the table.

He placed his food and drink down, sitting on the bench. Artimus and his son both sat in the chairs opposite him. Scrunching his face as he adjusted in his seat, he thought about how the lizock couple got the better end of the deal. The sofa was much more comfortable.

As Zelag picked up the turkey leg and took a large bite, Artimus spoke.

"About this lead of yours. I know you asked Sissera to fetch Shadiro about some counterfeit coins. She wisely thought that I might come speak to you first."

Zelag swallowed his first bite, shaking his head as he put down the turkey leg. He held up his hands, palms forward.

"Look, I promise I won't hurt any of your little family here, but I have it on good authority that Shadiro is the one who made the counterfeit coins. You must be a bit curious as to whether he's been swindling some of your own people. And disrupting the Republic's money supply…that must go against Marftaport's code of ethics."

Picking up his turkey leg and taking another bite, Zelag chewed as Artimus responded.

"Alright, I can appreciate your perspective," said Artimus softly. "But we will accompany you to ensure that your conversation remains…civil."

"Oh, playing the Constable again, are you?" asked Zelag, still chewing on his last bite.

"I'm being a good neighbor," quipped Artimus.

With a smile, Zelag put the turkey leg back on his plate.

"I would have no problem with you accompanying me to talk to Shadiro. But I'd remind you it would be to everyone's benefit if such a counterfeiter were put out of business. And also consider the fact that tracking down these coins would mean getting possession of Vistoro's long lost family pendant."

Artimus's eyes widened, his mouth hanging open for a moment before collecting his composure. He was good at concealing his surprise, but not good enough to hide it from Zelag. His son was even more obvious, his mouth hanging open for a few seconds.

"You've really found it?" Artimus Jr. asked.

Artimus just stared at Zelag; his eyes narrowed.

"And you're sure Shadiro will lead you to it?" Artimus questioned.

Zelag picked up his fork, spearing a piece of potato and bringing it up just short of his mouth.

"I have good reason to believe that the person Shadiro is working with is directly affiliated with the individual in possession of the pendant." Zelag took the bite, the tender mixture of garlic, butter, and assorted herbs igniting his tongue.

"So," Artimus replied, "you're not sure."

110

"Let me put it in terms you might better understand," said Zelag after swallowing his food.

"The Albino has the pendant. And I have confirmation Shadiro's involvement in his organization is at a top level. So, either way, he gets me close."

The two elves exchanged a glance, giving Zelag enough time to take another bite of the potatoes and some of the greens. This time, Zelag wasn't quite sure what they were thinking, but he was confident he had won them over.

"Alright," Artimus said after a few seconds pause. "If Shadiro is involved with The Albino, we want to know. That puts the entire city of Marftaport in danger. As soon as you're finished, we'll show you to him."

Zelag smiled, considering the food left on his plate. It would be a shame to let it go to waste.

"Just give me another minute," he said grabbing the turkey leg and taking another bite. Eating the rest of his meal as quick as he could, he reached into his coin purse and pulled out a silver piece; it was one minted in Marftaport.

"This should cover, right?" he asked.

"Yeah, and a nice gratuity!" Artimus Jr. uttered, his eyes wide and lips closed tight.

Zelag smiled, coming to his feet, and extending his arms towards the exit. He regarded his plate. There was still a bit of meat he could pick off the turkey leg, a few bites of potato, and some stray greens. But he had scratched that itch and was ready to move on.

The elves rose from their seats, turning about and walking for the door. As Zelag followed behind, he made sure to locate Arnona. She was currently speaking with a felite at a table to the right of the exit.

Stopping just inside her peripherals, he held up his hand and offered his best smile.

"Please, excuse me. I wanted to thank you for your service, Arnona. It was a real pleasure to meet you," he extended his hand. She smiled and accepted. Laying a kiss on the top of her hand, he gently twisted her palm up and deposited the silver piece before closing her fist around it.

"I hope to see you again," he said with a wink.

Not waiting around for her reaction, he whipped back to the exit and trotted to catch up with Artimus and Artimus Jr. As he stepped outside, he squinted and held up his right hand, attempting to block out the sunlight. Keeping his eyes low, he followed Artimus as his vision adjusted.

They were walking south along the road. The street was busy, much more than he remembered. When he had last been here, Sissera's Tavern and Keldor's Forge were the only two buildings here beside the tiny three slip dock and lighthouse.

In just five years, the docks had expanded out, a modest market had sprung up, and at least a half dozen new homes had been built in this dockside district. By the looks of it, a few more homes were already in the works.

"So, are we heading back to the town center?" Zelag asked, looking about at the open fields around the road.

"As luck would have it," Artimus replied pointing east, "Shadiro lives in that little cabin over there."

Zelag turned in that direction. There was a full field of overgrown grass and weeds between the road and the cabin, but if they cut through, they could get there in a couple of minutes.

"We shouldn't cut across," Artimus Jr. suggested. "It's just a few extra minutes if we walk around on the road."

With a sigh, Zelag nodded.

"Alright, but then you have to talk to me that much more. Tell me, has the Avatar shown his face recently?"

Artimus shook his head. "No, we haven't seen him since he left to 'help other children outside of Erathal'. I'm more concerned that he will be showing up soon."

"Oh?" Zelag looked back at the elf, cocking his head to the right, and narrowing his eyes.

"We had to defend a farm outside Paxvilla from a hájje attack just a couple of nights ago," Artimus Jr. interjected.

Zelag tensed up, bringing his gaze forward. He didn't want the others to see his face, because he suspected he was the one now that might be sharing too much. Taking a moment to collect his thoughts, he forced a grin and looked at the elves.

"What do you mean by 'hájje attack'?"

"He means a couple of contingents of hájje warriors -it was enough that we're keeping close tabs on the southern border of Paxvilla. None of us have even seen a hájje since we fought-"

"Don't say his name," interrupted Zelag. "I've come across a few in recent years, but that is unwelcome news. Going after farms could be the prelude to a full-fledged siege."

"That's my concern as well," Artimus replied. "It's a left at the road ahead.

They were heading east on the road now. As they approached this next road and started back north, Zelag could already see Shadiro's cabin a bit more clearly.

"Well, after I complete my current quest, perhaps I could hang around for a bit to help if needed. But I'm not playing the provincial part. It would be purely as a mercenary."

Artimus chuckled. "I wouldn't expect anything different."

Walking closer to the cabin, Zelag was able to get a better lay of the land. It appeared to be no more than a ten-meter walk from the road to reach the front porch, which consisted of a couple of wood columns and some plain wood planks. There was a barrel sitting to the right of the doorway, a simple unadorned wooden door. The porch itself wasn't more than a meter deep, making Zelag wonder why he even bothered having the egress to begin with.

The home itself featured an A-frame roof, with a chimney centrally located. Though construction was not one of his strong points, Zelag guessed by the pristine state of the windows and slate roof that construction had been completed recently.

"So, tell me one more thing before we knock," said Zelag as the group approached the cabin. "Does Shadiro have any friends or family?"

"No," replied Artimus, stopping, and grabbing Zelag's left arm. He stepped in front of Zelag, looking him sternly in the eyes. "You're not threatening him. We're doing this my way."

"We'll do it your way," Zelag affirmed, holding his hands up, palms out.

"Do you wish to do the knocking then?" he asked.

Artimus Jr. stepped onto the porch and knocked on the door. The three waited for a solid fifteen seconds, everyone looking around and fiddling as they waited.

Again, Artimus Jr. knocked, this time a bit more forcefully. "Shadiro, are you in there?"

After fifteen more seconds, Zelag let out a long sigh.

"Why don't I go look around. Don't worry, I'll call you before I do anything."

"Junior, you stay at the door. Knock again in a minute if we don't get you first. I'm following Zelag."

With an exchange of nods, Artimus and Zelag went left, stepping around the side of the home. Stomping through the patchy grass and dirt, they approached the first window on this side. And with a quick glance, they saw the window had been left open.

Artimus approached the window first. As he glanced in, he winced, turning towards Zelag.

"Feklar!" Zelag pushed Artimus aside, looking in to see for himself.

The entire home was disheveled, wooden crates scattered about. A variety of sacks and random scraps of parchment were strewn about the room.

And there was Shadiro by the fireplace, slumped over in a pool of his own blood, a knife planted in his chest.

CHAPTER X

Sarah looked around the cabin, averting her eyes as she looked past Shadiro's corpse. While she was no stranger to violence, most recently the skirmish with the hájje, this felt different. No one had ever been murdered in Marftaport. Which meant, of course, this was the first murder victim that Sarah knew.

This created an unexpected and unfamiliar sensation, a mixture of grief, guilt, sadness, fear, and something else she couldn't quite put a name on. It made her pause, thinking about the death she had witnessed in skirmishes past. Why should this one hit her so differently?

Shrugging it off to focus on the situation at hand, she looked around the cabin. The place was a mess.

It looked like a raging windstorm had blown through, leaving behind only destruction in its wake. Starting from the window on the left, there was a broken wooden chair. An array of crates and sacks were broken and scattered about the floor. Littered with torn pieces of parchment, and upon closer observation, with stray, counterfeit coins, it seemed the aftermath of the physical altercation might have been just as violent as the main event.

Artimus stood over Shadiro's body, pointing something out to his son. Aside from the damage to the window, the house structure looked mostly undisturbed. The simple wooden walls were undamaged, the fireplace seemingly untouched as well. Sarah had a hard time imagining how they would possibly track down the murderer.

George was off fetching Savannah, who Artimus insisted would be able to help. Meanwhile, it seemed the close study and examination of the victim was an integral part of the investigation. Really, as she thought more about it, she wondered why they had brought her in to begin with.

What could she possibly have to offer?

As if an answer to her thought, the door creaked open. But she dropped her gaze as she realized it was Zelag returning, and not her fellow Guild members.

"They were a dead end," said the shapeshifter, shaking his head. "It had to be another mage who killed him. Nothing hides footfalls so perfectly as a well-executed spell."

Artimus came to attention.

"Oh, do you have that much confidence in yourself now?"

Zelag frowned and shook his head.

"Even if your skill does exceed mine, I can tell when magic is involved. I've only ever lost tracks like that a handful of times. And each time, a mage of some sort was waiting at the end of the chase. I'll give you the real bit of speculation though. I bet it was another counterfeiter."

"That's not a bad theory," replied Artimus with a grin. "Was he doing it to steal the method, or to eliminate his competition? And what does this do to your search for the pendant?"

"Oh, this changes nothing!" Zelag clapped his hands together. "If I'm right, our killer is the holder of the pendant."

Sarah brushed her bangs out of her forehead, glancing around the room in hopes of finding something. These speculative games were always so boring to her. Why waste time guessing about what you might find when you could be spending that time finding what you're after?

She understood George was the same way and had heard his perspective more than a few times. It just still never seemed as exciting though, no matter what rationale they might have.

"Perhaps the killer is really just that good," interrupted Artimus Jr. "Or maybe you guys should stop making wild guesses and start focusing on the information we do have."

With a smirk, Sarah glanced back over. Artimus Jr. was always a wildcard. He would engage in theory at times, but mostly he stuck to practice. And just as Artimus Jr.'s comment seemed to bring an end to the discussion, the backup arrived.

The door creaked open again, Savannah stepping through and followed closely behind by George.

"And now the real fun can begin!" exclaimed Artimus, coming to his feet. "Savannah, I believe I know how we will track our killer, but I need your delicate touch."

119

George stopped, glaring at Zelag for a moment before looking around at the others.

"Should I notify anyone else? Maybe inform Vistoro and Tel' Shira at least?"

"I think that's a good idea," Sarah interjected.

She stepped forward, looking around at the others.

"I guess normally we might look for his next of kin, but Shadiro had only moved here recently. He didn't have any family here, and if anyone knew whether he had it elsewhere, it would be one of them."

"I think that's a good suggestion," replied Savannah. "But I'd just share it with Vistoro for now, in private. There's less chance for rumors to start if you can avoid letting anyone else hearing."

"Yeah, I like that," said George. "I'm going to go tell Vistoro and find out whether there's any family we should get in touch with."

George paused before leaving, scowling at Zelag before adjusting his gaze. Locking eyes with Sarah, he offered a broad smile and blew her a kiss. She returned both gestures as he turned and stepped back outside.

"So, what do you need me to look at?" Savannah asked.

"Yes!" Artimus waved his right hand, gesturing for Savannah to approach.

"Look at the mess of parchment, the broken chair, and the scuff marks here on the floor. This was not a hired assassin, but a clumsy and uncoordinated attack. The way the knife was stabbed into his chest -it's just sloppy!"

"Go on," Savannah encouraged. Sarah stepped in closer, hoping to get a better glimpse of Artimus and Savannah's investigatory process.

"Well, as I was just showing to our son, take a closer look at these two coins. Don't use your magic yet though!"

He held out his left, offering a couple of coins to his wife. Savannah took them both, holding them close and squinting as she examined them. Artimus crowded in next to her, nearly pressing his face against hers.

"Now look as you tilt both coins. Try to make sure you get some of the sunlight from the window."

Artimus clasped his wife's hand, slowly tilting it to the side. It was always so encouraging to see the two of them interact. Married for sixty years, and still able to share such a close bond. If they were alive long enough to celebrate sixty years in marriage, Sarah always prayed she and George would have that kind of bond.

"I see it!" exclaimed Savannah, her eyes glowing.

"So, if Zelag and I are correct, one of these coins was made by our late friend Shadiro and the other by his killer."

Sarah's eyes widened, and she stood with mouth agape. After realizing how she must have looked, she brought her hands to her face, turning away from the others and composing herself.

"Let's see what I can find then," said Savannah, putting a coin in either hand. Sarah wasn't sure which was which, so she didn't try to bother and keep track.

Savannah closed her eyes and Sarah watched intently as the magic unfolded. A faint glow started in Savannah's hands, as if emanating from her palms. As the glow died down, Savannah opened her eyes.

"You're right. One of these was made by Shadiro. The other one is calling me to the east, somewhere in the wilds of Erathal. I'm not sure where, but I can track him."

Sarah was in disbelief. All this time learning from Savannah and not once did she bring up this profound sense of divination.

"How did you do that? Can you teach me?"

Savannah looked at her apprentice and smiled. "Yes, it's quite a simple spell. I bet you would pick it up in a week."

So far, this was shaping up to be the most interesting and eventful week in Sarah's memory. She could hardly wait to follow through with this hunt.

But she couldn't leave her kids!

"I uh," Sarah started. "I definitely look forward to learning." She finished with a half-smile.

"Alright, if you want to guide me on the way, I can just take Savannah along," said Zelag, stretching his neck. "Should we start on the trail now?"

"Hold up," Artimus Jr. stepped over. "I've heard stories of your investigations back in Erathal City," he said looking to his father. "There's no way I'm staying behind now that we have an opportunity to actually investigate a murder."

"Yes," added Artimus. "And I am not sending Savannah off on her own."

"Fine, you can tag along. And you too, Little A."

Artimus Jr. scrunched his face.

"I should definitely stay behind to watch the kids," Sarah interjected. "But George could maybe get you part of the way there. Perhaps he could send you to Dumner as a starting point? Or perhaps to the old forest camp?"

"Maybe he can come along with us," Zelag suggested. "He could cut down our journey significantly, especially our return journey."

"This could still take a few days though," Savannah added. "I'm sure he doesn't want to be away from his children that long."

"Then it's good that he can use those portals of his," replied Zelag. "He can go home every time we need to make camp."

Sarah glared at Zelag.

"I know you wouldn't understand caring about anyone other than yourself, but some of us actually enjoy the time we get with our families."

Zelag's eyes widened as he turned towards her.

"I see you've grown some claws since I left. They look good on you."

Rolling her eyes, Sarah marched towards the door.

"I'm going to wait for George to return outside. You discuss your plans. But limit them to the four of you. My husband can decide for himself how much he wishes to assist."

Stomping outside, Sarah threw the door closed behind her. She looked around the tiny front porch and decided to keep walking. After putting a few meters between herself and the home, she stopped and let out a loud sigh.

Looking down at her hands, she took a deep breath and allowed herself to think more about the situation. She hadn't known Shadiro well at all. In fact, she hadn't even had a complete conversation with him. But it felt so odd to see him there, dead in his home.

Marftaport was supposed to be a safe haven, a place where everyone could live peacefully and watch out for one another. Seeing violence right here in her own backyard was jarring. And having to deal with Zelag's return wasn't helping matters at all.

Fortunately, as she started to drift into darker thoughts, she felt the faint call of magic. Looking up, she saw a portal form just outside the cabin. She walked towards it, coming up alongside as George and Vistoro stepped through.

"Ah, hey again beautiful!" George hugged Sarah, holding her for an extra moment. She squeezed him, hanging on as she looked at Vistoro.

"The others are inside. Perhaps George and I could stay out here for a moment though."

Vistoro nodded, his eyes communicating understanding. He didn't say a word, giving a quick knock at the door before going inside.

Sarah stepped out of the hug, clasping George's hands and looking him in the eyes.

"The shapeshifter wants you to go with them to help track down Shadiro's killer. He thinks they can get through everything more quickly if you help."

"Well, he's right about that at least," he said pulling back his right hand and stroking his chin. "But how are we supposed to track down the killer to begin with?"

"Oh," Sarah's eye lit up, momentarily forgetting about her concerns. "Savannah can apparently track the killer. He left behind an enchanted coin he made, which I guess is all she needs to follow it to the source."

"That sounds like some impressive magic! And look," George sighed, taking her other hand again and peering into her eyes. "I can deal with being around Zelag. Someone came into our community and killed one of our neighbors. I have to do something, right?"

Sarah pulled away and took a deep breath. She closed her eyes and nodded.

"You're right, of course. Just promise me that you'll be careful with him. I don't trust him."

"Nor do I! But maybe I can teach him that the world doesn't exist simply for his own personal gratification."

Sarah smiled and hugged George tightly. He held her close, giving her a squeeze and kissing her forehead.

"I'm so thankful to have a wife as kind and understanding as you."

"Not as thankful as I am to have such a wise and loving husband."

The couple held on for just a moment more before separating, keeping one another's gaze, and smiling. It was the sound of the opening cabin door that interrupted the moment.

Glancing over, Sarah watched Savannah step out first, followed by Artimus, Artimus Jr., Zelag, and trailed by Vistoro.

The group all gathered around in a semi-circle, Sarah and George keeping a bit of distance from them. After a few seconds of silence, Vistoro spoke up.

"We were just discussing our next move. George, I'd like to request you fetch Morn and Neman from Jaldor's farm. I will speak with Tel' Shira and call for a community meeting in the longhouse. In the meantime, I agree with the plan of action Zelag recommended."

Everyone turned and looked at George.

"George, we obviously don't want to pressure you," interjected Savannah. "So, if you even want to just bring us all to the farm when you fetch Morn and Neman, that will get us started well enough. But we would all appreciate if you joined us on this quest."

Sarah looked at her husband. He nodded.

"I will journey with you. But if this journey takes us more than a few days, I'll have to leave you to continue without me. And I'll need an hour to go spend some time with my kids and let them know I'll be gone for a few days."

Looking to Zelag as her husband spoke, Sarah watched carefully. He shifted his stance, but his face remained stoic. She wished she could read what he was thinking.

"That all sounds like a plan to me," said Artimus. "We'll need about an hour to gather some supplies."

"Oh, and I will go with you to fetch Morn and Neman," added Vistoro. "I haven't met Jaldor yet and would like the opportunity to do so."

"Of course, why don't we head off there now. Sarah, did you want to walk home, or should I drop you off there first?"

"I think I'll walk," replied Sarah.

She figured the walk home would give her extra time to think. The skirmish with the hájje had been bad enough, but now having someone killed this close to home still left her uncertain and, if she was being honest with herself, a bit scared. Walking home would help her process everything, at least that's what she told herself.

"Well, enjoy the stroll," said George, leaning over and giving her a kiss.

She smiled after, closing her eyes and offering a nod.

"I will see you soon," she said.

George nodded, lifting his staff, and pointing to his left, away from the group. Sarah stood and watched as he gathered the energy for the spell.

"Ixidor!" he exclaimed, opening the portal.

He glanced back at Sarah, tilting his head slightly to the left and raising his eyebrows.

"I'll think about that one," she replied with a smile. "Definitely not your worst one."

Grinning ear-to-ear, George motioned to Vistoro.

"After you!"

Vistoro stepped through, and George approached, pausing for a moment, and looking back at his wife.

"I love you, Sarah."

"I love you too."

ChAPTER XI

Erathal Forest, Abandoned Camp
15 Julla, 1149 MT

Zelag glanced back at the others, remembering why he preferred to work alone. Sure, it was nice to have George zap them about the continent. The idea of starting at the Avatar's old forest camp was brilliant, but now as they stood by the scattered remains of an old lean-to, he couldn't help feeling impatient. He'd make much faster time flying overhead as a roc.

After all, he only really needed Savannah to track the coin. But since his suggestion to travel alone with her met with so much opposition, here he was. And while George might get him home a bit quicker, as they passed through the camp, Zelag couldn't help but wonder if that benefit would be outweighed by his slow pace.

"It's amazing how quickly the forest has reclaimed this land," said Artimus Jr. as they strolled through some thicker foliage.

"It's been more than thirty years since we were last here," replied Savannah.

"Has it really been that long?" Artimus Jr. asked.

"I'm just happy I put us in the right place!" exclaimed George.

Zelag rolled his eyes, turning back towards the group.

129

"Let's just pick up the pace and get out of here. There's no sense in sticking around this decrepit place."

Turning back around, he marched forward, brushing aside some vines, and pushing into a clearing. He paused as he looked around, his heart skipping a beat as he remembered this place. The clearing was still devoid of any trees, but the grass and weeds had grown to be over two meters tall.

Through the thick grass, he could just barely discern the outline of chairs and benches. Most of them were broken and scattered, but there was no mistaking where they were. This was the old outdoor temple, a place where he had spent every morning for nearly a year of his life.

Savannah stepped into the clearing and knelt at the ground. Zelag considered her for a moment, watching as her aura intensified, a vibrant green light pouring from every pore of her body. The magic flowed out of her hand, coursing through the temple and permeating the grass. With a low hum, the grass retreated, shrinking back into the ground beneath. After only a few moments, the entire field of overgrowth looked like a well-managed field, the grass only a few centimeters tall.

Broken and rotted piles of wood were spread throughout the old temple. Benches were barely recognizable, but as he looked towards the old, gnarled seating, he could feel a pit in his stomach and a knot in his throat. His eyes twitched.

"Sixty years is still too soon to return," Zelag mumbled, stomping off to the east.

He didn't want to let the others see him.

Even after all these decades, this place was so deeply etched in his memory that he just couldn't shake it. He ducked under a large oak branch, considering for a moment how the tree had grown since he last passed through. The whole area was so overgrown and for a fleeting moment he felt like melding into the scenery -it would help squelch his feelings.

Branches and vines scratched at his leather armor as he pushed through the thicket and trudged further from the group. After a couple minutes of struggling, he made it out into another clearing. He paused here, more emotions flooding in as he vividly recalled what this looked like so many years ago. The tents, the people...

"You're thinking about her, aren't you?"

Zelag turned to Savannah, his mouth trembling. He could feel tears in the back of his eyes screaming to escape.

"How can I not? I avoid this place for a reason," he was struggling to steady his voice.

"You know," Savannah walked up alongside Zelag. "Did I ever tell you about Allessandra?"

Zelag tilted his head to the right and narrowed his eyes. What could this possibly have to do with his memories of Casandra?

"I didn't think so," she continued. "But you see, Allessandra is a fellow member of the Mage's Guild. She came to Marftaport about twenty years ago. And for the first ten years, I did everything I could to avoid talking to her. Because you see, she reminded me so much of Casandra."

131

"Blue eyes, ruby red hair, even the pattern of scales on her tail reminded me of Casandra." Savannah placed her hand on Zelag's shoulder. His instinct was to pull away, but something held him in place as the druid continued.

"Worst of all, she joined the Guild as a geomancer. And one day she confronted me about it. I won't bog you down with the details, but as I got to talking with her, I had to admit myself. Casandra wouldn't want me avoiding one of her kind simply because I missed her. No, she would want me to treat her with the same love and kindness Casandra showed every single person she met."

Zelag could feel the tears escaping his eyes. He pulled away from Savannah and wiped his eyes.

"And what's your point?" he spat.

"Casandra would want you to find peace. She'd want you to be happy. And as one of her mentors, I must say, I want you to be happy too. You carry a burden that no one else can imagine. Your entire species was taken from you. And the one person you really connected to afterwards was taken away from you so violently. I just hope you can open your heart again and realize there are others who care about you too."

With a shake of his head, Zelag sniffled and looked back at Savannah. She matched his gaze, her serene green eyes peering into his soul.

"You might care," Zelag said. "But I don't know if my heart is strong enough to bear losing anyone else. It's easier to go through this world alone."

"Perhaps, but it's not just me who cares. Remember the shenanigans you and Artimus Jr. used to get into when he was younger? How about the adventures you had with my husband and the sparring matches with Luna Freya, Morn, and Neman? We all care about you, and it might be easier for you to be alone, but what about us?"

"What about the Petersons?" Zelag quipped. "They would be happier to never see me again."

Savannah took a step towards him, her flowing hair blowing in the cool spring air. The scent of jasmine wafted through the air. The druid narrowed her gaze, looking at Zelag intently.

"That was your fault, and it was a big mistake you made. But Evorath teaches us forgiveness. And if you sincerely apologize to Sarah and George, I'm sure they could find it in their hearts to forgive you. You up and leaving didn't help anything, and it left us all worried about you."

"Maybe," replied Zelag breaking eye contact and looking past Savannah to the west. He saw some rustling, and a moment later Artimus came through, followed by Artimus Jr. and a few seconds after by George.

"I checked by the road," proclaimed Artimus as he walked up to Savannah. "And it looks like a single horse came through here not more than an hour ago. If it is our killer, it means he has been driving his steed hard. But it pretty much lines up with our estimates on Shadiro's time of death."

Zelag averted everyone's gaze and wiped his eyes. His eyes tingled as he concentrated to make sure there was no residual redness from the tears shed.

"That's still a lot of ground to cover for just two days. Could his horse really have kept up that pace?" Artimus Jr. asked.

"We're after someone who used magic to forge coins," Zelag said turning back to the group. "An extraordinarily fast horse means the scales fit the dragon."

"I guess that's true," replied Artimus Jr. looking down.

Savannah had looked down as well, clutching the coin in her right hand. Her aura again lit up, a calm and stable outpouring of green as her hand glowed. A moment later, as the light died and her aura normalized, she smiled towards her son.

"I can confirm whoever made this coin is to the southeast. He's not far, but I can feel he is on the move."

"Then let's get moving!" exclaimed Zelag with a clap of his hands. This conversation might have pulled his attention from memories, but the sooner they got away from this old camp, the happier Zelag would be.

"Hold on," Savannah stepped over and put her hand on his shoulder. "Allow me."

Once again, her aura lit up. Zelag watched the green energy pouring out from the forest around them and converging on Savannah. She held her hands straight out in front, palms open. His human eyes couldn't detect it, but his Preajin gifts allowed him to watch as green mist floated out from her palms, running through the trees. As the mist passed, the foliage spread apart, creating a path for them to follow.

Zelag squinted, stepping forward and watching the spectacle unfold. It was a miraculous sight, trees bending away, vines tightening around branches, and overgrowth shrinking from sight. The path kept expanding, stretching along for as far as his human eyes could see.

"Wow, mom. I've never seen you do that before!" Artimus Jr. exclaimed, walking up to the mouth of the new path.

"I don't think you'll see it again anytime soon either," she replied, her voice softer than before. "But I figured that would help us catch up."

Artimus stepped over to his wife, reaching into a pouch at his side and pulling out an apple.

"Do you need to rest?" he asked holding out the apple.

Savannah shook her head and accepted the fruit.

"No, let's get going. George can tell you, there was a lot of latent magic left here. I just used what was available. This should keep me moving fine," she finished holding up the apple and smiling.

"Great," replied Zelag. "Then let's move onward."

Without looking to see if the others were following, Zelag took off with a start. If he had been alone, he would have shifted into something quicker at this point. Perhaps a wolf, or maybe even a cougar.

As it was, he still needed Savannah to lead him to his prize. Once he had the pendant, he would come up with an escape plan. For now, he needed to stick with the party.

After marching for a few minutes, he took a brief pause and glanced back. Seeing the rest of the party trailing not far behind, he grinned and turned back around. This was just like old times. The only thing missing was Luna Freya and her snarky comments.

This march continued for the better part of an hour, and only then did they reach the end of Savannah's path. At this point, Zelag considered the light trickling in through the trees. By the looks of things, they had less than an hour of daylight remaining. Unsure which way to go next, the shapeshifter looked back to his companions.

Artimus Jr. was leading the march, with George far enough behind that Zelag had to wait a few minutes for everyone to reach his location. Tapping his foot impatiently, he let out a loud sigh as George finally arrived.

Fortunately, Savannah wasn't wasting any time. She had closed her eyes, channeling magic to track the coin maker.

"It seems our killer has stopped, likely to make camp for the night."

"How much further to go?" Artimus asked.

"You know it's not exact, but we're close. Maybe a few more kilometers through the trees here." Savannah motioned east southeast.

"Alright, it's my turn to do a little reconnaissance," said Zelag. "Keep going towards the killer. I'll find you outside his camp and let you know what we're up against."

He stepped forward, glancing back at the others and grinning. "You may want to look away if this still makes any of your squeamish."

Not waiting for a response, Zelag concentrated on the form of a fox. Small, nimble, and quick enough to make short work of a kilometer, this form always served him well for reconnaissance. The little whiskers, the bushy tail, the large ears; they all came into focus in his mind.

Then he thought of the internal anatomy, his bones beginning to creak as his body transformed. Heart, lungs, liver, all his organs compacted, his bones grew denser as they compacted, the popping of ligaments causing excruciating pain as his body kept shrinking to form.

His leather armor and various blades melded into his very essence. Over the decades, he had become proficient integrating these external tools into his form. But the side effect meant an even more painful transformation. Moaning as he went to all fours, he felt the steel of his blade softening and melding with his armor to create the orange fur.

Whimpering as he completed the transformation, he stood in place for a moment and panted. With only a brief glance at the others, he took off into the foliage.

The price of transforming was always worth it.

He dashed through the woods, ducking under gnarled branches, leaping over large roots, and squeezing through even the tightest of corners. As he ran, he paid close attention to the smells of the forest. This fox nose was quite proficient.

Ignoring the various fragrances of spring, he smelt the typical mixture of composting vegetation. Along the way, he passed a few fragrant mushroom patches, a menagerie of different bird droppings, and some dead animals. But as he darted east, he picked up what he was looking for, the unmistakable odor of horse manure.

As he drew closer to the smell, his nose picked up some other familiar odors. Whoever they were after was an elf by the smell of things. Pausing to sniff around, Zelag spotted his first visual clue.

There was a lot of grass around, some of it recently trampled by someone wearing boots. Slinking forward, Zelag spotted hoof prints next, and as the smells grew stronger, he knew his prey was not far ahead.

He listened intently as he crept forward, his bushy tail sticking straight out behind. There was some thick overgrowth just ahead, a large willow with branches stretching in every direction. Vines grew all around, with thick thorny bushes providing a natural barrier. But as he pushed forward, he peered through into a clearing.

This elf had to be the most flamboyant murderer Zelag had ever come across.

Standing in the clearing, scratching a brown draft horse behind the ears, was a short brightly clothed old elf. In fact, the clothing must have been considerably brighter than they appeared, because Zelag had never seen such a clash of colors through these fox eyes.

But there stood his target, a wide-brimmed blue hat set upon his head with a yellow ribbon tied across. With a matching yellow vest and scarf about his neck, the elf had to be at least seven hundred years old judging by the wrinkles on his face and hands. And he was talking to his horse.

"Yes, you are a good boy, aren't you? Oh, yes you are! Here, you deserve a treat for running so hard. You know when we get home, I'm going to treat you to a whole bushel of carrots!"

The elf nuzzled his horse, reaching around into the saddlebag and pulling out a carrot. As the horse crunched away, Zelag was tempted to make his transformation back to human form and capture this eccentric killer himself. But he needed to first make sure he was alone.

His nose told him that was the case, but to confirm he snuck around the camp, keeping careful to hide behind foliage as he did. The elf was still fawning over his horse, which left him distracted and allowed Zelag to make his search quickly, unconcerned about rustling some leaves.

Confirming there was no one else around, Zelag retreated a few meters through the thicket to the west. He barred his teeth and focused on his human form.

The pain of the transformation was a little less intense when growing, his bones cracking as they expanded and lost some of their density. His chest felt heavy as his ribs cracked open wider and his heart filled with more blood. Careful to focus on the separation of his leather armor and steel weapons, he did his best to stifle his moans of pain as he completed the transformation.

Coming back to human form, he stood up to full height and scratched behind his head.

"Stupid insects," he muttered, grasping a tick between his thumb and index finger before pulling it out from his neck. With a quick squeeze of the pest, he flicked it off into the grass at his feet, stroked his beard and looked at his hands. Everything felt right, the pain fading away within moments.

With a deep breath, Zelag looked back to the west. The others would likely be another few minutes at least. He might still need them, but he saw no harm in subduing this flamboyant old man in the meantime.

Drawing his short steel sword, Zelag burst through the brush.

The old man shrieked, stumbling away and causing his horse to neigh as it brayed back. Losing his balance, the old man landed just to the right of the horse. Zelag ran towards him, keeping his sword held back.

"Stay down," he ordered, eyes narrow.

The old elf held up his hands, nodding in agreement.

His horse snorted, backstepping and nodding towards Zelag.

"Shhh," Zelag whispered, lowering his blade, and holding up his free hand to try and calm the beast. The horse scratched at the ground, snorting.

"If you want to keep him, calm your steed."

Zelag offered his hand to the old elf, who hesitated for a moment before accepting. Pulling him up to his feet, Zelag took a step back and kept his sword trained on his enemy.

"Don't even think of fleeing."

"Oh, I -uh. No." The old elf stammered.

He reached for his horse, patting him on the side and shushing him.

"It's alright boy. You'll be alright."

As the elf patted his horse, Zelag realized this old man did more than just forge coins with magic. His body was alight with arcane energy, a smooth white magic flowing from his hand and calming the horse.

Which meant his next move was inevitable.

Watching the elf slow down his patting, Zelag saw the crafty old man shifting his gaze towards him. And his aura grew dark, a powerful green energy being gathered from the plants around him. With a shout, he turned and hurled a green bolt.

The green energy struck Zelag in the chest, dissipating immediately.

"I'm more than meets the eye," said Zelag with a smile. "And I'll let you have that one. But make another attempt to escape, and I will kill your horse. Understand?"

The old elf appeared in shock, his mouth hanging open and eyes wide as he took a couple steps back.

"Now sit back down," Zelag barked.

With a slow nod, the elf lowered to the ground, leaning against a tree and keeping his hands up.

Just as he did, Zelag heard some rustling from the overgrowth behind him. With a glance, he watched Artimus and his son come through, bows drawn. Taking in the scene, Artimus shook his head and lowered his weapon.

"You called it George," he shouted through the foliage.

Savannah and George pushed into the clearing next, eyes darting around to assess the situation.

"And who do we have here?" Artimus replaced his bow on his back, dropping the arrow in his quiver. "I never thought we'd cross paths again Ornathorn."

The old elf growled -a guttural noise that Zelag would have never expected. His face went red, his nostrils flaring as he glared at Artimus. After a moment, he broke his stare and began laughing.

"Artimus Atyrmirid. I thought I might run into your traitorous face." His voice sounded deeper than before, a maniacal tone taking over.

"We're going to have fun."

CHAPTER XII

Middle of Erathal Forest
15 Julla, 1149 MT

George kept his mouth shut tight, his lips curled as he looked between Artimus and this elderly elf: Ornathorn.

The old man was laughing maniacally.

When they left Marftaport that afternoon on the trail of a killer, George would never have imagined the killer to look like this. Bright blue pants, hat, and tunic accented with a yellow vest, scarf, and ribbon around the hat. But it was probably the hat that was most off putting.

He thought to himself that next time Sarah gave him grief about his tasteful pointed hat, he'd have to bring up whatever this monstrosity was that Ornathorn wore. It had a rounded top, the brim at least thrice as long as George's own hat. And the way the ribbon wrapped around and tied up in a bow made it look rather effeminate, or so George thought.

In either case, it wasn't, oddly enough, the elf's attire that made this discovery so shocking. It was his short stature and frail build. How had he even managed to kill Shadiro?

"He used magic to calm the horse and tried some sort of offensive spell on me before you all arrived," said Zelag, as if hearing George's thoughts.

Rubbing his chin, George focused on Ornathorn, trying to get a sense of just how powerful he might be.

Ornathorn himself didn't seem to have an unusually high amount of magic. But George could feel he had some powerful implements about his person. Yes, it was his rings, at least part of it. He wore five rings in total, one on each index and ring finger and an additional pinky ring on his left hand.

Immediately, he could tell both ring fingers were adorned with opals, a zircon on his right index finger, a moonstone on his left, and it appeared the pinky ring was simply made of gold. Together, this would help him store a fair amount of magical energy, but he felt more latent power around the elf.

"Is that derga spider silk?" George asked pointing to Ornathorn's ribbon.

Ornathorn ceased his laughter, looking at George with a deranged smile.

"Only the finest!" Ornathorn snickered.

"Alright, so what is this guy's story?" Zelag asked, looking at Artimus.

"I'm not sure. Last I saw him, he was a stablemaster in Erathal City."

"You're not sure?" Ornathorn leapt to his feet. George squared his stance, holding up his staff defensively. The others all took defensive stances as well, Artimus pulling out his mythril sword and pointing it towards the insane murderer.

Ornathorn stopped just centimeters from Artimus's blade.

"Of course, you don't consider the consequences your actions might have on other people," Ornathorn began.

"You remember how you left last time you saw me?"

Artimus narrowed his eyes, nodding after a moment.

"Yes, I rented a horse and carriage. And I made sure that you got both back, even if it wasn't me who returned them. So, what vendetta do you have again-"

Ornathorn threw his head back, laughing maniacally.

"What vendetta? You deserted your position in the Republic! And I provided you with the means to leave the city. You know I spent twenty years in the castle dungeon for aiding in your escape? No? Of course, you didn't, because you're a selfish son of a dragon!"

George had never seen this particular expression on Artimus's face. His eyes sagged, a frown forming as his face loosened and he looked down. As the experienced hunter took a step back and lowered his sword, George could only guess the expression represented shame.

"I'm so sorry Ornathorn. I had no idea."

"Ha! Ha, ha, ha!" Ornathorn leaned in, placing his hands on his hips, and wagging his head side-to-side.

"What else did you expect? You think the Chancellor just allowed all you deserters to go without punishment? You were the first of many to leave, which I'm sure you know. But when the others followed, that fat old tyrant Ulagret really cracked down. He knew it was too risky to go after you all directly. And what good would it have served?"

"But he found a way to deter others from leaving. I was one of the many who paid that early price. What better way to deter people from leaving than placing the blame for their departure on any friends, family, or business acquaintances left behind? In my case, the simple act of loaning you a horse and carriage meant I was stripped of my entire livelihood!"

George looked at the others. It felt like he could cut through the air with a knife, and he hoped someone else knew what to do.

"I'm sorry," started Artimus.

"Take your pity party somewhere else," interrupted Zelag. He stepped between Artimus and Ornathorn, puffing out his chest and pointing to the ground. "And sit your rear back down before I do it for you."

Ornathorn sneered, taking a step back and lowering himself back down to a seated position.

"Let's cut to the chase," Zelag continued, not paying any mind to the others. George could see Artimus was still having trouble processing what he had just discovered. In the years George had known the elf, he had never seen him hesitate, not in anything. But now, as he stepped away from Zelag and Ornathorn, it was clear Artimus was deep in thought.

Savannah went to his side, placing a hand between his shoulders. Artimus Jr. appeared just as dumbfounded as his father, his hands hanging halfway up his torso and looking at Zelag as the shapeshifter spoke.

"We know you killed that lizock, whatever his name."

146

"Frankly, I don't care how it went down or why you felt the need to kill him. If I were to guess, I'd say he had a superior forgery, and you were just cutting out the competition. But it's not you I'm interested in. And you know my traveling companions here don't believe in imprisonment or revenge. So, when I tell you we'll let you go free, you know I mean it.

"But here's the deal, while they might be a bunch of sanctimonious do-gooders, I'm just a mercenary after a payday. If you want us to let you go, you'll have to lead us to the big boss. I want The Albino."

Despite all his faults, George had to hand it to Zelag. He didn't mince words.

Ornathorn appeared to be thinking Zelag's offer over. His eyes were downcast as he twiddled his thumbs.

"If he knew I betrayed him, there'd be nowhere in Erathal I'd be safe. And if you understood the influence he has, you wouldn't be asking for him. What is it you want from The Albino?"

Zelag glanced back at George and the others. With a devious grin, he turned back to Ornathorn.

"If you don't lead me to The Albino, I'll force feed you your horse here. And I'll-"

"Zelag, no!" Artimus stepped forward, shaking his head.

"I told you; we're doing this our way. We're not going to kill his horse or torture him in any way. But Ornathorn, we do care. Why did you kill Shadiro?"

147

"Eh, fine." Zelag said with a sigh. "George, Savannah, let's have a chat while Artimus tries 'his way' of getting Ornathorn's cooperation. Because I'm sure that will work."

Zelag rolled his eyes, arms wide as he approached George and motioned for Savannah to follow.

George wanted to listen as Artimus asked questions. And the last person he wanted to huddle up with was Zelag. But something in his gut told him to follow.

"You keep an eye on your old man," said Zelag as the trio stepped to the far edge of the clearing.

Zelag went to wrap his arms around both Savannah and George, but the wizard pulled back, holding up his right hand.

"You can say what you need to from there."

"Alright. Understandable. Look, if I can't torture this crazy old guy, there's no way he's betraying The Albino. You guys have heard the stories -that's just not someone you betray. But here's what I'm hoping. Can you somehow keep track of me?"

With raised eyebrows and pursed lips, George rubbed his chin and looked at Savannah.

"You could track a runestone, right?"

George considered the question.

"I suppose so. Why do we need to track you?" He glared at Zelag, cocking his head.

"What if we let this lunatic escape and I trailed after him? He'll lead me to The Albino, and then I can call you in to help take care of things."

George stepped back and rubbed his chin. Holding up his right index finger, he shook his head.

"I'm not so sure about that last part. Tracking the stone might be easy enough, but there's no way I know of for you to communicate when you need us back."

Savannah scrunched her nose, twirling her hair between her fingertips. George recognized this as her thinking face.

"Zelag, I'm not sure we can really stick with you beyond this point."

"What do you mean?"

George wondered the same thing, stepping back and looking at the druid with wide eyes.

"I mean we tracked down the killer. And based on what he's told us, I'm inclined to bring him back to Marftaport and offer him the opportunity to make penance."

"But this is our opportunity to stop The Albino!" Zelag pleaded. "And we all know this isn't the first time he's caused suffering to that community of yours. Especially with this hájje situation at hand, wouldn't it help to know that you're safe from at least one threat?"

Savannah closed her eyes and shook her head.

"The Collector is a threat to everyone. But what exactly are your plans here anyway?"

149

"I intend to reclaim Vistoro's family pendant," replied Zelag.

"The pendant Vistoro sold to help start Marftaport? That pendant? Are you intending to return to it whoever it now belongs to?"

"I'm not the one to say who something does or doesn't belong to," retorted Zelag. "But I do know I was hired by a lizock representative to retrieve the pendant and return it to the Lizock Kingdom, where it belongs."

George looked back at Savannah.

"By a lizock representative? You mean someone from the castle?"

He glanced back at Zelag.

"If it's being returned to the King, where else would the representative be from?

"I don't know," replied Savannah, looking off into the distance and twirling her hair. "But there's something not adding up. I want to get Tel' Shira's insight on the situation."

George nodded along. This seemed like a reasonable approach. And it had the added benefit of allowing George to go home to his family.

"It kills you doesn't it!" the shrill sound of Ornathorn's voice pierced their conversation, pulling George's full attention back to Artimus.

Artimus Jr. had taken up a flanking position, hand on his sword but maintaining a relaxed posture.

George moved closer to the conversation. He noticed Savannah and Zelag suspended their debate as well, creeping in behind him.

"I simply don't believe you," Artimus replied. His voice was strained, his tone showing he had not overcome the initial shock of Ornathorn's claims.

"Yes, you do. You're just afraid to admit it. There is no redemption for me, no going back. I am who I am. And I thank you for getting me started down this road. Without you, I'd still be an obscure stablemaster serving a self-righteous tyrant."

Ornathorn cackled, clenching his fists, and looking to the sky. "But instead, I get to serve one of the most brilliant leaders to ever grace this world. Your master has abandoned her own world. My master commands the very shadows of Erathal."

Artimus shook his head, stomping away from Ornathorn. Artimus Jr. kept his eyes trained on the killer.

Zelag marched back in, winking at Artimus as he approached Ornathorn.

"Alright, so we all acknowledge The Albino is not to be crossed." He declared. "I wonder what he's going to do when rumors of Ornathorn's betrayal start circulating. I don't imagine he'll be too happy about that."

"As if he'd believe wild rumors. He has many eyes and ears -they would not be so easily fooled." Ornathorn looked around nervously, blinking rapidly and speaking with an erratic tone. Zelag had always been good at extracting information from others, at least in George's experience.

"You sure you're willing to take that chance?" Zelag asked with a smile. "Because in my line of work, I imagine a lot of those eyes and ears are listening. And I know how to give a rumor some credibility. I can't wait to tell everyone how you're planning to challenge The Albino."

George paused to consider the ethics of this tactic. But even if he disagreed with the methods, there was no way he could prevent Zelag from following through with his threats.

"I guess we should just let him go then," George interjected. "Maybe if he runs back to The Albino fast enough, he can convince him your stories are untrue."

"Yeah, we have no real use for this murderous little coward," replied Zelag. "George, perhaps you can drop me back at Paxvilla with one of your portals. I know that some of the town guards are in The Albino's employ, though I know they just call him 'The Collector' there."

George kept his eyes on Ornathorn, and he could see Zelag was doing the same. And if the old murderer was trying to hide his fear, he was failing miserably. His face was stretched out in terror, his eyes wide and mouth trembling. He even winced at the mention of 'The Collector'.

With shaking hands and an unsteady voice, Ornathorn chimed in.

"Alright! I get it. I'll um. He can't know I've betrayed him. But what is this...? What is this 'portal' you speak of?"

Zelag crossed his arms and nodded towards George.

152

"George here has developed a way to travel across vast distances through the ether. He's the wizard, so maybe he can explain the process to you. But I can be in Paxvilla in the blink of an eye spreading stories of your betrayal. Or you could tell us where The Collector is, and George can send us there instead."

Ornathorn looked at his hands, his eyes lighting up. George could practically see the neurons firing as his hands stabilized, and his face tightened. With a deranged smile, he looked between the two.

"I am due back in two days. I cannot delay my return without running into trouble. But if you leave me here to travel unmolested, I'll provide his location. However, I need Artimus to promise you will keep your word. And that you will not let him know I was involved."

George glanced back at Artimus. The elf was shaking his head, rubbing the bridge of his nose with eyes closed. After releasing a long sigh, he opened his eyes and lowered his hand, offering an affirmative nod.

"I promise none of us will reveal your involvement. You can go free. But I ask you to follow one additional caveat. You will never return to Marftaport unless it is to offer repentance for your crime."

With a sinister chuckle, Ornathorn nodded in response.

"Very well Mr. Atyrmirid. I will never return to your little community."

Ornathorn reached down into one of his vest pockets.

153

Both Zelag and Artimus Jr. adjusted their stances, hands on their swords as they watched Ornathorn remove a small stone.

"This is the key you'll need to find The Albino's castle. It is shielded from the naked eye, sitting at the northern edge of the Marta Plains. Look for the tree that doesn't belong and insert this stone into the keyhole to open your eyes. But be warned: getting inside is the easy part."

"The northern border of the plains…that's nearly 200 kilometers," exclaimed Zelag.

"Ah, but I have a solution for that," replied Ornathorn holding up his right hand.

"George, was it? Come here. I will show you where you need to send your portal."

Glancing around at the others, George looked to Savannah for guidance.

"Zelag, what shade of magic was Ornathorn using when he calmed the horse?" Savannah asked.

"White."

"It should be safe. I'd guess he can share his thoughts. Zelag, just make sure whatever he does to George is that same white magic."

Zelag nodded.

With a nervous gulp, George approached Ornathorn. He stood with his hands at his side, closing his eyes as Ornathorn placed his palm on his forehead.

CHAPTER XIII

Jaldor's Farm
15 Julla, 1149 MT

Jaldor looked around nervously at all the guests. He didn't want to be an ungracious host, but feeding all these people was a lot of extra work. Not to mention it created the most uncomfortable atmosphere in his small farm home.

Irontail had been kind enough that he and his fellow centaur were all eating outside. But it seemed Mojo and the two younger barghest, Luna Freya, and the massive troll Oogmut were all too aloof to consider they were causing an inconvenience by crowding inside.

Of course, these thoughts made Jaldor feel a bit guilty. If it weren't for all those gathered, his farm and family would have all met their end. But there had been no activity since the initial attack. Perhaps the hájje really weren't coming back. A comforting thought, but one Jaldor doubted.

Luna Freya belched, leaning back in her chair, and extending her claws to pick at her teeth.

"If you don't decide to join us in Marftaport, you'll have to share this chicken recipe. That was the tastiest bird I've ever eaten!"

"It is delicious," Morn added.

"Yeah, really good," blurted Neman between bites.

Glancing at his wife, Jaldor watched her finish chewing. She put down her fork and smiled, brushing her curly hair back.

"I learned the recipe from Jaldor's mother," she said nodding towards Ruth, who was seated just a few chairs down.

"Oh, I can't take too much credit," Ruth replied, not taking her eyes from her plate as she carefully cut her potato.

Even after all these years, her black skin weathered and wrinkled with so many decades of farm work, she still had a youthful enthusiasm to her voice. Her gray/white hair was cut to her shoulders, her brown eyes glowing at the compliment.

"You see," Ruth continued, spearing the piece of potato, and holding it up. "Our chickens get some extra treats that help make their meat that much tastier. It's really David who came up with the idea. Have you not shown them the larvae boxes you have set up out back?"

Despite the fact that he was actively chewing a piece of chicken, David shook his head and replied mid-bite.

"No, I didn't show them. Why would they care about boxes full of insect larvae?"

Jaldor noted the specks of chicken fly from his father's mouth. The grizzled old farmer had spent a lifetime on this farm, which had left him frail and weakened. He was hunched over in his seat, his weathered skin seeming to lose color every day. While his mind was still sharp enough, Jaldor feared his body wouldn't last much longer.

Luna Freya chuckled, an odd clicking sound accompanying her laugh. Since Jaldor hadn't met any other felite, he guessed it was normal for them.

"Oh, you old curmudgeon," Ruth shook her head.

"Anyways, those larvae keep our chickens nice and fat," Ruth continued. "Most chickens are nothing but bones and muscles. That extra bit of fat is what you're tasting."

"Well, when you do decide to join us in Marftaport," interjected Mojo his grizzled old tone rough and discordant, "maybe we can convince you to raise some more chickens. You'll probably find no shortage of people willing to help around the farm if it means getting this tasty meat."

Jaldor considered the old barghest's words. With his various scars, weathered and matted fur, and a morbid choice in jewelry, he was the most intimidating of his group. But over the last couple days, Jaldor had come to recognize his wisdom and kind heart.

"Just remember, we still haven't decided," replied Samantha. "We all have to be on board with the move, or we're staying put."

"And I had more questions for the elves," added David, letting more particles of food fly as he spoke.

"Daddy," Jaldor looked to his left, smiling down at his daughter. Her green, innocent eyes sparkled.

"Yes Mary?"

"I think it would be fun to live with these big monsters."

Jaldor's eyes widened. He could feel the color leaving his cheeks. But the clamor of laughter that followed a brief pause allowed him to relax. With a light sigh, he looked around.

Even Oogmut, who had talked the least of all the guests, was chuckling. It was a hearty and somewhat disturbing noise, but as the troll slapped his chest a couple times and shook his head, he let out a final snort.

"I think it would be fun to have a little girl like you around," he said, his voice low and slow. "And we could make sure you and your family are always safe."

Mary giggled, smiling ear-to-ear.

"See daddy? They are fun and nice monsters."

Luna Freya coughed, shaking her head and chuckling.

"Dinner was delicious. Thank you again," she said. "I'm going pay a visit to the outhouse and then check on Irontail and the rest of the four-legs before Mary here causes me to laugh too much more. Mary, don't ever change."

The felite stood, her chair hitting the wall. She looked around, frowning and pushing behind Morn and Neman towards the door. As she got to the end, she looked up at Oogmut.

"Mind letting me through old timer?"

Oogmut looked down and grinned. The two stared at one another for a few seconds before Luna Freya sighed and threw up her hands.

"Before I get old maybe? Please!"

Oogmut stepped aside, bumping into Jaldor's seat.

"Oh, I'm sorry Jaldor," he apologized.

"Don't worry about it."

Luna Freya shook her head, scooching past and opening the front door. Jaldor glanced back after her, dropping his fork as he saw a couple of familiar faces at the door.

Standing just outside was Artimus, and standing right next to him, Savannah.

"Look who's back!" Luna Freya exclaimed. "Now, if you would step aside. I've got an appointment with the outhouse."

Savannah brought her hand to her face and shook her head. Both she and Artimus parted, allowing Luna Freya to slip through outside.

"Well, that pleasantness aside," said Savannah after a pause. "I'm sorry to see we're interrupting dinner. But when it's convenient, maybe those of us who don't live here can gather outside to discuss a few things."

"I'll be happy to join," Jaldor's father shouted, raising up his right hand. He smiled.

"It's good to see you both again!"

Artimus and Savannah exchanged a look, both returning the smile.

"It's good to see you too David," said Artimus.

"I just still can't believe that you look the same after all these years. Did daddy tell you Mary? I met these two elves when I was just about your age!"

Mary giggled.

"No gampa. You told me! They rescued you."

"Yes, they did," replied David with a satisfied nod. "None of us would be here today if they hadn't helped us get to safety."

"We just did what any reasonable person would have done," Savannah suggested with a smile. "Morn, Neman, Mojo, Oogmut…maybe you can join us outside?"

Jaldor stood up, regarding the few scraps left on his plate. "I think I will join you while they finish up if you don't mind. I'd like to discuss something myself."

"Of course," Artimus said motioning outside. "Please, join us."

Offering a quick smile towards Samantha and a reassuring pat on the head to Mary, Jaldor stepped outside. He shut the door behind him, stepping a few meters away from the home before turning to address the elves.

As he turned back towards them, he realized there was another, unfamiliar face with them. This new face appeared human, with tan skin and an unkept brown beard. His bright blue eyes told the story of a man who had seen more than his fair share of bloodshed. Standing just a few centimeters shorter than Jaldor, the man appeared to be no more than a few decades old, around the same age as Jaldor.

160

"Oh, this is Zelag," offered Savannah, as if anticipating his question.

"Zelag. It's nice to meet you. I'm Jaldor, the caretaker of this farm," he said extending his hand.

Zelag regarded his hand for a moment before accepting, his grip firm as they shook hands.

"First, thank you again for what you've both done. I owe you and your friends everything I have." Seeing Artimus open his mouth as if to respond, Jaldor held up his hand. "Please, allow me to continue. I don't know if you've heard, but Paxvilla has officially closed its borders. And apparently, there is some talk about the town that they are expected food shortages thanks to the recent attacks.

"But since that night, no other farms have been attacked. And according to the guards I spoke with, there's been no additional signs of hostile activity. Is there a chance that, thanks to your interference, the hájje have reconsidered their plans to attack?"

"No way," blurted Zelag immediately. "I've been keeping tabs on those snow skins since we killed their creator. If they're sending armies out of their fortress, they're preparing for something bigger than attacking a few little farms."

"For how long?" Jaldor gaped.

"He's older than he looks," interjected Artimus. "And I fear he's right. Before we came here, we checked in with Tel' Shira, the one who foresaw the first attack here."

Jaldor could feel the hair on the back of his neck stand on end. There was a knot in his stomach, and as a cool breeze blew past, the faint smell of cow manure filling his nostrils, he felt sick to his stomach.

"What did she see?" he asked, gulping down some air.

Artimus and Savannah exchanged a look. Although he didn't know either of them very well, he knew the look. It was the look he'd give his wife when he was about to tell Mary there was nothing to worry about; even though there most definitely was.

"I don't know if Vistoro explained it, but he plays a big part in interpreting many of her visions. A lot of time, it's not so clear cut," said Savannah.

"But they think there's going to be an attack?"

Artimus closed his eyes and nodded. "We might as well tell him everything we know."

Savannah frowned. "You're right. So, they are still not sure where there is going to be an attack, or exactly how big it will be. But they are fairly certain whatever is going to occur will be happening in five days."

Jaldor looked around at the others, hoping they would have something to add. His mind raced, trying to consider the reality of another attack. As he was struggling to think of a response, another participant entered the conversation.

"So, the rumors are true," came the deep voice of a centaur. Irontail trotted over, extending his hand to Zelag.

"It is good to see you again Zelag. What has it been? Two years?"

"Two years?" Artimus and Savannah both looked at Zelag, mouths open and eyes wide. They turned and looked up at Irontail.

"And why didn't you ever let us know you had seen him?" asked Savannah.

"I made him promise not to. Otherwise, he wouldn't have seen me that recently either."

"I'm sorry," interrupted Jaldor. "I don't want to spoil your reunion, but I can't let you stop there. What else did your seer report?"

Savannah lowered her head, eyes closed as she spoke. "Like we said, it's usually vague. But she sees darkness growing from the hájje kingdom. Yesterday, they sent a couple of scouts down that way to check, but we won't hear back for at least another day or so."

"Maybe you should prioritize that scouting trip," Jaldor suggested. "Have your friend George create one of those portals and you can have a closer look."

"We may just do that," replied Artimus. "But there's another opportunity presenting itself right now that we have to consider."

"And what's that?" asked Jaldor.

"There's a man called 'The Collector' that we're after," answered Savannah. "He's built an empire on theft, coercion, and

163

murder. Everything he owns is stolen and anyone he views as a threat is eliminated. He threatens the peace and security of everyone in Erathal. We've tracked him down and have a chance to put a stop to his operation."

"Is he involved with the hájje attack?" Jaldor was trying to make the connection. He didn't understand how they could consider anything but the imminent attack on Paxvilla.

"No," Zelag clapped his hands together. "But our window of opportunity is closing. We have to make a move as soon as possible if we hope to maintain the element of surprise."

"Yes," interjected Artimus. "If you are ready to commit to coming to Marftaport, we'll be happy to allow you to listen in to our planning. If not, I'd ask you please grant us privacy to discuss our next move."

"You won't leave us undefended?" Jaldor asked.

"No, of course not," replied Irontail. "I will remain behind with my warriors to ensure your farm is safe."

Hearing the creak of his front door, Jaldor turned back to witness the other visitors leaving his home. It was jarring to watch Oogmut leave, the troll ducking low and still just barely clearing his head through the doorway.

And as the party converged, Jaldor was finally able to admit the truth. His world would never be the same.

CHAPTER XIV

Zelag stepped through the portal, sweeping his gaze around to take in his surroundings.

This was definitely the Marta Plains. And it was a brilliant place to build a secret castle.

The air around here was thick, a permanent, dense fog coating the entire southeast peninsula. All the flora and fauna of this area were made to kill, including some of the most lethal mushrooms in the world. In fact, the last time Zelag had come this way, it had been to harvest some piscoshrooms.

Now, looking about, he was reminded just how eerie the setting was. Sticking to his human senses to avoid overwhelm from all the latent magic floating about, he could only see a few meters away, which was filled with nothing but overgrown patches of grass, dead trees, and his fellow travelers.

The air smelled a mixture of stinkhorn mushrooms, damp wood, and a hint of rotting flesh, likely from a nearby dead animal. As the rest of the party came through the portal, George stepping through last, they all wore various looks of disgust and apprehension. Oogmut was the only exception, his face stoic as he looked about. George seemed to notice this fact as well.

"This really doesn't bother you, does it?" the wizard asked looking up at Oogmut.

The wrinkly old troll looked down and smiled, the gaps in his teeth creating a skin-crawling expression.

"This isn't so different than the swamp I grew up in. Aside from my fellow trolls living in Marftaport, this may be the only place left in Erathal that any trolls call home."

"Well, it's good we have you here then," said Luna Freya. "I don't really feel like fighting any trolls." She pulled out her gauntlets, clasping one after the other on her hands.

The other party members were all preparing as well. Artimus Jr. inspected his sword, making a slight adjustment to his belt. Mojo was inspecting some pouches on his waist while Morn drew his axes and Neman his swords. As the portal closed, George even started stretching.

"Alright, let's get ready," said Artimus pulling out his bow and preparing an arrow. "They could already be watching."

"So, which of these is the tree that doesn't belong?" Artimus Jr. asked, squinting through the fog.

George stepped forward, walking past the group towards an old dead tree. "That's the clever part. If you don't know where to look, you won't see it."

With a wave of his staff, the tree pulsed with life, leaves growing out from every branch. As the black bark turned brown and came to life, it revealed a small hole perfectly centered on the trunk to fit the stone. Savannah smirked as the others looked upon the tree in awe.

"So, it was a mirage," observed Zelag stepping forward and removing the stone from his pocket. "I guess I should have been looking for that. Are we all ready?"

Zelag glanced back, looking to the party to ensure everyone was prepared. Oogmut stood at the rear, with Artimus and Savannah only a meter before him. Mojo, Morn, Neman, Luna Freya, and Artimus Jr. all formed a loose line next, and George was immediately behind Zelag.

"Maybe you should step back George."

"Oh, right." George looked around. Holding his staff sideways, he ran back to stand next to Oogmut. As he took his position, Zelag looked back at the tree. Placing the stone inside, he spoke as instructed.

"I come to serve The Collector."

With a flash of light, the area before him erupted to life. Fog cleared away in a circle, as if opening a large window. A stone path appeared just a few meters past the tree. The path was lined with small rose bushes, leading up to a wide staircase. And that is where things got impressive.

Zelag stood in awe as he beheld the gigantic fortress. It was massive. The outer curtain walls were nearly six meters high and stretched out at least sixty meters on this front face. Two larger towers, at least nine meters tall, were set on either side of the stairs leading up to the front gate. These towers featured arrow loops and machicolations, with crenelations to keep the defenders safe from outside assault.

The front gate featured two massive doors, which were conveniently left open. Its portcullis was also conveniently withdrawn. Looking beyond this main entrance, Zelag noted the batters of the wall, with additional towers and battlements placed every six meters or so.

"This thing is better protected than Paxvilla's Castle," muttered Zelag, trying to wrap his head around how anyone could have built such a massive fortress without the support of a large population.

Shaking his head, Zelag looked back at the others, who were all similarly impressed. Most were hanging with mouths agape, eyes wide as they tried to take everything in.

"Alright," shouted Zelag in a muted tone. "I think you all have to file onto the path before I remove the stone."

It took everyone a few moments to get their wits about them. But after some fumbling, everyone proceeded forward. After George, who fell to the back, stepped onto the stone path, Zelag pulled the stone from the tree. Looking with his natural Preajin senses, he could see the window closing. Unsure of how important it was to slip in before the veil was restored, Zelag dashed onto the path, the window snapping shut behind him.

Zelag paused as he glanced behind. For in the place of the ugly and dank Marta Plains, it appeared they were now on a large plateau overlooking the ocean. This tracked with what he knew of The Albino's obsession with beauty.

Now over the initial shock of the castle's scale, Zelag turned back and kept his eyes training all around for any signs of activity. It seemed their timing was perfect. Or at least that no one was currently outside the castle walls.

Everyone circled around, making a loose huddle at the base of the large stone steps.

"Alright," said Zelag stepping forward. "We follow the plan. It seems our informant left out some key information about the scale of this place, but that doesn't change the strategy."

He paused, looking around to make sure everyone was focused. Predictably, it was Luna Freya whose attention seemed to be straying.

"Luna, focus in! Morn, Neman, Mojo, you three are to remain outside with George. If you are discovered, you know what to do. The rest of you, let's reassess when we're through this first gatehouse."

With an exchange of nods, the party proceeded forward. The three barghest and George followed up the stairs, stopping just outside and taking position to the right of the gate. As the rest of the group proceeded in, Zelag continued to get a lay of the land.

As he feared, a second gatehouse came into site. These inner walls were at least 50% taller than the curtain walls, with similar battlements. Getting through the first gatehouse, Zelag glanced to either side.

Again, it seemed timing was on their side as he didn't spot any movement. But he was surprised by what he saw. Beyond the steps leading up to the towers, there were substantial stacks of lumber, and dozens of large crates and barrels. More unexpected were the various buildings between the inner and outer wall. This wasn't just a retreat or a last defense for The Albino and his men. This was a permanent residence, a community for his gang to live.

In terms of the inner gatehouse, the construction was like the outer one, but it appeared the walls might be even thicker, which was impressive considering the curtain walls were at least three meters thick.

"Alright. Savannah, Oogmut, Artimus, and Little A." Instructed Zelag. Luna Freya chuckled at the mention of 'Little A'. "You all stay outside these gates. If you want to do some recon on these smaller structures, go for it. Just make sure to stay out of sight. Luna, it's you and me beyond this point."

"Just look old times," she quipped with a toothy grin. "Let's see if you've gotten any better."

Zelag ignored her remark and continued forward. He crept as softly as he could, his leather boots inaudible to his ears.

"I can still hear you," Luna whispered as she stepped out ahead. She slunk low to the ground, squatting on her hind legs and keeping her hands held up close to her chest. Her tail stuck up behind her, offering counterbalance.

"You haven't changed at all, have you?" Zelag whispered in response.

"I mean, I haven't abandoned my family like some jerks might do. But I've gotten even better at everything, which I know is hard to believe. Don't worry though. I'll make sure you can keep up."

Zelag shook his head. He wasn't going to let Luna's arrogance bother him. Though, her first remark did sting, whether he would admit it to anyone or not.

The pair continued through the second gatehouse, making their way towards the inner courtyard. But as they reached the edge of the gatehouse, Luna nodded to her right. She pressed up against the wall, motioning towards Zelag.

Nodding in acknowledgement, Zelag slowed his approach and came up alongside her.

"I hear something," Luna whispered.

Zelag nodded, considering what he could see from this vantage point. Again, he was surprised and impressed by the scale of this place.

Just before him was a wide-open courtyard, with a winding path leading towards a central keep. The path leading to the keep was well-manicured, with flowers and trees lining the way. But there were stalls set out along the path as well, all currently covered with tarps.

Glancing to the left, he noted more permanent structures, and had a guess at what Luna was hearing. They even had their own farming operation. No more than fifteen meters from their location, Zelag spotted a pen with pigs. And beyond that, he could see a mill and some small fields of grain.

"I was never really part of your family though," whispered Zelag after taking in the scene.

"What?" Luna looked at him with her face scrunched.

"We all thought of you as family. You just never wanted to stick around and commit to that. And then what you did to George and Sarah…not cool man."

"Alright, alright," whispered Zelag shaking his head. "Let's forget about it and focus on the mission."

"I wouldn't expect you to be able to have a real conversation anyway," Luna shrugged. Zelag clenched his fists.

"But look here," she continued. "If they have their own farm, stalls for merchants, and everything else that got here, I don't think we need to stay hidden. I bet we could walk right into the keep without anyone asking a question."

"You're probably right," Zelag mumbled. "I wonder if I should take an extra precaution though."

"If you change into Ornathorn, I think that might violate Artimus's word."

"I know," said Zelag standing up. "So, I have to do something a bit risky. I've only done this once before, so keep an eye out for anyone. It might take me a minute."

Zelag took a few steps back, keeping close to the walls. He closed his eyes, focusing on his lizock form. Transposing Shadiro's features over this form, he tried to make the necessary connections. With a deep inhale, he considered how this might affect the overall energy of his body in this form, trying to account for the shorter stature and less muscular build of Shadiro as he began his transformation.

Usually, he relied on studying the living creature to assume its form. Imitating a complex life without doing so could result in not only a painful transformation, but severe injury. He took on the very essence of his shape, becoming that thing. Without a living reference for Shadiro, he had to try this way. And as expected it hurt. A lot.

His bones creaked and organs stretched, an additional chamber coming out from his heart. Lungs shrunk down, merging before splitting into three smaller lungs. His body felt like it was on fire, his skin blistering and blackening as he clenched his jaw, trying to keep himself from screaming.

He yelped in pain as the tail extruded from his back, his spine stretching out. Ribs became denser, toes webbing together, and fingers elongating. What was usually a discomfort was instead the most painful transformation in recent memory. And as his extra eyelids took shape, he clenched his fists and moaned.

With every bit fitting into place, he felt a searing pain in his chest. Sure enough, the wound that Shadiro had when Zelag found him was trying to come through. He focused on the healthy form of his nameless lizock face, especially thinking about a whole, functioning heart. And letting out one final gasp, he stumbled against the wall, breathing heavily.

His skin cooled, opening his eyes and heaving as he looked down at his hands, wiggled his toes, and wagged his tail. Everything seemed to be working. And with a quick pat of his clothes, he confirmed his armor had also made the transition without issues, fitting to his new form. Most important, his sword still hung on the belt at his side.

"Next time, remind me not to watch," said Luna, her face drawn back, and lips shut tight as she looked at Zelag.

"Sorry, I was too focused on not killing myself to think about how bad I looked in the process."

"Touché. I guess I'm your bodyguard for this ruse?"

"Yeah, just stick about a meter behind me, maybe a bit to the right."

"Oh, is that how a bodyguard follows?"

Luna shrugged, eyebrows raised before she exhaled and relaxed her face.

"Alright, no one asked for your sarcasm," replied Zelag shaking his head. Scratching behind his head, he stepped out into the courtyard. As usual, his lizock form was plagued with dry skin, which kept him scratching as he walked.

Fortunately, Luna Freya took her part in this play seriously. So, as they meandered down the path to the keep, she kept her lips sealed. Zelag looked around as they walked, trying to be subtle, glancing sideways to get a better lay of the land.

He recognized quickly that the exterior walls had to be wider than he first thought. And by the distance of this path, it was even longer than that still. There was another field off to the east, which looked like it was growing vegetables at a quick glance. To the left, he spotted what appeared to be a collection of houses, likely for some of the transient members of this hidden little community.

Of course, the castle keep was another impressive feat by itself. The structure was at least thrice as large as Vistoro's manor, large stone walls and expansive windows showing whoever lived inside had expensive taste. With massive turrets on either side of the keep and a central tower positioned towards the back, it looked like it could house at least a few dozen people. And it was well fortified too, battlements matching those on the two layers of outer walls.

Zelag approached the main entrance, which consisted of massive mahogany double doors. To his surprise, the right door creaked open upon his approach.

Pausing and placing his hand on his blade, he regarded Luna. She had also assumed a more guarded stance, coming up next to Zelag and regarding the door.

A large troll was behind the door, pushing it open. The troll was massive in stature, nearly four meters tall and clothed in full steel plate armor. It was even uglier than most trolls Zelag had encountered, face scarred and malformed, its left eye sitting at least six centimeters higher than its right. With a crooked nose and pale gray skin, it appeared no more than a beast of burden. And judging by the chains attached to its hands and feet, it was being treated as such.

Ignoring the pity he felt for this creature, Zelag was just thrilled to see they wouldn't have to go much further. For behind this troll, speaking with a young, tan-furred barghest was their target, The Albino.

Clothed in a purple robe tied with a gilded braid, the pale-skinned human strode through the doorway, motioning with his hands as he spoke. He wore his signature shoes, bright blue gator skin boots fashioned to resemble the head of the beast killed to make them. Walking with a pep in his step, his red eyes glowed with ambition.

Judging by the size of the barghest by his side and the studded armor he wore, Zelag guessed this was hired muscle. The twin swords hanging at his sides supported that theory.

With a subtle nod to Luna Freya, Zelag continued forward, keeping his head down but leaving his eyes fixed on The Albino and his guard. As the target drew near, Zelag looked up and stopped his advance.

"Good morning," he called with a wave.

The Albino stopped in place, looking at Zelag and Luna. He steepled his hands, tapping his index fingers together a few times and looking them over. After a few moments, he looked Zelag right in the eyes and pointed towards him.

"You're not who you appear to be."

"I told you we couldn't underestimate him," Zelag moaned, reaching for his sword.

"I'll get the dog," declared Luna.

She dashed towards the barghest, her stance low and claws pulled back as she prepared for the attack. The barghest drew his swords, growling as he charged towards his foe.

Luna leapt into the air, flying over her opponent. The barghest attempted to adjust his approach, his momentum forcing him to stumble as he attempted to swing both swords overhead and intercept her. Taking advantage of her off-balance foe, she landed on all fours and sprung back to her feet, swinging a wild uppercut.

Her attack landed, causing the barghest to reel back and fall. He kept his grip on his swords, but at the cost of leaving himself vulnerable to another attack. Zelag's attention was pulled away before he could confirm Luna finished the job.

The Albino, though initially too shocked to react, had composed himself and pulled out some sort of musical instrument. It was small and circular, fitting perfectly between his two hands. As he brought it to his lips and blew, it released a startlingly loud, high-pitched note.

Zelag winced at the noise, which reminded him of a banshee. And with a quick glance at Luna, he realized it was enough to halt her attack as well. She and the barghest had ceased their struggle and were now covering their ears, bent over in pain from the noise.

Within another moment, the sound began to overwhelm Zelag as well, his vision blurring. He could feel pressure building in his head, the pain running down his neck and causing him to go down to one knee. Struggling to think of a defense, he decided to try something drastic.

With a scream, he took both his index fingers and shoved them into his ears. The loud pop from his bursting ear-drums left him disoriented for a few seconds, but as he felt the warm blood flowing from his ears, he looked back at his enemy and smirked.

His head still hurt, but the overwhelming sensation from the banshee flute had faded. Coming back to his feet, Zelag drew his sword and approached The Albino.

Realizing his attack was failing, The Albino lowered his instrument and took a few steps back. He was mouthing something, but with his hearing impaired, Zelag couldn't tell what. It didn't matter.

Not wanting to give his enemy time to react, Zelag lunged forward, swiping with his sword. His swing landed true, cutting clean through The Albino's left hand. Though Zelag couldn't really hear it, he assumed The Albino screamed in pain as he fell to his knees and clutched his dismembered limb.

Offering a quick glance back at Luna, Zelag confirmed she had maintained the upper hand, a notion that made him smile considering his own situation. In either case, it appeared she was done with her enemy, his body limp and unmoving as she rose to her feet.

"I can't hear," Zelag shouted, pointing to his ears. "But I'll carry him if you watch my back."

Luna nodded, which was good enough for him.

Without delay, Zelag knelt by his dismembered foe, tossed him over his shoulder, and ran back the way he came.

CHAPTER XV

Luna smiled as her attack worked and the barghest tumbled back. She extended her claws, savoring the moment as she went in for the kill. Then came the sound from the underworld. She cried out in pain as the shrill sound filled her ears. What kind of awful weapon was this?

Falling to her knees, she retracted her claws and clasped her ears. Usually, she appreciated her felite hearing. But in moments like this, she would have preferred to be a troll, or something less sensitive to such shrill noises. Her entire body felt like it was being torn apart, an intense pain radiating all over as she tried to drown out the sound. Her vision blurred, and for a moment, she thought she might lose consciousness.

And then it stopped.

Blinking a few times, she took a deep breath. The pungent smell of her opponent helped clear her head, lashing her tongue a few times as she stood back up. It seemed the barghest was not so quick to recover, only just beginning to come back to his senses.

"Why would you do that to yourself? What are you?" The Collector asked. Zelag approached him with sword drawn, blood dripping from his ears.

"That's commitment," murmured Luna Freya, focusing back on her foe.

Just as the barghest went to reach for one of his swords, Luna pounced. With claws extended, she pierced the dog's chest, and swiped at his throat. As the life left his body, her attention was pulled away yet again.

"ARGH!"

The Collector let out a blood-curdling scream.

Luna had to blink a few times to ensure she was seeing correctly. She grinned and considered the severed hand on the stone floor. Zelag wasn't messing around.

"I can't hear," yelled Zelag, pointing at the blood coming from either side of his head. "I'll carry him if you watch my back."

"You are one crazy feklar," Luna said with a nod.

As Zelag knelt and pulled The Collector up over his shoulder, Luna Freya did a quick scan of the courtyard.

Zelag ran past, The Collector still crying in pain. But as Luna expected, that shrill noise drew some unwanted attention.

One by one, people were filing out of all the structures around the courtyard. Barghest, elf, felite, lizock, and human alike were all coming out to check on the commotion. And those they seemed confused at first, it didn't take long before they realized what was happening.

Luna sprinted after Zelag, cursing as the mob converged on them.

She caught up to her ally in just a few seconds, passing in front before considering the situation.

Slowing her pace to ensure Zelag wasn't left behind, she did a quick scan of the area. None of the approaching enemies would catch them in time, at least she didn't think they could. But there was a bigger threat to consider, the gatehouse.

"Zelag, pick up the pace!" she yelled, forgetting for a moment that he couldn't hear. "Oh, right."

She looked inside the gatehouse, where she spotted two more trolls. They looked identical to the first one tending the keep's door. And they were intending to close Zelag and her inside.

"Come on." She mumbled, keeping stride next to Zelag. There was no way she'd leave him behind, even if he might do so were the roles reversed.

Holding her breath, she ran just a bit in front of Zelag, clearing the first portcullis before it came down. But there was no way to make the second.

Screeching to a halt, Luna stumbled and stopped just short of the second portcullis as it slammed shut. Zelag made an even less graceful stop, dropping The Collector and stumbling right into Luna.

"Dammit Zelag!" Luna shouted. "We need some assistance here!"

Scrambling back to her feet, Luna did a quick assessment of their situation. No one else had made it into the gatehouse, which was helpful. Zelag was still prone, his face reminiscent of someone who had just been kicked by a donkey. The Collector was laid out unconscious just a couple meters away.

181

Artimus Jr. came up to the portcullis, glancing inside.

"I'll fetch George to get you out. Just hang tight. We have some opposition to deal with here."

Luna shook her head and stepped over to Zelag, her mind racing as she considered her options.

"You deserve this," she said with a smile.

Crouching over his face, she farted.

Zelag's eyes dilated, his tongue lashing out as he came to his senses and scrambled to his feet. Luna moved just out of the way, standing up straight and gesturing with her hands. She pointed to him, put her hands together, and then spread them apart.

"Transform. Fix your ears." She spoke slow and loudly, hoping he'd put things together.

With a scowl, he shook his head and took a few steps back. After glancing at The Collector, he started his transformation.

Luna looked away this time, turning back to try and see what was happening on the other side of the portcullis. She could hear the clamor that came with a violent exchange, but the thick iron bars obscured her view.

"Don't think I won't return the favor," came Zelag's voice. Or more specifically, his human voice.

Luna turned back with a smile. She shrugged.

"You appeared dazed. Was I supposed to leave you?"

"What did you even eat this morning?" he asked with a sour face, sticking out his tongue. "I can still smell it."

"Don't judge a lady. It's not my fault you can't handle yourself. We got The Collector at least, so just wait until George arrives. He'll get us out of here in no time."

"Well, I hope he comes soon," replied Zelag. "Because I think we're about to have company."

Luna closed her eyes, hearing the clanking of chains as she turned back towards the inner portcullis. Opening her eyes, she confirmed her fears. As the portcullis rose high enough, a wave of enemies filed in.

There were dozens of them. And in these close corners, there was no way she and Zelag could hold them all at bay. Worse yet, it seemed they had their most menacing soldiers at the front of their ranks.

"Maybe you should have transformed into someone more useful. You got a dragon yet?"

"Maybe you should just fart on them. That might be noxious enough to knock a few out."

"Oh, ha, ha."

The leading soldiers, twin brown barghests, growled as they approached. These were feral, more muscular than the one Luna had dispatched in the courtyard and armed only with their claws. Of course, this meant they were vulnerable, no armor or additional weapons for protection.

Fanning out from these two, an even greater threat revealed itself. It was a trio of felites, two black and white and the third orange with black spots. This third was the largest in stature, even bigger than Luna. He held a two-handed sword and took position between the two barghest. The black and white ones took position on either side, pulling out bastard swords and chuckling as they closed in on Luna.

"Maybe we can just throw their boss at them?" suggested Zelag as they came nearer.

He reached for The Collector, grabbing his intact arm, and pulling him closer.

"And we got what we came for," he continued, reaching under The Collector's robes, and pulling out the pendant. With a swift tug, he removed the pendant and placed it into one of his pockets.

Despite the humorous nature of Zelag's suggestion, Luna paused to consider it. Just a few more meters before the enemy was upon them.

"Let's do it," she shouted, crouching down and grabbing The Collector's legs.

Without hesitation, Zelag grabbed both arms. The two were in perfect sync, swaying back and forth once before coming back against and releasing the body forward.

They flung The Collector, sending him flying towards the center of the approaching enemies. All five of them hesitated, their eyes wide as they held their arms up. Keeping his sideway orientation, The Collector landed right in the center, causing the orange and black spotted felite to stumble back.

Trying to lighten the load, the two barghest reached in to help as well, causing them to fumble. That was all the opportunity Luna needed.

With their attention on their master, Luna charged forth and extended her claws. Zelag moved almost as quickly, drawing his sword and stabbing the felite on the right. Meanwhile, Luna slashed at the left one's throat, causing him to stumble back and clutch at the wound.

The nearest barghest had already recovered from dealing with his unconscious leader. He snarled at Luna, lunging forward and throwing a left hook. Ducking under the punch, Luna stepped to the side with eyes wide. It appeared the orange and black felite had turned to flee, The Collector held in his arms.

"Hey!" she shouted, pulling out a knife, and throwing it in one smooth motion.

Landing true, the knife stuck in the larger felite's thigh, causing him to trip and fall on top of The Collector. The barghest moved back in, this time snapping at Luna's left arm. Only narrowly avoiding the bite, Luna took another step back, her tail sweeping against the portcullis. She hated fighting in confined spaces.

Her opponent wasn't going to give her a second to think. He followed up with a slash, his left claw coming down towards Luna's face. Instinct kicked in, and Luna extended her claw overhead, palms facing towards the enemy.

She dropped to one knee, intercepting the attack with her left. She reached around with her right and slashed at his arm, drawing blood. Unfortunately, her commitment to blocking his first attack made her vulnerable to his follow up.

The barghest swung with his right, grabbing onto Luna's shoulder, and digging in with his claws. With searing pain in her shoulder, she glanced to the right, noting Zelag was still on the offensive. With a quick slash and seamless follow-through with a stab, he dispatched the second barghest. There was no way he was going to dispatch more enemies than her.

Releasing a primal roar, Luna stood back to full height, withdrawing her right hand and clasping onto the barghest's claw. Repositioning herself to grasp both his arms, Luna darted in head-first, headbutting her opponent square on the nose. With a yelp, the barghest stepped back.

Not allowing him time to recover, Luna pounced, digging both claws into her foe. Her momentum caused the barghest to fall back, landing flat on the stone. Without hesitation, Luna delivered a swift jab to his head, the final blow.

Looking up, she reassessed their situation. The rest of the mob was converging on them, and if they didn't do something soon, they'd be overwhelmed by sheer numbers. But while Zelag might have just been after the old dragon pendant, she was more interested in The Collector himself.

"Did someone ask for an exit?" George called from behind the portcullis.

"Not a moment too soon," Zelag replied.

"No, wait!" Luna shouted.

The orange and black-spotted felite had come back to his feet. He removed the throwing knife and tossed it aside. It seemed his master was regaining consciousness as well, letting out a low moan and rolling onto his side.

"We came for The Collector, and I intend to leave with him," continued Luna. "Zelag, you pull him through the portal. I'll come through as quickly as I can."

Not waiting for his response, Luna leapt for the enemy felite, her claws out. Much like herself, it seemed his large stature didn't impede his speed. He intercepted both of her hands, clasping her wrist, and barring his teeth. Her shoulder ached, the raw flesh from the barghest's strike causing her to wince as she struggled against the stronger foe.

"You won't be getting out of here alive," he growled, his deep menacing voice causing her hair to stand on end.

"That's no way to treat a lady," she grumbled, struggling to push back against her muscular foe.

Firming up her left foot for stability, she kicked with her right, aiming for her enemy's groin. Finding her mark, she watched as the larger felite's eyes dilated and he let out a high-pitched whine.

"And this is for thinking you could touch me," she said with another kick. This loosened his hold on her wrists, allowing her to pull away. In that moment, she observed two important things. First, George had opened a portal. Second, Zelag grabbed

The Collector. Propping him up, he pushed him through the portal. He didn't delay a moment before following behind.

Luna didn't want to leave without a proper sendoff. She regarded the two-handed sword her felite counterpart had dropped. With a smile, she grabbed the blade and swung in a wide arch, decapitating the black-spotted felite.

"Never forget the black terror, Luna Freya!"

Throwing the sword towards the remaining mob, she dove through George's portal.

CHAPTER XVI

Zelag closed his eyes, running his hands through his beard as he listened to the others debate.

The afternoon sun was beating down on his back, the eclectic smells of Vistoro's courtyard filling the air as a soft breeze swept through. And if this circuitous conversation wasn't bad enough, the dull pain in his ears caused his entire head to ache, the pain radiating out from behind his nose.

Standing nearest the home, Zelag considered the others gathered. Oogmut was just a couple meters away, cradling the unconscious Albino. Artimus and Savannah were standing side-by-side just a few meters to the east. Mojo and the barghest brothers had taken position to the south and Artimus Jr. and Luna were to the west. Vistoro was standing in the center of the group.

"All I'm saying," insisted Vistoro, "is that this was not what we formed this community for. Going after Shadiro's killer was one thing, but it's not our job to police the world. Who are we to render judgement on someone who has done none of us any harm? What threat is he to any of us?"

"We can't just be considered with ourselves," objected Savannah, stomping her right foot and clenching her fist. "We've been hearing stories about this 'Collector' for decades now.

Dozens of us who call Marftaport home have been harmed by his syndicate."

"But we can't even confirm that!" retorted Vistoro, throwing his hands out to the side. "All we have is hearsay and vague stories. For all we know he's just a cover, a unique face to keep attention away from the real villain."

"That would be a clever strategy," interrupted Artimus.

Zelag sighed as loudly as he could, exaggerating his breath and rolling his eyes in the process.

"He's the villain alright. You should see the sway he has in Paxvilla -practically has as much influence over the town guard as their Regent. From what I've gathered, he has some sway in Ulagret's court as well. And the Lizock Kingdom is crawling with his people."

"Having a lot of followers doesn't necessarily mean you are a villain." Replied Vistoro.

"Then let's consider it in simpler terms," interjected Luna, a hint of condescension in her tone. "He was using trolls as slave labor. Or do you think the trolls operating his doors and gates volunteered to be chained up?"

Vistoro frowned, glancing at the others.

"You're right, of course. But unless Tel' Shira has a vision from Evorath telling us to keep him detained, I'm not going to be a part of imprisoning him here."

"And that's understandable," replied Savannah. "I propose we keep him in the Mage's Guild dungeon for now."

"You have a dungeon in that tower?" Luna asked, her eyes lighting up.

Savannah shook her head.

"It's not really that kind of dungeon. We have a code of conduct that comes with Guild Membership and there are a couple of sins that could land you time in the dungeon. But mostly we just use it for experimenting with spells. Some of our members delve into some unpredictable magic, so having a controlled environment is important."

"And that's the reason I haven't joined their guild," replied Mojo.

Oogmut snorted, stifling a laugh.

"What?" Mojo asked, looking up at the troll.

"Oh, nothing." Replied Oogmut. "I'm sure your lack of guild membership has nothing to do with your conduct."

The barghest brothers sniggered.

"Enough," interrupted Savannah. "This isn't the time. If there's no objections, I'd ask Oogmut to come with me to the tower. When George and Sarah arrive, tell them to join us there."

Everyone looked around nervously. After a few seconds of silence, Artimus spoke up.

"Then I say we proceed for now. I'm going that way as well. We can regroup after The Collector is secured."

"Yes," replied Vistoro with a nod. "Why don't we all reconvene for dinner this evening?"

191

With an exchange of nods and some verbal affirmations, the group splintered. Mojo and the barghest brothers started south immediately, likely heading back to the rendezvous with George to be sent back to Jaldor's farm. Artimus, Savannah, and Oogmut all started south after them.

"Luna, Artimus Jr." Vistoro added before they had a chance to leave. "Why don't you both join me inside? I have a couple other things to discuss with you."

"Only if it includes some food," replied Luna, rubbing her injured shoulder. "You know how healing magic always leaves a pit in my stomach."

Zelag shook his head, starting off south after The Albino and his escorts.

"I'm going to follow you," he called ahead.

Artimus glanced back and nodded.

"Think we can't manage one unconscious demagogue?"

"If he wakes up," Zelag spoke jogging to catch up, "you might be glad I'm around. I told you; he has some unique, mind-altering magic."

"Does that mean you're sticking around?"

Did it?

Zelag really wasn't sure.

But he'd agreed to deliver this pendant to his employer. Could he really justify breaking that agreement?

"So, you're going to stick around for dinner, right Zelag?"

Lost in his own thoughts, it took Zelag a moment to recognize it was Savannah speaking. But her soft, feminine voice was unmistakable.

"Um. I'm not sure," Zelag stammered.

"You'd be welcome to." Continued Savannah. "I'm sure Vistoro could extend your usual accommodations."

"I wouldn't want to cause anyone discomfort at dinner," Zelag replied after a moment's pause.

"You know," Oogmut replied glancing back at Zelag. He looked at him for a couple strides, his eyes gazing right through the shapeshifter before turning his attention back front.

"Did I ever tell you about my water-dwelling friend Shelly? We've been friends since I was a small child," Oogmut's tone raised as he spoke.

"You mean the friend you always talked about that no one else in Marftaport has ever met?" Zelag asked, rolling his eyes. Artimus and Savannah exchanged a grin.

"Shelly is a shy turtle," replied Oogmut defensively. "But that's not important to the story. You see, many decades ago, when Shelly and I were both still young, we had a bit of a spat. The details don't matter, but the sad thing is…it was all my fault. And because I had hurt her feelings, I spent nearly three years without visiting her."

"Well, that's a different story at least," interrupted Zelag. "But does this have something to do with The Albino or have you gone senile in the last five years?"

Oogmut snorted, letting out a hearty laugh.

"Who's to say? I may have gone senile years ago. But no, that's not what the story is about. You see, when I finally went back to Lake Algarath, I made camp at our old meeting spot and stayed there for a fortnight before Shelly came back to shore. And you know the first thing she said when she saw me?"

"I don't know. What do imaginary giant turtles ever say?"

Oogmut shook his head and sighed.

"She asked me why I had come back. And I told her the truth: 'I missed you, and I'm sorry for what I did.' The next thing she said is something I teach all my students. And I remember it exactly as she said it. Her sea green eyes looked so full of sorrow and regret as she looked at me and formed a smile and said: 'That's all I wanted to hear. I forgive you.' And to this day, we continue to be great friends."

"I appreciate the sentiment," Zelag replied, following the others as they turned left on the road to the Mage's Guild tower. There were a few elves having a picnic by the pond to the north, but otherwise the road was only sparely populated.

"But I'm not sure George and Sarah are going to be as understanding."

"Maybe," Savannah interjected, not turning to look back at Zelag. "Or maybe if you were sincere and promised not to violate their trust again, they would feel your sincerity. I know you always consider them 'children' but let me remind you to the three of us, you're just a child too."

"And do you trust me?"

Oogmut answered first, stopping mid-stride, and turning to look down at Zelag.

"I don't know. Can you be trusted? Tell us, what was the real reason you were interested in this Collector? I noticed you didn't bring up Vistoro's old pendant to him."

Artimus and Savannah both stopped and looked at Zelag as well. The old investigator appeared to be studying his face, and the druid just seemed curious to hear his answer. She twirled her hair between her fingers, her eyes soft.

Though his first instinct was to lie, Zelag felt something he hadn't felt in the last five years. Guilt. And thinking about the conversation he had just the day prior, he could almost feel Casandra standing behind him, whispering in his ear.

"They're our family."

His lips quivered as he fought the uncertainty. He had never accepted that to be true. But as his gaze passed from the elves to Oogmut, he looked into the troll's eyes, contemplating the question and the intent behind it.

He saw only compassion.

"I have a source in the Lizock Kingdom," Zelag started, speaking slowly to maintain his composure.

"I've been doing jobs on and off for her for decades now. When I left Marftaport for good five years ago, I got heavily involved in her organization. Without going into detail, I was tasked with retrieving this pendant to pay off a debt."

Zelag bit his bottom lip, breaking Oogmut's gaze and looking down.

Artimus stepped towards Zelag, his boots clanking on the cobblestone street. He stretched out his arm, placing his hand on Zelag's left shoulder.

As Zelag looked up and met his gaze, the elf smiled.

"Let's get The Collector to the Tower and we'll discuss this more on the way. But I appreciate your honesty. Family doesn't let family suffer alone, so let's see how we can help."

Zelag nodded, releasing the breath he didn't realize he was holding.

As the elves turned to proceed, Oogmut stood in place, looking down at Zelag with a wide smile.

"To answer your earlier question, yes. I even trust you enough to bring you with me next month when I pay Shelly a visit. Since Lake Algarath has become too populated with Erathal City on one side and Hajjeona on the other, she's been heading more inland for her visits. I think she'll really like you."

Returning the smile, Zelag nodded.

"I guess I'll have to make sure I'm around for that."

Giving Zelag a soft pat on the head, Oogmut turned and proceeded east. The group walked for a couple of minutes without speaking, getting to the north road before continuing. Though it was still off in the distance, Zelag could see the Mage's Guild Tower up ahead.

"So, what kind of debt are we talking about?" Artimus asked, keeping his eyes on the road ahead as he stretched out his neck.

"The kind that if I don't repay soon will make this face unusable."

"And I know you enjoy the human form. Perhaps you could find another that works for you?"

"No." Zelag replied immediately. He took a deep breath.

"I've become so used to this body that it would just be so much trouble to learn a new one." Strictly speaking, this was true. Every new form took time to fully adjust to and understand. Of course, there was another reason Zelag preferred not to say.

"You should embrace a troll form," offered Oogmut. "I'm sure one of the people here will volunteer to let you use their likeness. It might include some stipulations that you participate in pranks with them though. You know how young trolls can be."

"Maybe we should consider ways to help him keep what he's comfortable with," suggested Savannah.

"I think turning over the pendant may be the only way for that," said Zelag scratching behind his head.

"Well then maybe that's what you do," replied Artimus. "But before that, perhaps you'd be willing to chat with Tel' Shira and Vistoro to get their insight."

Gazing at the road ahead, Zelag considered this suggestion. With recent events, perhaps it was time to return to Marftaport and work with these idealists, at least temporarily.

197

"I have a lot to think over," said Zelag after a few seconds of silence.

"Does that mean?" Savannah started.

"Yes, it means I'll stick around for the rest of the day. But no promises about tomorrow."

Artimus and Savannah exchanged a look. With a subtle nod to his wife, Artimus looked back at Zelag and smiled.

"Fair enough."

Looking ahead, Zelag considered the Mage's Guild tower. The tower itself looked just as he remembered, the symmetrical design and pale stone construction stretching into the sky. It had bright green double doors perfectly centered on the front of the tower. Aside from the artistically curved arch, the doors themselves were uniquely crafted, narrow, and tall, which made it almost appear as one large door from this distance. Matching windows completed the exterior construction, with corbels adding dimensionality and visual appeal.

The one thing that had changed was the landscaping around the tower. He distinctly remembered there being hedges, but now it appeared they had cleared the area. Instead, there was just the single willow tree, which had been left behind when the land was originally cleared.

Zelag considered the tree, noting a couple lizock sitting under it and enjoying the afternoon air. Looking back towards the tower, he spotted another unfamiliar face, a small satyr coming from the tower.

198

"Ahoy!" the satyr called, waving towards the group. Her voice was laced with honey, high pitched and almost disturbingly cheerful.

"Good afternoon, Ygabb," Savannah waved in response.

Ygabb was short, even by satyr standards, measuring no more than 1.3 meters by Zelag's estimation. She had splotches of brown and tan fur, with a streak of white between her asymmetrical horns. She wore a simple red robe and a small red, pointed hat adorned with a single violet flower. A small choker with a ruby in the center accented her outfit, and at her waist hung a short sword with a scabbard painted the same shade of red as her outfit. Skipping towards the group, she wore a wide smile on her face.

"It's a beautiful day to enjoy the outdoors, isn't it?" Ygabb asked. She stopped right in front of Oogmut, the comical difference in their height forcing Zelag to smile as this tiny satyr looked at up the massive troll.

"It is pleasant," replied Oogmut.

"Yes, I just wish we could spend more time enjoying it," followed Savannah. "However, we have urgent matters that might keep us indoors for the afternoon." She nodded towards the unconscious Albino.

"Ah, yes!" Ygabb squeaked. "Who is this unfortunate fellow? Do you need any help tending to him?"

"That's a bit of a long story," Artimus interjected. "But I'm sure Savannah can catch you up at the next Guild meeting."

"Yes," added Savannah. "And no, thank you. George and Sarah will both be joining us. But what you should know is this man is extremely dangerous. He uses mind magic."

Ygabb bleated, her eyes widening as she looked around. "So, one of you?"

"Removed his hand?" Artimus interrupted. "Yes, Zelag here did that." He motioned towards the shapeshifter.

"Zelag? Hmm…" Ygabb stroked her beard, looking down contemplatively. "Wait, are you the Zelag that used to live here?" she asked looking into Zelag's eyes.

"The one and only. But I'm sure whatever stories you heard are exaggerations."

"I'm sure," Ygabb giggled. "But I'd love if you found time to have some tea with me if you're sticking around. Meeting a real live Preajin has always been a dream of mine. I was always told that stories about your people were myths growing up, so it would just mean the world if-"

"Yes, I'm sure we can arrange something," interrupted Savannah. She glanced back at Zelag, raising her eyebrows and mouthing an apology.

With a sigh, Zelag nodded.

"Agreed," he added with a forced smile. "After current crises are resolved, we'll have to find an afternoon to chat."

"Oh, that's wonderful!" Ygabb shrieked, hopping up and down and flailing her arms. "Anyways, I should leave you to it. Here, let me get the door at least."

Spinning around, Ygabb drew a wand from inside her robe and flicked her wrist toward the Tower door. The doors creaked open, revealing the interior.

"Thank you," offered Savannah. "We'll see you later Ygabb."

Oogmut didn't even wait for Savannah to finish speaking. He stepped past Ygabb, starting for the door. The others followed suit, all filing inside the tower.

Though he rarely visited the Mage's Guild Tower in the past, Zelag was pretty sure the interior had changed significantly. For starters, it appeared all the torches had been replaced with glowing rune stones, much like the ones used in Sissera's Tavern. Additionally, the atrium had been spruced up some, portraits covering the walls on the left and right. It appeared they were portraits of all the current guild members.

Wooden floorboards creaked as the party stepped through the atrium. Zelag considered the stone staircase ahead, which, just as he remembered, only appeared to lead upstairs. It seemed this was still their destination, as Oogmut, Artimus, and Savannah proceeded through the doorway and towards the steps.

Oogmut stopped once inside, looking to the barren wall on the left of the staircase. He bent over and placed his hand on one of the stones, which was about chest height for Zelag. After holding his hand there for a few seconds, he drew his hand back and with a pointed index finger drew an invisible symbol on the wall. It was hard to distinguish exactly what he outlined, but as he finished the outline, the stone glowed.

Focusing on the stone, Zelag looked past the physical, his mouth dropping open as he figured out what was happening. The glow extended, but Zelag could already see the result.

This entire wall was a facade, solid to the touch but magical in construction. As the glow expanded, Oogmut stepped forward, stepping through the ethereal barrier of arcane energy.

"So that's where you hide it," murmured Artimus as he followed behind Savannah. Zelag kept to the rear, stepping through the barrier, and proceeding down the steps.

The staircase down was made of matching stone to the one above, but it was about a meter wider. Oogmut stopped near the top of the steps, waiting for Zelag to pass. As he did, he placed his hand back on the barrier, infusing some of his own energy into the wall and causing it to resolidify.

"Is that really secure against enemy mages?" Zelag asked as the group descended the steps.

"As far as we know," replied Savannah. "But you can see it, can't you?"

"Yes, though I don't think anyone else in Evorath can see like I do. Can't others detect that it's just a facade though?"

"Maybe one day," replied Oogmut, shifting his grip on The Albino and hoisting the unconscious criminal over his shoulder. "But before we reveal the entrance to new members, we always have them try to find it themselves. So far, no one has been able to."

"And no one who helped fashion it knows of a way to detect it," added Savannah. "That is, except by already knowing it's there and entering the correct password."

"For what it's worth," said Zelag, glancing around the sparse corridor as they descended. "I've seen my fair share of hidden rooms and passages, and this one is the most unique. Even seeing it there, I couldn't breech it without the password, could I?"

"Nope," replied Savannah. She flipped back her hair and glanced back at Zelag. "And no one nonmagical can breech it really. Part of the password involves casting a spell."

As she said this, they reached the bottom of the steps. This area was still void of any decorations aside from glow stones on the left and right walls. The landing area was a rectangle, about 20 square meters in size. And before them was a solid iron door. But his Preajin eyes revealed something about this door that his human eyes would have missed. Glowing with a prism of multi-color arcane energy, this door was perhaps the most heavily enchanted entryway he had ever encountered.

"You really pulled out all the stops," Zelag rested his hands on his hips, looking the door over. Inspecting further, he realized there were no visible hinges on the door.

Oogmut and Savannah went to opposite ends of the door. They looked at one another before holding out their hands in sync and drawing some sort of rune in the air. A semi-circle, a triangle, an X shape -once again, Zelag couldn't follow along with the pattern.

"Aethri bonum firigatti zu relbo." Savannah and Oogmut chanted in sync. And as they uttered the last syllable, the ground shook and the door ascended, retracting in the ceiling.

"My ancient elvish is a bit rusty," admitted Zelag. "But that sounded like gibberish."

Savannah looked at him and shrugged, a faint smile on her face.

"No one will be guessing that passphrase," Oogmut chuckled.

The Albino moaned, dampening the collective mood and causing everyone to fall silent. Exchanging somber glances, the party all stepped through the open door.

CHAPTER XVII

Marftaport, Mage's Guild Tower Dungeon
16 Julla, 1149 MT

Sarah held George's hand, focused on maintaining steady breath as they descended the stairwell. The cool, damp air, combined with the spartan design of the steps, always made her a bit uneasy. She never liked the idea of being underground much either, which is why she clutched onto her husband so tightly. There was no way she'd be trapped if he was there to portal them out through the ether.

"Do you think they've already started?" she asked, keeping her eyes down, counting each step as they descended.

George rubbed his chin, furling his eyebrows as he glanced up. He then proceeded to look at his free hand, counting his fingers and mouthing out gibberish.

"I have no idea," he teased with a shrug.

Looking at his smiling face, Sarah gave him a squeeze and offered a nervous grin.

"It's just that this is all so different than anything we've dealt with before. Repelling hájje attacks and now imprisoning some evil mastermind. How far is this going to go?"

George gazed into her eyes, stopping their descent before they rounded the final turn. He took her other hand, holding on and just breathing for a few seconds.

"I wish I was powerful enough to magically fix the world for you. But the truth is, I don't know what to expect and I'm as scared as you are. Knowing that you're on my side, fighting for our family…that's what keeps me going."

Sarah smiled, leaning in and hugging George. She held him for a few seconds, grasping him tight. She wished to cling to that moment, to hold on and forget about the troubles of the world. And for those few seconds, she did just that.

"Together," George continued, "we'll make it through anything."

After another moment, Sarah drew back, still smiling.

"Alright," she said determinedly. "Let's see what everyone is up to."

Turning round the corner, the couple proceeded down the stairs to the dungeon. With the iron door already opened, they were immediately greeted by the inside cells. The dungeon itself was only slightly larger than the landing, but it was divided into four cells and one staging area.

Stepping into the dungeon, Sarah's attention was drawn to the noise in the back left cell, where she spotted their allies, along with the now conscious Collector. Oogmut was standing at the far corner, looking down at the prisoner. Artimus and Savannah were both standing directly in front of the prisoner, while Zelag was positioned nearest the cell door.

The Collector had been shackled to the wall by his one remaining hand. He sat in the corner, cradling his other wrist and averting eye contact.

"That's really quite the castle you've built," said Zelag, pacing back and forth.

"We've all heard whispers about your grand estate, but even the wildest stories didn't do you justice. Like my friends already told you, we're willing to let you go, but only if you are willing to cooperate. So, I'll ask again. How many of those people are there willingly?"

Sarah and George approached the cell, standing outside in the staging area. From that vantage point, Sarah was better able to see The Collector. He was frowning, his eyes fixated on the stump of his wrist.

"I recognize you," he muttered after a few moments. "You almost stole that pendant from me in Paxvilla last year. You're a shapeshifter, like one of those demons in the Xyvor, aren't you? That's why my magic has no effect on you; you are an actual embodiment of magic."

Zelag glanced back at the mages. Sarah immediately averted her gaze.

"What I am isn't important. Who you are is what we're interested in. Does anyone work for you by choice?"

The Collector looked up from his wrist, a sinister grin forming on his face.

"Oh, how I envy you," he exclaimed, his voice sharp. "To be able to mimic any form you choose. No concerns for aging, no vulnerabilities to magic. If I had your talents, I would have saved the whole of Erathal by now."

"This is a waste of time," interjected Artimus. He looked at Oogmut and shook his head.

"Maybe you're right Oogmut. Perhaps we should just go back in force and blow the cover on his castle. Zelag can drop a few rumors about the location and let the Erathal Republic arrest him, or maybe the Felite Confederacy -they're closer after all."

The Collector threw his head back, laughing maniacally and rattling his chains.

Sarah looked around nervously, wishing she hadn't left her staff upstairs. She noticed Artimus move his hand to the sword at his side and Savannah took a step back. As The Collector's laughter died down, the rest of the group all exchanged nervous glances.

"You are all so naïve," The Collector murmured. "You just don't get it," he continued, his voice growing louder.

"The world can't be at peace. Chaos is violence and destruction. Without central order, without a controlling hand, Evorath will be torn apart, divided."

Sarah rolled her eyes, but it was Savannah who spoke up first.

"How sad for you," she proclaimed. "I'm sure you have a lot of reasons to believe that, but it's simply not true. I know you weren't even alive when Marftaport was established, but did you know the main reason we were left alone was because people who would have, and could have, destroyed us early on believed as you do? They thought a society without compulsory authority would crumble, collapsing under its own disorder."

The Collector tugged on his chain, pulling himself to his feet and glaring at Savannah.

"If I wished it, I could march my army here and wipe your little community off the map," The Collector's words were like poison, spewing from his wicked mouth.

"You see," he continued. "You don't have a clue about what's really going on in the shadows. You're so ill informed that you believe I'm the authority behind it. But you see, I'm just another cog in the wheel of power."

Sarah gasped, throwing her hands over her mouth, and shaking her head. The others all looked around at one another as well. Even Oogmut, whose expressions always seemed so foreign to Sarah, wore a clear look of surprise.

"Trying to shake off responsibility?" Zelag asked, taking a step towards the prisoner.

The Collector cackled. He looked at Zelag.

"Keep me down in this dungeon of yours and you'll learn the truth soon enough. Though I might add, it seems a little hypocritical. I'm pretty sure chaining someone up against their will violates those ethics you so proudly claim."

"Ethics?" Artimus stepped in between The Collector and Zelag, holding his arm out to block the shapeshifter. He positioned himself so his face was just centimeters from The Collector, his tone stern.

"Who are you to speak of ethics? Someone who enslaves people and violates their free will. Allowing you to roam freely would be unethical. So maybe we will keep you locked up down here. Maybe we'll ensure you eat well enough that you live for many years to come, spending them all tied up in this prison. Or maybe you can finally make a correct choice."

Artimus paused, glancing back at Savannah. With a nod, he turned back to The Collector.

"Tell us, who is the real authority behind that hidden castle then? If it's not you, who?"

The Collector withdrew, standing to full height and looking around. Sarah made sure to avert her gaze as his eyes passed over her. She stepped closer to George, placing her left hand on the small of his back.

"What an eclectic group you have here," said The Collector with a smile. "But that's part of your story, isn't it? Absolute liberty in a community of all races. Everyone is welcome, so long as they respect and care for their neighbors. That's pretty much what you claim here, is it not?"

"We don't just claim it," replied Oogmut, his voice booming. "We act as children of Evorath all should."

"What would you know of being a child of Evorath?" The Collector asked. "And what do they know?" he nodded towards George and Sarah, his red eyes enflamed.

Sarah shifted uncomfortably, looking down at her brown turnshoes and pausing to reflect.

"They are both valued members of our community," replied Savannah. "And even if they weren't created by Evorath, they are as much of her children as anyone else here. You just don't get it. It's not about where you were born, what you look like, your upbringing, or even the troubles of your past. It's about your heart now, your kindness, and your willingness to treat others with love."

"Oh, so is that the secret then?" The Collector asked, glancing down at his missing hand. "And does this sort of violence represent treating others with love? Since I've lost my hand and heard your pleas, can I now be sanctified in your eyes? You people twist and distort the Xyvor, claiming to live for Evorath while sowing chaos and disorder."

He threw his head back and cackled.

"You're a pitiful creature!" Sarah blurted, stepping into the cell. "You disguise your torment with barbs and treat others as your plaything because it makes you feel significant. But deep down, you loath yourself. And because of that, you loathe seeing anyone else content in this life."

Savannah strode over towards Sarah, offering a nod before looking back at The Collector.

"And what harm have you caused others with that hand?" Savannah asked. "You asked if dismembering your hand was an act of love. The truth is, we ask ourselves those questions all the time. How can we do better? How can we come closer to Evorath's vision? We may not be perfect, but at least we try. Have you ever tried to even consider someone beside yourself?"

"Oh, no. Of course not. How could someone like me think about someone other than myself?"

Sarah narrowed her eyes, tilting her head slightly to the right. She couldn't tell if he was being sarcastic or not.

Artimus threw up his hands and let out a loud sigh. "We're not going to get anywhere with this."

"And you won't," replied The Collector. He looked back at Artimus, his eyes wide as he stared at the old elf.

"Whatever magic I am capable of, you must realize it is nothing compared to what my master can do. And we both know the hájje threat is growing. According to our network, they've been mobilizing thousands of troops, an army unlike any Erathal has seen before. Centuries from now, The Demon Wars will be a historical footnote compared to the war that's coming.

"And while you all sit here and waste your talents trying to live in some warped society of absolute freedom, my people are working to ensure our own survival. While your insignificant little community rots away with the rest of Erathal, we will continue to thrive. Because no matter what empire rules this land, we'll be in the shadows of Erathal, influencing everything."

Sarah felt sick. She closed her eyes, taking a step back. George came up behind her, grabbing her right hand with his own and placing his left on the small of her back.

"You're making one fatal mistake," Zelag interjected, stepping over to The Collector.

"Oh, and what is that?"

"You're forgetting your audience. It occurs to me, if what you say is true and you really aren't the master of the shadows that everyone believes you to be, then all you are is an actor. And judging by your performance here, not a very good one."

The Collector smiled, his eyes roaring with intensity as he stared directly at Zelag. Sarah could feel the tension in the air and the prisoner's hostile intentions.

"But if I am just an actor," The Collector spoke slowly, annunciating every syllable as he spoke. "Can you trust anything I have to say?"

"We don't have to," replied Zelag nonchalantly. He looked away, examining his right hand, the same hand he had cut off The Collector. "But you've already told us enough."

"Alright," he looked around at the rest of the party. "Let's leave our new informant here to think about how he wants to live the rest of his life. I think we should regroup and discuss what we've learned away from present company."

Sarah wasn't sure why Zelag felt he had the right to take the lead. She was surprised he had even stuck around this long. Was he really any different than this man they now had in shackles? She wondered but held her tongue.

"Yes, perhaps we'll return tomorrow," suggested Savannah. "Oogmut, if you would be so kind as to lock up. Meet us outside when you're done."

The Collector laughed as everyone else left the cell. Oogmut remained behind for a moment while the rest of the party proceeded outside into the landing.

"He's telling the truth," Artimus said as they stepped past the threshold, out of earshot thanks to the enchantments in place.

"Yeah," Zelag agreed. "There is someone else pulling the strings. But that's not what is most important to us now. It's his comment about the hájje that interests me. He's afraid of them."

Artimus nodded.

"Yes, despite appearances, he is terrified," he agreed. "Which leads me to believe whoever is in charge doesn't have any influence in the hájje court."

"Exactly," replied Zelag. "So, I suspect the hidden nature of his castle isn't to keep him from lizock, elvish, or felite authorities. But rather to ensure they are isolated from the war that is to come."

"But who is the real puppet master?" George asked. Sarah was wondering the same thing.

"I don't know," replied Zelag. "But I know how we can find out."

"Absolutely not," Savannah interjected.

"I hadn't even-"

"You're not impersonating The Collector. Sure, you've apparently encountered him before, but how much do you really know about him? If he is an actor, and not the criminal mastermind we've been led to believe, it means anything we think we know about him could be wrong."

"But we can extract what we need to know. Let me have Mojo's help. We'll get him to sing like a bird."

"Let's not discount his suggestion," Artimus suggested. He held up his right hand as if anticipating objections. "I'm not saying we just go for it either. But we should consider all our options. I say we discuss it tonight at Vistoro's. Perhaps we should even bring in some other members of the Mage's Guild to consider alternatives."

"Will you be patient enough to wait for us to decide our next move as a family?" Savannah asked, giving Zelag a stern look.

"Yes, I can manage."

"What did I miss?" Oogmut asked, stepping through the threshold.

"They agreed to just let me kill him," quipped Zelag. Sarah shook her head. She never understood his dark sense of humor.

"I object to that plan," replied Oogmut, a look of concern on his face.

"He's just joking," George said. "He's always had a sandy foundation."

"Alright, so does it require two of you to close this iron door?" Zelag asked, motioning back towards the entryway. He looked suspicious, but Sarah wasn't sure why.

"Yes," Savannah replied immediately. "Oogmut, Artimus and I needed your help with something. Sarah, George, would you two mind securing the dungeon?"

"No, that's fine," replied Sarah.

"Perfect!" Savannah exclaimed. "We'll see you all at dinner then." Her tone was rushed, an unusual urgency in her voice.

Oogmut and Artimus followed her lead, proceeding up the stairs. George walked over to the right side of the door, looking back at Sarah as she proceeded to the left. Zelag stood in place at the center, rocking in position while the others departed up the stairs.

"Is there a reason you're not going with them?" Sarah was not in the mood for dealing with this shapeshifter's shenanigans.

"Yes, there is actually. And I'm not sure how to best address it. But, before you close things up, I wanted to have a word with the two of you."

He glanced between Sarah and George, avoiding eye contact and twiddling his thumbs as he did. If Sarah didn't know any better, she'd think he was nervous.

"About five years ago," he continued, his voice a bit shaky. "I really messed up. And the truth is, I spent these last five years avoiding Marftaport because I was ashamed. So, I wanted to tell you both that I am sorry. I don't expect or deserve your forgiveness, but I want to assure you nothing like that will ever happen again. I violated your trust and have regretted it every day since."

Sarah looked down at her shaking hands, her eyes trembling. She clenched her fists, looking across the room at her husband to see his reaction. He appeared shocked, his mouth agape and eyes wide as he stared at Zelag.

There were butterflies in Sarah's stomach, and a knot in her throat. She tried to process this, uncertain whether she could even trust the shapeshifter's sincerity. But then she reminded herself of Evorath's teachings on forgiveness. If Zelag was sincere, she had to give him a chance.

Looking closer at him, watching him rock back and forth, the way he averted her eyes, and the frown on his face. He was a good actor, but was he good enough to fake this level of sincerity? Still questioning this in her head, her husband was the first to speak.

"Zelag, I." He paused, looking down at his feet and then glancing over to Sarah, his eyes pleading. "Can we? I just don't know. Thank you!"

He looked at Zelag and nodded. "Yes, thank you," he restated. "We've been waiting five years to hear that. Sarah, do you care to say anything?"

Sarah was fighting back tears. She was still torn. Part of her wanted to hate Zelag, to deny him the satisfaction of forgiveness. And yet, the other half of her wanted to let this wound heal, to let go of the past.

"You can't do anything like that again," she said, her voice shaky. "And I mean it. Not just for George and me. I need you to promise that you won't impersonate anyone in this community again without their explicit consent. I don't care what rational you might have to do so. If you can agree to that, they maybe, in time, I can offer forgiveness."

Zelag nodded, a faint smile on his face. His mouth was shaking as he turned away and threw his hands over his face. Rubbing down over his face, he looked back at her with a larger smile, his eyes red.

"Thank you, Sarah. I promise, I will never do anything like that again. Nor will I impersonate anyone here without their direct consent."

This was a strange sensation. Amidst all the uncertainty and chaos right now, it felt like a weight was lifted from Sarah in that moment. A tingling in the back of her head and neck, and a release of tension she hadn't known was there.

There was still a voice in her head that told her she couldn't trust Zelag. How could he change? How could he be trusted? But for now, she was able to push that voice aside.

She would focus on healing.

CHAPTER XVIII

Marftaport, Vistoro's Manor
17 Julla, 1149 MT

Zelag sat upright, yawning as he stretched out his arms. He had forgotten how comfortable the beds were here. His usual accommodations either consisted of sleeping in the dirt or in a flea-ridden bed at a shady tavern. But the soft, plush mattress in the guest room of Vistoro's manse was a welcome change of pace. And with recent events, he wondered if he might actually stick around for a while.

Standing up, he stepped over to the end table. He picked up his sword belt and tightened it around his waist. He then proceeded to open the drawer, removing his various knives, and placing them in their respective positions in his armor. Lastly, he collected his various pouches and his coin purse.

Pausing as his hand hovered over Vistoro's pendant, he reflected on the conversations last night. The people of Marftaport were truly unique. Or at least his family was.

Sniffling, he wiped his nose and massaged his temples for a moment. He proceeded to the door, sitting down at the stool there and fastening his boots. As he stood up, he closed his eyes and took a deep breath.

"I'm going to really try this time," he muttered to himself.

Twisting the copper door handle, Zelag stepped into the hallway, looking down the long, narrow corridor. He proceeded

219

left through the hall, taking his time, and admiring some of the new Tor Noga paintings hung along the wall. Reaching the grand stairway, he took another moment to pause and listen.

There was some faint noise coming from upstairs, footsteps across the wooden floor and what he could only guess was Tel' Shira's wheelchair.

Proceeding down the steps, he took a moment to admire the craftsmanship of the railing and banisters. For someone who had left behind his royal lineage, Vistoro sure did cling to his luxurious architectural design.

Reaching the bottom of the staircase, Zelag continued through the double doors to the foyer. He heard some noise coming from the left, likely from the kitchen. Seeing no one else around, he continued outside. The cool spring morning air greeted him, the smells of various flowers allowing him to relax as the sun warmed his skin.

He couldn't remember the last time he took time to just enjoy nature and being outdoors. And he wasn't sure why, but something inside told him this morning was the time to remedy that. So, he proceeded left, heading towards the path through the hedges.

As he turned and reached the end of the path, he stopped and stared towards the shrine. It must have been his instinct driving him, for he started walking towards the shrine without thinking about it. Before he knew it, he was standing before the statue of Evorath, looking over her features before gazing up to the mural painted up above.

Of all Tor Noga's sculptures and paintings, this was Zelag's favorite. It was an abstract rendition of the first story of creation from the Xyvor. Featuring a larger-than-life image of Evorath reaching her hand out over her creation. With various hues of blue, eddies of black and white, all coming together to form the beautiful, green world of Evorath.

Though he preferred to keep his appreciation for such art to himself, he couldn't help but feel a sense of awe and wonder as he beheld it. The soft brush strokes conveyed a deep sense of care and emotion. And while it might appear chaotic on the surface, Zelag could tell every color, every line, every stroke, was deliberate.

Lowering to his knees, Zelag clasped his hands together and started to pray, whispering under his breath.

"Evorath, please help me to keep these people safe. Provide your divine protection as we fight against the forces of evil that have invaded your world."

He looked up to the statue, gritting his teeth and considering recent events.

"You were the last person I expected to see here!"

Zelag jumped to his feet, glancing back at Luna Freya, who was standing just a few meters away. She had to be the only one in the town who could sneak up on him, or so he thought.

"Oh, I was just paying my respects," Zelag lied with a faint grin.

"On your knees? Sure. And I definitely won't tell anyone else that you were out here begging for Evorath's mercy," Luna replied sarcastically. She winked, touching her pinky and thumb together and curling her other three fingers over.

"Begging for mercy? Really?" Zelag asked. "Good luck getting anyone to believe that."

"Yeah, you're right," Luna shrugged. "Maybe I'll just tell them you were praying to be as skilled a fighter as me. That's much more believable, though never achievable."

"Oh yeah," Zelag held up his fists, lowering into a fighting stance. "Nonlethal match to prove it?"

Luna lowered her stand, squaring off against Zelag. She held up her hands, palms forward and in at a slight angle.

"So, no teeth or claws then?"

"And no weapons for me," agreed Zelag.

"You're on!" Luna took a few steps back, waving her fingers to invite Zelag to advance.

Smiling wide, Zelag approached slowly. He kept his feet both pointed towards Luna, but didn't wish to charge in. So, he took one deliberate step after the next, keeping his eyes narrow and focused on Luna's feet.

"You afraid to go for it?" she asked standing her ground.

"I'm not foolish enough to try and breech your defenses," Zelag countered. "I remember how you fight."

"It's been five years though. Who knows what new tricks I've learned."

"Not enough!"

Zelag lunged forward, shifting his gaze to Luna's shoulders and feigning a jab. As she shifted to block, he adjusted his attack vector, attempting a leg sweep. Luna stepped back, bringing her instep up to catch him in the shin, effectively blocking his attack while delivering a counterattack. Before he had a chance to react, Luna continued her counteract.

She jabbed with her right, striking Zelag in the throat. Stunned by the swift response, Zelag tried to retreat, backpedaling as he choked, struggling to breathe.

Luna wasn't going to let that happen. She ran after him, leading with a flying front kick and knocking Zelag to the ground.

"Have you gotten worse at this?" Luna asked, standing up tall and relaxing her stance.

Zelag coughed, massaging his throat for a few moments before standing back up.

"I think." He paused, clearing his throat, and slapping his chest. "I think you've just gotten a lot better."

"Well, that's what you get going around Erathal doing Evorath knows what. I keep up my training every day."

With a few blinks and nod, Zelag cleared his throat again, finally feeling like he could breathe properly.

"I guess I'll have to step up my game."

"I'd say. Morn and Neman even put up more of a fight than that!"

Zelag clutched his right side, making an exaggerated expression of pain.

"Ouch. That hurts more than the strike to the throat. But I'm going to call rocpiss on that one."

Luna shrugged. "When we join them at Paxvilla you can find out for yourself."

Shaking his head, Zelag glanced back at the shrine. He wondered whether all the clandestine work he'd done over the past few years really had softened his fighting skills.

"Do you still join Vistoro for breakfast most days?" Zelag asked, turning back towards Luna.

"Sometimes, but I wasn't thinking I would today. With all that's going on, it feels like a good morning hunt is in order. Want to get your blood pumping a bit and join me?"

Zelag scratched his bread, considering the request. He was no stranger to hunting his food, but after eating some of the great meals the past couple of days, he was sort of looking forward to getting the royal treatment for breakfast.

"Yeah, why not?" he exclaimed.

"Excellent. In that case, let's make things interesting."

Chapter XIX

Zelag stepped out of the portal, looking around to see where George had deposited them. He had assumed his lizock form, his scaly skin itching as usual as he got his bearings. Glancing back, he watched as Luna Freya, Artimus Jr. and Goerge stepped through, the portal closing moments after.

"How close are we?" Luna asked, glancing around, her face scrunched in a look of disgust as she sniffed the air. "It smells like something died around here."

Zelag had learned decades ago that the lizock sense of smell left much to be desired, so he took her word for it. He could sense, however, how humid it was. Rain was coming.

"Not as close as I hoped," he replied, pointing southeast.

"Half a day?" Artimus Jr. asked. "An hour's walk? Perhaps even less?"

"Yes, but I doubt we'll beat the rain." Zelag looked around, considering the cloudy sky.

"Stay close to me. The closer we get, the more 'unique' the locals will become. Best to avoid eye contact, or even to look at anyone for too long, or at all if you can help it. And good luck with the stench Luna. Consider this my revenge for earlier."

Not waiting for a response, Zelag strode southeast.

225

He could hear the others following close behind, George's staff providing a measure of their pace as it clacked on the road. With a brisk pace, Zelag stayed on the road they arrived at, keeping his eyes down. The homes around them were in disrepair, many of them with missing doors or windows. The close groupings of these homes didn't help matters, with piles of trash and detritus scattered about.

They passed very few lizock along the way. A young boy and girl playing with a dead fox. A beggar sitting just off the road beside a pile of debris. And a group of muscular lizock with tribal markings on their arms, chests, and face, likely heading off to intimidate, coerce, or do any otherwise unsavory act to an unwilling participant.

"Did you hear that?" Luna asked after a few minutes.

Zelag glanced back. She had taken position right behind him, with George next, and Artimus Jr. taking up the rear. At least Little A had enough sense to keep an eye on the wizard.

"The thunder in the distance?" Zelag asked. "No, but I can feel it." Lizock ears weren't too good either, but there was something about this form that allowed him to feel vibrations more distinctly. It was a unique sensation.

"You feel it but don't hear it? Lizock are weird," said Luna, her voice carrying a hint of disbelief. "Can you tell what direction it's coming from?"

"It's headed our way, from where we're going. If all of us can keep up this pace, we might just make it to the tavern before we get soaked though."

"You hear that, George?" Luna shouted. "Keep up!"

"Oh ha, ha. I'm keeping pace just fine," called George, his voice sounding a bit labored.

"Alright, good. Now let's keep quiet," instructed Zelag. "We're getting into Melora's territory now."

He pointed towards the charred remains of an old library. One of the cornerstones of the foundation was still left intact, a rune carved into the side. It featured a circular shape with three wavy lines attached to the top and two small dots just beneath.

"Is the hydra rune her tribal symbol?" George asked in a hushed tone.

"Yes, and she has an unhealthy obsession with them, so please don't bring it up."

Happy the wizard didn't respond, Zelag continued forward. The group kept their pace for the next few minutes. And to his delight, they didn't come across anyone else on the road. But Zelag could feel the moisture in the air increasing. And as they walked, the light seemed to grow more dim, the sky being darkened by storm clouds.

"It's a left up ahead," said Zelag, pointing to a small wooden post at the center of a two-way split in the road. Both directional signs had fallen off the post years back, a fact that Zelag found revealing about the Lizock Kingdom's priorities.

Just as they turned onto this road, passing by the abandoned lumber mill, a crash of thunder sounded out above. And as Zelag felt the first drops of rain falling against his scales,

227

two large lizock stepped out from a hovel to the right of the road. They were enforcers for Melora.

Aside from the fact that Zelag had encountered them before, they were easily recognized by the hydra brands on their chest. These brands were just right of center, a symbolic gesture to indicate their hearts belonged to Melora. Their matching leather harnesses, complete with ritualistic knives completed their tribal demeanor, leaving no doubt of their allegiance.

Though similar in height and build, the one on the left was a bit shorter and appeared bulkier as a result. The one on the right looked leaner, with a few centimeters in height to stretch out his muscles.

"What do we have here?" Asked the taller one, his gruff voice was like a knife being sharpened on a whetstone.

"Yeah, what business does an elf, a felite, and a human have with a lizock?" followed the stout one, his voice humorously high-pitched.

"They are with me," Zelag replied, trying to contain his frustration with the delay. The rain was still light, and there was a chance they'd avoid the downpour if they hurried.

"And who are you?" the tall one asked.

Zelag rolled his eyes.

"You've seen me at least a dozen times. I'm Zelag, and I'm returning from an important task for Melora. So, move aside and let my friends pass."

As he said this, he reached into his coin purse, pulling out a couple of the counterfeit ulagrets and flinging them to the pair of enforcers.

The two meatheads scrambled, catching the coins, and smiling as they stepped to either side of the road. With a slight bow, the short one spoke.

"Enjoy your day, mercenary."

Offering a reassuring nod to his friends, Zelag continued forward, walking at an even faster pace than before.

The occasional drops of rain were getting more frequent, and with another thunderclap, Zelag glanced back and pointed at the tavern, which was just beyond a couple of delipidated shacks.

Of all the structures in this district, Melora's Tavern was the only one in good repair. But that didn't mean it was an attractive building. The large, three-story tavern must have started its life out as a small, single-story home of sorts. Over the years, the front door had been covered with brick, leaving no exterior entrance to the ground level floor.

The second floor had been added and stretched out a good three meters (or more at some points) beyond the first story. Constructed of oak, it featured an asymmetrical design more consistent with the style used hundreds of years earlier.

The third story had been added in the last few years. Zelag had seen this one at various stages of construction. And since it was built using pine and featured a more modern design, it amplified the general unappealing look of the building.

"That's our destination. The main entrance is up those steps around the side there," he nodded towards the angular staircase, which wrapped around the front before leading around the right side to the banded oak door.

As he pointed this out, another crash of thunder echoed through the street. Zelag closed his eyes, anticipating the downpour.

"Keep close!" shouted George, running over and holding his staff overhead. To Zelag's delight, he watched as the rain fell all around them. But it seemed George had learned a new trick.

Squinting, Zelag could see the faint glow of white magic pouring out from George's staff. It created an invisible canopy over Zelag and the rest of the party.

"Huh. I guess you're no longer a one trick pony," muttered Zelag, smiling at George.

George shook his head, continuing towards the tavern entrance. It wasn't exactly the most comfortable, but the others continued along with him, keeping close together as they stepped.

"If I'm never this close to any of you again," said Luna as they started up the steps, "I'll be a much happier felite."

"Is that so?" quipped Artimus Jr. "What does 'much happier' look for a grumpy, unfriendly felite anyways?"

"It means I won't smack you for asking dumb questions."

"Fair enough."

"Oh, just open the door," grumbled George.

Zelag pulled on the tavern door, stepping aside to allow the other three inside. George slipped past last, lowering his staff and releasing the spell. Zelag clutched the door handle and pulled it shut behind him, getting only a light dusting of rain in the process.

Wiping down his arms, Zelag looked around the tavern. As expected for this hour, only a few shady characters were about, along with the same bartender he had seen on his last visit. That would make things easy at least.

"Well look who's already back!" the bartender exclaimed as she noticed Zelag. "I thought you'd be away for a fortnight. Couldn't resist coming back to see me, could you?"

"Girlfriend of yours?" Luna asked sarcastically.

Zelag smirked, glancing at Luna.

"You know every bartender around Erathal wants me as a boyfriend. But let's just have a seat at the center of the bar," he whispered. "Allow me to do the talking and we should be able to slip out in no time."

"OK, but don't flirt too much with your lizock girlfriend. That's just gross."

Shaking his head, Zelag walked up to the bar, his tail dragging across the wood floor as he pulled out a stool and took a seat. Glancing side to side, he waited until the others had taken a seat before addressing the barkeep.

"You know I did miss those sparkling eyes of yours. But I'm afraid I need to see Melora again. Is she in her office?"

Luna made an exaggerated gagging sound, as if she was choking on a hairball. Zelag passed her a glare, but she just responded with a toothy smile.

"She's meeting with someone else right now," said the barkeep, nodding back towards the closed office door. She leaned in, putting her elbows on the counter, a not-so-subtle way to bring attention to her bosom.

"We can all enjoy a drink while we wait though," she winked, her tongue darting out just long enough to signal interest in Zelag.

"Maybe we should serve ourselves and the two of you can get a room," interjected Luna. "I used to tend bar back home."

The barkeep looked over Luna, examining her closely. She finished by glaring at the felite, darting her tongue aggressively before dismissively glancing up towards the ceiling.

"Let's just all have a drink," suggested Zelag, slapping down a real silver piece. The last thing they needed was for Luna to start a brawl.

"So, a bog whiskey for you," the barkeep said turning back to Zelag and batting her eyelashes. "What will you friends be having?"

George was looking over the selection. "Is that one a cider?" he asked pointing at a green bottle.

"Oh no," the bartender shook her head. "That's Melora's signature ale."

"I'll take one of those," interrupted Artimus Jr.

"I guess I'll have one as well," added George.

"And what about you," the barkeep asked, her tone caustic as she looked back at Luna.

"Oh, you can count me in for one of those bog whiskeys," replied Luna sternly, flaring her eyebrows.

"As you wish," the barkeep wore a devious grin as she went to retrieve the drinks.

"Well, at least we beat the brunt of it," said George, glancing around the tavern. Thunder shook the tavern, the sound of pouring rain swelling as it pelted against the roof.

"Yeah, the weather somehow feels appropriate for the setting," Artimus Jr. replied.

"Ugh. It was like this yesterday too," the barkeep interjected, returning with glasses and the two bottles. As she poured the drinks, Zelag kept his eyes on the hallway leading to the office. He said a silent prayer to Evorath, wishing for the meeting to conclude so they could get this over with.

"...and I just think that's ridiculous," the barkeep finished. Zelag gritted his teeth, realizing he hadn't been paying attention.

"Yeah, absolutely," agreed Zelag with a nod. "Let's have a drink to less of that ridiculousness in the future."

Zelag lifted his glass, giving it a quick swirl before taking a swig and placing it back on the counter. If there was one benefit to this form, it was the fact that he could even tolerate such a caustic liquid. But that didn't mean he liked it.

Of course, Luna didn't seem to have trouble with it. She swallowed her entire glass in one big gulp, her whiskers twitching and eyes dilating almost imperceptibly as she tapped the glass back on the countertop. Tilting her head to the left, she pursed her lips and exhaled.

"Not exactly the whiskey you cats are used to, is it?" the barkeep asked with a smirk.

"Definitely not," Luna replied returning the smirk. "I think even the barghest make better drinks than you lizards."

Luna had always been a bit hotheaded, but Zelag couldn't figure out why she felt the need to antagonize this bartender. Was she trying to start a fight?

Clearing his throat, Zelag reached over and grabbed Luna's glass, turning it upside down.

"Perhaps my friend here should stop. She's had far too much to drink today already."

"What? That was my first drink all day!" Luna objected.

Zelag kicked her leg, glaring at her in hopes that she'd take the hint. Luna slid back off her chair, licking her lips and baring her teeth.

"I think this ale is fantastic," Artimus Jr. exclaimed in a particularly cheerful tone, cutting through some of the tension.

"Oh, yes," agreed George. "Definitely a unique and delightful taste." Zelag could tell George wasn't sharing his true thoughts. He looked like he had just been surprised with something sour when he was expecting sweet.

"Well," the barkeep popped her hips and held up her right hand, index finger extended. "I think Zelag's right about your cat friend. No more drinks for you today."

Zelag watched Luna. Her left eye twitched, her ears pulling back and tail wagging behind her. With clenched fists, she stepped towards the bar.

The creak of the office door cut through the noise of storm, coming at just the right moment. Perhaps Evorath had heard Zelag's prayer after all.

"Ah, it looks like the meeting is over," Zelag exclaimed, pushing back from the bar, and dropping to his feet. He glanced at Luna to make sure she was standing down. Seeing her tail fall flat and fists open, he let out a sigh of relief.

The entire party watched as an unexpected figure exited the office. Whatever tension was there moments before was replaced with a new, very real fear.

A hájje walked out of the office. Standing two meters tall, this dark elf was lean and powerful, his barrel chest and sinewy biceps bulging in his black leather armor. The armor itself covered him from the neck down, and featured mythril studding on all his vital areas, the blue glinting in the candlelight. His boots echoed throughout the tavern as he walked.

Featuring the usual pale skin and void black eyes, the hájje had a pointed nose and square chin. His long black hair was pulled back into a perfect ponytail. A bastard sword hung at his left side, a large dagger on his right, and various other pouches spread about his waist.

Zelag kept his hands at his side, palms open and stance wide as he watched the hájje approach. He looked beyond the dark elf's physical features, which was even more terrifying. This hájje's dark and powerful aura was eerily like Yezurkstal's, a realization that made Zelag sick to his stomach. This had to be one of Death's children.

Focused on keeping his breath steady, Zelag remained as still as he could. He could feel the nervous energy coming from his allies. With a side glance, he noticed both Artimus Jr. and George had come to their feet as well. Despite their collective apprehension, everyone remained steady.

Melora walked just behind the hájje, her eyes widening as she spotted Zelag and the others standing just beyond the bar. She quickly looked back to the hájje, her face obscured as they reached the end of the bar.

"I will send word when the next stage is in motion," she said, her slimy voice causing Zelag to shudder.

The hájje glanced over at Zelag and the others, smirking as he spoke. "Thank you Melora. It has been a pleasure, as always." He slathered his words on like smooth honey.

Continuing out from behind the bar, the hájje paused as he passed Zelag and the others. With a subtle nod and a smirk, he continued towards the door. Thunder rang out in the air as he opened the door, followed by a flash of lightning.

The hájje held up his left hand, channeling magic and conjuring up an umbrella in his hand.

"I'll see you soon Melora."

Letting out a long exhale, Zelag turned back towards Melora. He realized in that moment how tense he'd been, his muscles feeling like he had just let go of a heavy load.

"Zelag," Melora spoke from behind the bar. "I didn't expect you back so soon. Who are your friends?"

With a quick glance at his allies, ensuring everyone was on the same page, he turned back to Melora and smiled.

"No one as significant as your friends I would think. But they did help me procure something for you. Something that I think concludes our business."

Reaching into his back pouch, Zelag released the clasp and pulled out the royal pendant. He held it up by its chain, allowing it to dangle for a few moments.

"But before I hand it over, I must know. This has nothing to do with your business with the hájje, does it?"

Melora smiled, stepping over to look at him directly from across the bar. She made direct eye contact with Zelag, her aura remaining calm and steady.

"Of course not," she said.

Nodding, Zelag placed the pendant on the bar top, glancing to either side at his allies.

"In that case, I take it our debt is settled?"

"I'm a lady of my word," replied Melora picking up the pendant. Her aura darkened as she did, her eyes alight with a scheme. In that moment, Zelag knew he had made a mistake.

He kept his focus on Melora, but using his peripherals, he looked to either side of the tavern, hoping to account for the other guests. Weighing his options, he decided there was only one path he could take.

"Well," Zelag started, preparing himself. "The hens need to roost, so I think it's about time my friends and I depart."

With a quick glance to ensure George reacted, Zelag leapt for the bar, reaching over, and snatching the pendant back from Melora's hands. Luna lifted two barstools, throwing them across the room at two of the thugs. George opened a portal just to their left, and Artimus Jr. didn't waste a moment, leaping through. Luna followed just behind, and Zelag dove through next.

Blinking rapidly and shaking his head to overcome the dizziness of the travel, Zelag watched as George ran through the portal, allowing it to snap closed behind him.

The sound of chirping birds, the shade of a beautiful oak, and the tranquility greeted them back in Marftaport as they all looked around at one another.

"What was that for?" Luna asked, holding her arms out and scrunching her face.

"Melora was lying about the hájje. Whatever she wants this pendant for, it has something to do with them."

Zelag watched everyone's auras darken. They all stood around, eyes drooping and faces filling with dread as they considered the implications.

Suddenly, Zelag's own life didn't feel all that important.

CᎮAꝐTEᏒ XX

Zelag sat in the left corner of the meeting hall, watching as all the various mages found their way to their seats. It was a simple room, the familiar runestones lining the stone walls to provide lighting. A wooden platform was built at the front along with a central podium. The rest of the room consisted of the ugly yellow carpet and five rows of wooden chairs, increasing by two chairs in each room to include a total of seventy-eight seats.

Seeing the dozens of mages filing into their seats, Zelag realized he had sorely underestimated how many mages called Marftaport home. Excluding Sarah, who was not present, Savannah and George, who were standing before the stage, he had counted at least forty-seven so far. And more were still filing in, taking seats throughout the room.

What was even more surprising is that he recognized less than half of them. He could tell from all the new construction around town that the population had grown since he left, but he never imagined this many mages would be among their ranks.

"Ahem, mind if I sit here?" came an excited voice from his left. The shrill, sweet voice was unmistakable, leaving Zelag to force a smile as he turned her way.

"Of course, Ygabb. Please, have a seat." He gestured towards the seat just next to his own.

"Oh, thank you Mr. Zelag! I didn't expect to see you here. So, I hope I'm not assuming overmuch when I think that you might have an idea why they called this emergency session. You see, I was planning to take a nice moonlight stroll tonight. So, I hope this won't take too long. Then again, I know these things can really drag on when some of the older mages start bickering over nuances and subtleties."

Zelag tried to maintain a steady demeanor as Ygabb's words poured from her mouth. But he was having trouble even keeping up with her random, incoherent thoughts.

"And that makes me think of this one time when we had a special meeting called and it was actually in the middle of the night. Turns out, it was just Morgana, she's the lamia just over there," Ygabb pointed, but didn't pause to breathe as she continued her word vomiting.

"And she's a really skilled geomancer, but like not the most friendly of sorts. I'll introduce you if you'd like though. But anyways, where was I? Oh, right! She somehow got confused and called the meeting because she thought there was some catastrophic quake about to happen. I think she must have had too much to drink, or perhaps ate a bad mushroom. By the way, do you like mushrooms? I grow my own because I really enjoy having mushrooms in just about everything I eat."

"That's all very fascinating," Zelag interrupted, jumping in as Ygabb finally took a breath. "And yes, I do have some insight into why this meeting was called. But rather than spoil it for you, perhaps we should focus upfront. I think the meeting is about to start, don't you?"

Ygabb jumped to her feet, clicking her hooves on the floor as she looked around.

"Yeah, I think Sarah is still missing, and Oogmut, and I don't see Lu Nora anywhere, or Tu Mora for that matter! Oh, wait! There they are. You may be right though," she said plopping back into her seat.

Zelag made a mental note to avoid Ygabb whenever possible in the future.

"So, Zelag," Ygabb started with a wide smile.

Shaking his head, Zelag pointed up front and held his index finger over his lips to signal her to be quiet.

"I think they are about to start," he whispered.

"Oh, you're right!" she exclaimed in a hushed tone. "Sorry. I'll be quiet now. But we'll talk more after!"

Closing his eyes, Zelag offered a slight nod before facing Savannah and George, both of whom had taken the stage.

"Good evening," Savannah started, her voice amplified by an enchantment placed on the podium.

"Thank you all for making the time to gather on such short notice. But as everyone knows, times are turbulent right now. And I'm afraid we have an alarming update that some of us agreed called for an immediate meeting to discuss."

An elderly elf in green robes was seated front and center. He adjusted his position and cleared his throat loudly.

"Oh yes," Savannah smiled.

"So let us begin, the emergency Mage's Guild meeting session on the 17th day of Julla, the 1149th year of modern times. We commence, as always, and ask Evorath to extend Her blessings over this meeting and our discussions tonight."

Savannah paused, looked down for a few moments before continuing.

"Tonight, we have the esteemed Elorius acting as scribe for Guild recordkeeping. Thank you for your diligence Elorius,"

Zelag leaned forward, squinting towards the elf in green robes. He could barely see through the crowd, but now realized the elf had a parchment and quill in his lap. However, to Zelag's surprise, the quill was writing on its own. The elder elf simply looked at Savannah and nodded as she spoke.

No one could say these mages lacked creativity.

"Now, let us come to the matter at hand," said Savannah, casting a quick glance at George before gazing back across the room.

"First, as many of you have undoubtedly heard, the Hunter's and Warrior's Guilds have both called similar meetings. And of course, the High Priestess is gathering all the clergy of Marftaport. Tel' Shira's vision of an imminent hájje attack has been confirmed by our scout, Katas."

Savannah motioned towards a brown lizock in the front row, clothed in a simple leather garment.

"But the reason we have called this meeting is because we have evidence that suggests one of the major lizock syndicates is allying itself with the hájje. And as many of you are painfully familiar with, the Lizock Kingdom is, unofficially, run by the major syndicates."

"And what does this have to do with us?" interrupted a weaselly, disheveled looking elf in the third row. His tattered robes were stained with what looked like bird droppings.

"Yes, and what about Shadiro? What is happening with the inquiry into his murder?" asked a homely elf in the second row. It looked like her sackcloth dress hadn't ever been washed.

"On the matter of Shadiro, we have some new information, but believe it would be prudent not to act on it until after we've ensured Paxvilla survives this imminent hájje attack," Savannah replied.

"And how about the prisoner down in the dungeon?" asked the homely elf, her voice rising in pitch. "We can't just hold him indefinitely."

Even without considering her aura, which was agitated, Zelag could tell Savannah was losing her patience. She was tapping her fingers on the podium, glaring down at the annoying elf, and biting her lower lip. After taking a deep breath, she responded.

"Let's try to stay on topic. The subject of this meeting is the situation with the hájje. With that in mind, I'll have George give a bit more context, as he's been more directly involved with these recent discoveries."

Savannah glanced at George and stepped back from the podium. George stepped up.

"As Savannah said, I've been working to follow up on the situation with the Melora syndicate. I witnessed, firsthand, her conclude dealings with a hájje. And not just any hájje. We have good reason to believe this hájje was a direct son of Yezurkstal."

The air was sucked from the room. After a few moments of shock, the mages erupted into side conversations. Zelag couldn't make out anything coherent amongst the uproar. But he did hear plenty of mentions of 'death', 'hiding', and a few 'not get involved'.

"Listen everyone!" George shouted over the clamor. "Let's focus in. We're here for solutions, and a panic now is not going to do us any good."

With the voice amplification offered by the podium, his words were sufficiently loud to cut through much of the noise, causing the uproar to die down. But a few stragglers decided they'd take the opportunity to speak.

"What exactly are they planning?" called a feminine voice from the right.

"Are we expecting the lizock to join the attack on Paxvilla?" came another voice from the left.

"Is he a necromancer as well?" questioned the weaselly elf from earlier.

"These are all great questions," George continued unperturbed. Zelag had to hand it to him. He had really grown his confidence over the last few years. Maintaining a straight face and even tone, the wizard seemed in control of the crowd.

"And to help answer these questions, I'd like to invite a special guest up to speak more on Melora and the situation with her syndicate. Zelag, would you please join us up here?"

"Oh, that's so exciting," Ygabb whispered to Zelag with a wide smile. "I always get so nervous speaking in front of crowds, but I'm sure you'll do great."

Not wanting to let her off on another tangent, Zelag jumped to his feet, walking briskly to the stage. He could feel everyone's eyes on him as he did, some discordant murmurs spreading about the audience.

Stepping onto the stage, Zelag approached the podium. George backed away, allowing him to take his place on the stage.

"Good evening," the shapeshifter started, shaking off some unexpected anxiety. "I know most of you do not know me, but for those who do, you understand that my people, the Preajin, have some unique gifts."

The room erupted again, people bursting into side conversations. Zelag could make out enough to recognize that most of the newer members were questioning his heritage. The homely elf from earlier stood up and pointed at him.

"You're a liar! Preajin are nothing more than a myth fabricated by worldly authorities."

At least it seemed most of the audience didn't share this sentiment. Several mages burst into laughter at this suggestion. Others called her out, at least one mentioning her 'sandy foundation' and others simply calling her 'crazy'.

245

"Prove it!" shouted a masculine voice from the middle of the room. Zelag couldn't quite place who said it.

George approached the podium again.

"Rein it in! There are enough among us who've witnessed Zelag's gifts firsthand. Most of you are sounding more like bureaucrats than anything right now!"

Zelag smirked as the uproar quieted, mages all settling back into their seats. As the few remaining murmurs died down, Zelag continued.

"Thank you, George. One thing I think the myths of my people downplay is our ability to see the world of magic. Where you see a simple emerald, I see that stone's stores of green magic. More than that, I can see every one of your life forces, your aura if you will. As many of you know, I was there during the final battle against Death," Zelag paused, closing his eyes as the thought of that day haunted him. The room was silent, and seeing everyone's attention on him, Zelag continued.

"Even though I wish I could, the truth is I could never forget that monster's aura. It was unique, powerful, and downright terrifying. And I hadn't seen anyone whose aura was remotely like his, not in power, nor in overall composition. That is, I hadn't seen one until early this afternoon.

"The hájje I saw was undoubtedly one of Death's direct offspring. And he had more power in him than any of you in this room." Zelag paused, casting a glance towards Savannah.

"Which is saying something, because there are those among your ranks who are quite powerful."

246

"Of course, while this hájje may have tremendous power, the power Melora yields is of a different sort. Her syndicate has influence over the entire southeastern district. Beyond controlling most of the slums there, she has an abundance of resources and materials, and all manner of unsavory members among her ranks.

"Her organization has continued to grow decade after decade because she leaves no room for disloyalty. Each of her enforcers is branded with her mark, which magically binds them in service to her. Some of the smaller operations in the Kingdom are run by those bearing that brand. In other words, her influence extends well beyond her direct syndicate.

"Effectively, she controls a quarter of the land within the Kingdom, making hers the largest syndicate. Where she leads, many of the smaller ones will follow. And as Savannah already alluded to, the real power of the Kingdom lies in the land. So, if she is allying herself with the hájje, it means the entire Kingdom is likely to follow."

A few murmurs spread throughout the chamber again. Katas stood up and raised his right hand.

"So, what exactly are you suggesting we do about this? From what I could discern in my scouting efforts, the hájje army is quite substantial. But it is just that -a hájje army."

Savannah stepped up to the podium, nodding toward Zelag, who took a step back.

"That's the perfect transition to the real purpose behind this meeting." She spoke. "We believe the attack on Paxvilla is just a gambit, a precursor to much larger plans."

The room was silent, everyone looking at Savannah.

"Before the final battle with Yezurkstal, he systematically attacked many of the smaller villages throughout Erathal. It seems reasonable that his children would take the same approach. And with the growth of our community here and the expansion of the three major sovereignties, there's not really many isolated settlements left in Erathal."

"But what about Dumner?" asked a green-skinned lizock in the back right corner of the room.

"What about us? Aren't we less defended than Paxvilla?" shouted the weaselly looking elf from earlier.

"We have to assume," Savannah spoke over the other voices, "that they have as much intelligence as we do. And if they have the proper intelligence, they know very well that either Dumner or Marftaport would put up much more of a fight than Paxvilla. The humans have a fortified position, but we have magic and physical might that they lack."

The room quieted down, listening as Savannah continued.

"And that's why it's imperative that we step in. Each of you has your own choice to make. Tomorrow we will be mustering all volunteers by the eastern borders of town and start on the way to Dumner. Our plan is to join centaur volunteers and continue to a farm just outside Paxvilla for deployment."

"Are you suggesting we march off to war?" asked the weaselly elf. His whiny tone got more annoying every time he spoke. And the inflection he put on the word 'war' reminded Zelag of a dying seagull.

"I'm suggesting we don't allow an entire city to be mercilessly slaughtered." Savannah glared at the weasel-elf.

"Have we tried sending a representative to talk with the hájje?" asked a new voice, deep and gravely. Zelag scanned the room before spotting the speaker. It was a dwarf, tall for his kind and wearing green robes.

"If they are allying themselves with the lizock, it means they aren't beyond reason. Perhaps if we know what their ultimate objective is, we can convince them there is another way to obtain it."

Zelag narrowed his eyes, looking more closely at the dwarf and trying to figure out why he looked so familiar. The red beard, the gray eyes…he looked like Keldor's son. When did he start practicing magic?

"That is an excellent point," Savannah replied. "And one we have considered. Tel' Shira insists it will make no difference, but part of our defense strategy in Paxvilla involves an attempt at negotiating. There's only one road they can take, and we'll make sure to have representatives ready to discuss terms, assuming they are open to them."

Savannah looked around the room, as if anticipating more objections. To Zelag's surprise, it seemed there were none, the room remaining quiet for a few seconds.

"So, anyone who wishes to join the defense force we will meet on the eastern border about one hour after first light tomorrow and depart mid-morning. The Petersons are staying to mind the prisoner, but it is recommended anyone else who remains behind consider ways they can protect Marftaport in case of attack. If there are no objections, this concludes our meeting for this evening. Thank you all for attending."

Zelag looked around the room, praying there were no objections. But as he feared, the homely elf woman stood, raising her hand and clearing her throat.

Savannah rolled her eyes, biting the bottom of her lip and nodding towards the elf.

"Yes, Karenella?"

This was going to be a long night.

CRApTER, XXI

Jaldor stood up, whipping the sweat from his forehead as he observed the progress. Banging of hammers and driving of nails rang out across the field, other volunteers still working away at the fence. The young farmer was amazed how quick and efficient everyone was.

This massive cedar fence was a major improvement compared to what he was used. Round 15-centimeter logs, enchanted for longevity, had been placed every couple of meters, establishing the entire fence line. All this left was for them to finish the railing, which leveraged similarly sized runs of cedar split in half circles.

"I hope it's up to your standards," said George, leaning on his staff and holding his right hand over his eyes as he looked out along the fence.

Jaldor glanced at the wizard, offering a smile and nod.

"This is brilliant. You've seen what I had before. I'm glad your people suggested cutting the logs down the middle like that too -allowed us to get a lot more fence. And you're saying the magic will keep it in pristine condition like this?"

"Oh, absolutely!" exclaimed George. "You'll want to make sure someone comes out every decade or so to check the enchantment and make sure there's no issues. But I'm sure your great-grandchildren will be using this same fence."

"That's amazing," Jaldor muttered, shaking his head.

"And all this space!" he continued spreading his arms wide. "My cows were so used to being crammed in just a single acre back at the old farm."

"Well, we're hoping you'll expand your operation once you get things going," replied George rubbing his chin. "Thirty acres in total, split almost perfectly in half; I don't know a lick about animal husbandry, but I imagine the only trouble you'll have is breeding the cows fast enough."

"My family and I are just so grateful for everyone's generosity. No one in Paxvilla would do work like this without payment upfront. It's…" Jaldor trailed off, uncertain what else to say. Why were they being so charitable?

"It's really no big deal," replied George, shrugging it off. "Like I've said, you're introducing a valuable commodity to our community. I had never had anything as delicious as that hard cheese you shared with us the other night. And those little breakfast discs your wife made…what did you call them, pan cakes? Those things were amazing!"

Jaldor laughed, bending down, and picking up the bucket of nails and his hammer.

"Yes, pancakes," he said, walking over to the next stack of fence rails. "Do you mind helping with these?"

"Of course!" George aimed his staff at the cedar rails.

252

Taking a step back, Jaldor watched as the first rail floated up, wobbling a little before settling in and aligning with the last post he'd nailed in. Without delay, the farmer lined up a nail and hammered it into the first post. He walked along the second, third, and fourth posts, putting two nails in each.

Without having to ask, George raised the next rail into place, allowing Jaldor to repeat the process. Jaldor had figured out that George was not exactly proficient at using this sort of magic. Every time he lifted one of the cedar rails, he would take a moment to stabilize it and put it into place. Some of the other mages working on the fence were able to do two or three at a time, but he struggled to raise just one.

Still, he couldn't complain. This was a lot quicker and easier than doing all the work by hand and George's slow and deliberate approach meant Jaldor didn't have to continue talking about anything. And on a cool spring afternoon like this, it was nice to just work with his hands in silence.

After securing all four rails on the posts, the duo proceeded to the next section and continued there. Before he realized it, Jaldor was approaching the final section, where they'd be placing another gate. One of the volunteers, a dwarf, was working on assembling that gate.

"Keldor, we don't usually see you helping out with these builds," said George approaching the dwarf.

The gray-bearded dwarf looked up at the wizard, wearing a smirk. Jaldor hadn't met a dwarf before today, but in the short interactions he had so far, this one was exactly what he expected.

"The people moving here don't usually make cheese!" the old dwarf exclaimed, his face lighting up. Despite his wrinkled, weathered skin, the old dwarf had a youthful exuberance about him. He reached for the leather wineskin at his waste, taking a swig. Judging by the strong smell of spirits about him, he had already consumed most of its contents.

"Did you get to try some of my cheese?" Jaldor asked, raising an eyebrow.

"Aye. This wizard's wife gave me a sampling. And you just remember who supplied all these nails you're using, and not to mention the hinges for these gates. I may even be tempted to smith you up some new and improved farming implements for a few wheels of cheese."

Placing the hammer and bucket of nails down, Jaldor nodded.

"That sounds like a fair deal. I'll tell you what. I'm sure I have a few kilos of hard cheese that are properly aged. After we finish these fences and get the cows into their new home, I'll fetch whatever is ready. I figure that should offer you and the others a bit of initial payment at least."

"Well let's get this gate up then!" Keldor cheered.

Taking a step back, Jaldor watched George point his staff at the gate. The wizard squinted, slowly raising the gate up. As with the rails, it took him a few moments to stabilize, but with some slow and steady movements of his staff, the wizard was able to drop the gate into place. With it settled in place, Keldor stepped up and drove in the pins.

He was done in a flash, three strikes for three pins. Especially considering his seemingly inebriated state, this dwarf was nothing if not impressive.

"And that finishes this enclosure! Who'll be placing the enchantments on the thing?" Keldor asked, wobbling as he reached down for his wineskin.

"I think that would be Foetidus," replied George, motioning towards a weaselly looking, unkempt elf sitting under the shady oaks in the distance.

"Well let's go get 'em so you two can fetch those cows and, more importantly, those hard cheeses!"

Jaldor chuckled, pulling open the gate and stepping inside. He looked out at the green pasture, taking a moment to appreciate the beauty of this land. The grass was already high enough to offer ample food for his herd.

The clicking of the gate shutting behind him turned his attention back to the others, who were walking towards Foetidus. Walking with long strides to catch up, Jaldor considered the fence along the way. Everything looked so perfect, the posts and rails all aligned and sturdy. Even without any enchantment, he was sure this could hold his herd in for many years.

"Foetidus!" Keldor called ahead, waving towards the elf.

Foetidus looked up, glancing across the field. He waited until the trio was closing in before he wiped his hands on his tunic and rose to his feet. It was hard for Jaldor to read his expression, which somehow looked like a cross between amusement and constipation.

"Ready to walk the perimeter and apply that enchantment of yours?" Keldor asked.

The disheveled elf looked around, first turning towards the house being framed to the north before looking back around at the fence line.

"Is it really done already?" he whined.

"Aye," responded Keldor. "George is going to take Jaldor back to fetch the cows. So, let's get moving."

With a loud sigh, Foetidus took a low bow.

"Urgo!"

Keldor shook his head, grumbling under his breath as he started off towards the fence. Foetidus regarded Jaldor, looking him up and down.

"Your bovines better appreciate how much is going into this home of theirs."

Turning abruptly, the elf marched after Keldor.

"Urgo?" Jaldor asked, turning towards George, and scratching the back of his head.

"It's just an old elvish word. Basically means 'yes, sir', but in this instance, I'd say Foetidus was being sarcastic."

"That much I gathered. Shall we go through one of those portals and get the exodus underway?"

"Urgo!" replied George with a grin. He lifted up his staff and pointed it just past the two oak trees. The quartz in his staff glowed and he called out "Ixidor!"

The blue portal opened in a circle before them. Though he had traveled back and forth this way a few times, Jaldor still felt a hint of nausea as he stepped through, walking right out into his cow pen back at Paxvilla.

The smells of fresh grass and milled lumber were replaced with the familiar, unmistakable odor of cows. Though he had lived with it his whole life, Jaldor noticed this immediate method of travel always brought the smell into sharp contrast. After glancing back to confirm George had followed him through, Jaldor proceeded towards the fence line.

Beyond the difference in smell, the contrast in fence quality was a reminder of why this was the right move for his family. He reached the eastern gate, looking at the various patch jobs and cockeyed posts along the way. Retrieving his length of rope, he proceeded to the nearest cow.

His daughter had named this one Fluffy, because she had an unusually fluffy coat. Her shaggy brown fur was without blemish or color, and her milk was always a bit heavier on the cream. Combined with her easy-going demeanor, this made her an excellent young heifer for cheesemaking.

"Is there anything you need me to do?" George asked as Jaldor tightened the halter around the first cow.

"You said you'll just do one at a time right?"

"Yes. I'm afraid holding these portals open for too long can take a lot of energy."

"I imagine so!" exclaimed Jaldor, scratching behind his head. "So, how about you just make sure you keep each portal

257

open until I go through and come back? It might take me a few seconds to remove the halter, but I'll try to be quick."

"I can do that," replied George. "Are you ready?"

"Yes, sir. Or, I guess I should say, urgo!"

George smirked, holding up his staff and pointing just in front of Fluffy. "I hope you'll forgive if I don't call it out every time, I cast the spell."

"It makes no difference to me." Jaldor shrugged. He had assumed the declaration was part of the spellcasting.

As the portal opened, Jaldor stepped through, pulling softly on the rope and leading Fluffy through. Coming out the other side, he looked back and blinked a few times as his vision cleared. Fluffy had stopped halfway through the portal, her hind legs still on the other side.

"Come on girl," Jaldor called softly, giving another tug on the rope. With a low moo, Fluffy stepped the rest of the way through. Not taking a moment to delay, Jaldor stepped back and patted her on the side as he removed the halter.

"Now go on out there and enjoy your new home!"

Fluffy took another couple steps away from the portal, far enough that Jaldor was comfortable to step back through. As he came back out at the old farm, he took a deep breath and shook his head. George lowered his staff, and Jaldor glanced back to see the portal close.

"That wasn't so bad," said Jaldor cracking his knuckles and looking around.

"Not bad at all!" exclaimed George. "Let's keep that up and we should have no problems."

Jaldor nodded, proceeding towards the next closest cow, one of the newest members to the herd. This little one was even easier to manage, quickly leading her through to the other side and returning for the next one.

And progress remained steady for the next twenty minutes. Haltering cow after cow with his rope, he led each through the portals without issue. That is, until he reached his bull, Noah.

Though Jaldor usually found him amenable, it seemed all the transportation of his heifers had him on edge. For as Jaldor approached with his halter in hand, the bull kept his distance, stomping away.

"Come on Noah," Jaldor called after him, fiddling with the rope in his hand. He tried moving in more slowly, puffing out his chest and taking each step with care. It was a fine balancing act, trying to assert himself as the stronger authority while not wishing to startle the creature.

But after a couple attempts, Noah let him move in. Maneuvering around the horns, the farmer affixed the halter and gave a firm pat to Noah's side.

"Good boy. Let's go get your girls."

As the portal opened before him, Jaldor stepped through, keeping Noah at his side to lead him on. Despite his initial trepidation, the bull meandered through, snorting as they came out the other side and scratching at the green grass.

Letting him off the halter, Jaldor patted Noah one last time before stepping back through the portal. George was standing just on the other side, a smile on his face.

"That was remarkably easier than I anticipated," the wizard admitted, rubbing his chin.

"It was a little easier than I expected too," Jaldor replied with a chuckle.

"How long does it take you to milk all those cows anyways?"

"About two hours, usually a little less. The harder part is all the work that comes after milking."

"I bet! Well, let's go ahead and collect those cheeses you have ready. Anything else we should get while we're here?"

"Just that and all the milking buckets. You sure your people will be able to get the stanchions in place before tomorrow morning? I'll need to milk them all then, even if we don't get to process it as usual."

"For sure," replied George, starting off north towards the house and cheese cave. "And I'll be back here at sun rise tomorrow to ferry you and your family to the new home too. We'll get you out of here before the enemy arrives."

"I hope so," murmured Jaldor, following behind. And as they walked towards the cheese cave, the decades of memories on this farm all flooded into his mind.

He would never forget this place.

CHAPTER XXII

Paxvilla, Road Outside Jaldor's Farm
20 Julla, 1149 MT

Artimus Jr. looked south, squinting towards the approaching hájje army. The sun was sinking in the sky, clouds casting shadows over the road. Clinging tight to the reins of his mount, the young elf's thoughts were only on the battle ahead.

He glanced to either side, his mother and father both seated to his left on their respective steeds. To his right was the Paxvilla delegation, a well-muscled but otherwise average bearded man clad in an amalgam of steel chain mail and plate armor covered by the standard white tunic with blue shield and eight-point star. Behind him were two similarly armored men, with Irontail taking up a defensive position just to their rear.

With the flag of Evorath hoisted above, Artimus Jr. hoped the familiar green tree and prolific roots would be recognized by the hájje. Having no prior experience with these dark elves, aside from the recent skirmish, he wondered whether they'd even recognize the traditional call for treaty. He shivered, considering the banner blowing in the cool spring air.

One way or another, he knew this would be one of the most significant moments in Erathal history. And that thought left him paralyzed, his heart heavy and hands shaking. Life in Marftaport had not prepared him for this.

With eyes glued on the approaching army, he felt a great weight lifted from his shoulders as the bulk of the enemy came to a stop. Their ranks were unlike any he'd witnessed before, more than a dozen wide, and hundreds deep. And at the front of their army were deployed demonic behemoths, large beasts of burden ready to lay siege to the thick walls of Paxvilla.

As the bulk of their army came to a stop, a handful of their soldiers continued forth, drawing into view. Still a few hundred meters in the distance, their features grew clear as they approached. Of the five approaching soldiers, four were covered from head to toe in steel plate mail with full cross helmets. Even their steeds were fully armored.

But Artimus Jr. was more interested in the one soldier stationed in the middle of the group. She was beautiful.

Certain his eyes were playing tricks on him, he blinked a few times, hoping to clear his vision. But as the snow-skinned, black-eyed beauty led her delegation forth, the young elf found himself entranced. Covered in custom ebony armor, she sat confidently upon her black mare. An adamantium blade hung by her side, the green blade shimmering in the setting sun as she marched towards him.

Without any head covering, her long black hair was left flowing behind her, wafting in the wind as she rode. Recalling stories of his parents' romance from his childhood, Artimus Jr. felt dizzy. This hájje made his heart skip a beat, her soft features igniting a fire in his soul. How could this aggressor stir such longings in his heart?

As the delegation grew nearer, Artimus Jr. closed his eyes, taking a few deep breaths and refocusing his mind.

"You alright Junior?" his father asked. The stern, confident tone of his voice helped quiet Artimus Jr.'s heart.

"Yes, just steeling myself against whatever may come," he lied. He could tell it was not convincing.

"Don't worry," interjected his mother. "We'll be having dinner back in Marftaport before we know it."

The group fell silent as the hájje delegation drew near, the air growing thick. Artimus Jr. could feel the tension in the air as they drew within a few meters.

"We recognize your signal and entreat as a courtesy," uttered the beautiful hájje as they came into earshot. Her voice was soft and melodic, even more beautiful than her symmetric features.

"Then we beg you," started Artimus Jr.'s mother, her voice more formal than he was accustomed to. "Please hear the delegation from Paxvilla. They wish no ill will upon your people and wish to call for an end to hostilities. Let's stop this before it's too late."

The hájje's face twitched, her stoic demeanor faltering for a brief moment. What was that that Artimus Jr. saw? Was it uncertainty? He wondered.

"Their wishes are irrelevant," the hájje replied, her voice cold and resolute. "We claim this land, formally known as Paxvilla, in the name of the hájje. It was my father who brought these humans to Evorath. It is therefore my right to claim this land. If you wish to live, I suggest you go back and tell your people to lay down their arms."

263

"And we'd advise you do the same lass," interjected the head of the human delegation. Artimus Jr. still found his strange accent so foreign. "We bow to no pale devils, no matter what unjust claim you might imagine having on our land. It was our ancestors who were forcibly taken to this land, and it was them who laid claim here. If you want a fight, you'll find our forces are more than ready to give you one."

The hájje closed her eyes, her red lips curling into a faint smile. "Then you choose death," she pulled on the reins of her horse as she uttered the words, turning about and trotting back towards the rest of her army.

Artimus Jr. kept his hand on his sword, clasping the handle and keeping a close eye on the other hájje. Fortunately, they observed typical protocol, making an about face and following their commander. With a sigh of relief, Artimus Jr. glanced back at the others.

"That went about like I expected," said his father with a shake of his head.

"Aye," replied the Paxvilla delegate. "Let's send these demons to the afterlife."

As the rest of the group turned to gallop back to town, Artimus Jr. hesitated for a moment, glancing back one last time at the hájje commander. There was a pit in his stomach. And though he had been in dangerous situations before, he found this one felt different. Galloping back towards the city walls, he wondered for the first time whether he'd make it through the coming days.

CHAPTER XXIII

Paxvilla
20 Julla, 1149 MT

Zelag examined the bow in his hands. It had been a few months since he last used a bow, and knowing the task ahead, he wished he could wait at least a few months more. But as the hájje army amassed before the gatehouse, there was no time to linger on those hopeful thoughts. It was time for action.

Pulling back the string of the bow, he aimed towards the sky, ready to do his part in the hailstorm.

"Fire!" screamed the human commander, his grizzled voice echoing off the stone walls as Zelag let his arrow fly.

The hundreds of arrows all soared through the sky, arching up before coming down like a hailstorm. But in this instance, the hailstorm looked much closer to reality. As the arrows sliced towards the ground, they met some unexpected opposition.

Red flashes illuminated the sky as each arrow hit an arcane barrier, lighting up the sky like fireworks. Leveraging his unique vision, he attempted to trace the origin of the barrier. There was no way a single mage was generating that large of a protective field.

As Zelag scanned the display of magic, in fact, he realized the amount was much greater than one. There were at least two dozen hájje cloaked in scarlet robes spread evenly throughout the enemy ranks.

"Ready!" shouted the commander.

Carefully protected at the center of contingents, the enemy mages were channeling a dark magic, each one aligned with others. The arcane energy itself made Zelag's heart flutter, stifling memories of the battle with Death.

"Aim!"

Zelag considered his bow, bringing an arrow close to his face to examine an arrowhead. He let them both go, falling harmlessly on the stone. These would never penetrate that magical barrier.

"Fire!" the whoosh of arrows soaring into the sky filled the air.

Looking about, Zelag caught Artimus's eyes before walking over to address the problem.

"We're not getting through that barrier. They have at least two dozen mages holding it up. We need to get inside their ranks and take out some of those mages if we hope to have a chance. With those massive demons on their side, they'll get through these walls in short order."

Artimus shook his head, replacing his arrow in its quiver.

"I'm getting too old for this. Let's get the party together and charge out through the gates. I'll get working on convincing them to let us out. You two, get the other party members."

Artimus didn't hesitate for a moment, shuffling away through the formation. Some of the human soldiers shared various glances. Most of them appeared frightened or confused, but Zelag could swear some appeared hopeful.

"Alright Little A! You get the barghest brothers and the two old timers. I'll get Irontail, Luna, Savannah, and the rest of their volunteers."

Artimus Jr. nodded, not even flinching at the 'Little A' comment. He took off towards the steps, which would take him back to ground level. With a moment's pause to consider the remaining human archers, Zelag followed right behind.

Leaping down the last few steps, he veered left towards the flanking army. While the many human soldiers prepared to reinforce the main gate, some of Marftaport's best were poised to use the side exit from the walls to the west. As he sprinted through the Paxvilla ranks, he thought about what form might best serve him for this encounter.

Perhaps a nimble cougar would be a good choice. Or maybe turning into a bulwark to stampede through their ranks. No, this human form was the most versatile, allowing him the most flexibility in the heat of battle.

Reaching the secret western wall exit, Zelag pulled the lever and leaned against the stone wall, straining as he pushed it open. Stepping out on the other side, he looked out at the Marftaport forces, trying to spot Irontail.

There were only a few other centaurs who joined the defense. So, when Zelag spotted the centaur standing next to

Luna Freya, towering over everyone around him, the shapeshifter scrambled through the crowd.

"Irontail!" he shouted, waving his hand overhead.

The centaur pivoted around, glancing down towards Zelag. "Oh, Zelag. What is it?"

"Change of plans," Zelag replied.

He paused to catch his breath, closing his eyes for just a moment before continuing.

"The enemy has some massive barrier at work thanks to a large grouping of mages. We can't do anything from the walls. We need to charge in now and disrupt the barrier. Otherwise, we'll lose the defensive advantage. Without that, there's no way any of us are making it to tomorrow."

Irontail glanced around at the others. Luna cracked her neck, stretching out her arms and proceeding to crack her knuckles.

"You sure this is the best way?" Irontail asked, his deep voice weighed with the burden of so many lives.

"Artimus didn't object."

"Then I say we do it," came Savannah's voice from behind a couple of lamia druids. She stepped past the two of them, striding towards Zelag with determination.

"Listen up," Irontail shouted, his voice reverberating off the walls. "Let's regroup to ensure we're equipped for quick, precise movement. Smaller groups for taking out these mages holding up the barrier. This means every group needs aerial defense capabilities, because we might find ourselves in the path of a hailstorm."

"Uhm," the somehow still cheerful voice of Ygabb pierced the air. "Let's not neglect the importance of someone who can handle large numbers of enemy soldiers. Each group should also have a heavy to help diminish their number advantage."

"She's right," interjected Luna with a smile.

"I guess that means we can't charge in together big guy!" she clapped Irontail on his left flank, marching east, presumably to find a different assault team.

A pair of lizock twins looked at one another and shrugged before marching west.

Savannah seemed uncertain where to go, her eyes wavering and looking down as she stood frozen in place.

"That means you too Savannah," affirmed Ygabb. "Maybe Zelag and I can round out your group!"

Savannah turned towards Zelag, arching her eyebrows. Zelag shrugged in reply.

"I suppose now is a good time to really see how long I can really maintain it without losing focus," replied Savannah, glancing down, and twirling her hair between her fingertips.

"Excellent!" Ygabb jumped in place, bleating in excitement. "Just wait until you see what she can do!"

Scratching his beard, Zelag forced a smile and nodded.

"I'm excited to find out," he lied.

In truth, he was nervous. Though this human form had come from a world plagued with this sort of open warfare, Zelag had always preferred more intimate settings for his violence. There were too many unpredictable elements on the battlefield.

But with steady breathing and a calm demeanor, he followed Savannah and Ygabb as they moved further away from the western city wall's secret exit. Interesting enough, he had discovered this exit not too long ago while on a covert mission within the human town. He hoped his act of surprise upon hearing the plan had been convincing.

In total, it seemed Marftaport had managed to muster more than one hundred soldiers. Considering the skill and expertise of most of those soldiers, Zelag conservatively figured that could account for at least five times as many Paxvilla guards. With these small attack groups, they might actually be able to disrupt the barrier, or so he hoped.

"Are you going to change into something else?" Ygabb asked as they walked, her high-pitched voice piercing through the chatter of the other groups organizing.

"No," Zelag replied. "Every second counts in the chaos of this type of battle. This human form is well-suited for it."

Zelag kept his eyes down as they walked, working to keep his balance on the uneven terrain. The ground was unstable, littered with holes and loose rocks left over from the building of the wall. And as they walked towards the southwest, he couldn't help but be reminded of his adventures with Casandra. Shaking off the memories, he glanced towards the approaching army.

"Have you fought in a battle like this before?" Ygabb questioned, her cheerful tone a bit diminished.

"No," Zelag uttered.

He considered leaving it at that, but hearing the apparent concern in her voice left him feeling obligated to continue.

"But Savannah has, and many others here have as well."

"Oh, yeah!" Ygabb's voice rose in pitch. "Savannah, you ready to show Zelag the ace up your sleeve?"

Savannah glanced back, offering a faint smile. She reached into the small satchel hanging at her side and pulled out what looked to be a small carving. Looking at it closely, Zelag could see the totem was filled with green magic.

"It's really nothing new," she said, blushing as she held up the totem. "I just figured out a way to channel an animation spell through this totem. It allows me to tie my subconscious to the animation."

"And what does that accomplish?" Zelag scratched his beard, arching an eyebrow as he considered the implications.

"Primarily, it means my animation will be capable of independent action."

Zelag's eyes widened.

"So, you're creating a golem of some sort *and* you'll be able to cast other spells? How long can you maintain that?"

Savannah tightened her lips, shrugging and holding her hands out to the side.

"I'm not sure. I've stored up a good deal of magic in the totem. And it will collect any latent energy it can from the environment, so hopefully it will last as long as we need it to."

"Your confidence is so reassuring," quipped Zelag, not trying to hide his sarcasm.

"The Command is 'spread no falsehood', isn't it?"

Zelag smiled and shook his head.

"Well, let's see it then."

Savannah nodded, brushing her hair back before tossing the totem on the ground unceremoniously. She closed her eyes, gathering some arcane energy around her. Zelag watched as she focused this energy on the totem.

The ground erupted, dirt showering up as rock, root, and soil all congealed around the totem. It began to form a bipedal form, thick arms and legs jutting from its wide torso. As the animated mass took form, it stood over four meters tall at full height, casting a shadow over the group.

Seeing things as only he could, it was like the totem acted as the golem's heart, magic branching out from there and connecting the rest of the body, just like blood within his current form. It was magnificent, which he intended to express. But just as he opened his mouth to say so, he was interrupted.

"Listen up everyone!" Irontail's voice boomed through the field, the murmur of conversations whispering away in the wind as they came to an end.

"Remember, your primary job is to make sure everyone in your unit lives to see tomorrow. After that, your objective is to take out the mages generating this barrier. Follow your unit leads and you'll make it through the day."

Irontail drew closer as he spoke. Zelag watched him step through the crowd, making his way to the front of the gathering. Once there, he pointed south towards the hájje army.

"We'll close that distance faster than you think. If this is your first battle, remember to focus on one thing at a time. Your biggest enemy out there is your own mind. Don't let it get the best of you. And whatever this day may bring, remember what we are fighting for."

The veteran centaur lowered his gaze, pausing for a moment of silence. As he looked up, he lifted his massive sledge up over his head and shouted.

"Charge!"

Luna roared, sprinting towards the hájje infantry line.

She would have preferred to have her adopted parents at her side, or even the Peterson's. But Bel' Mora was a competent mage. So long as the twin lizock warriors kept her safe, Luna could focus on tearing through the enemy ranks.

Her attack group had split off towards one of the easternmost contingents, running through the open field towards the enemy. The bedlam as some of the other attack groups engaged the enemy already filled the air. Battle cries were drowned out by screams of pain and thuds of bodies.

Keeping her attention on her group's target, she leapt towards the front line; a row of hájje soldiers wielding both sword and shield, clothed in matching plate armor.

With mythril claws extended, she landed atop the nearest soldier, knocking him back onto the hájje directly behind him. As the two enemies tumbled over, Luna tore the shield from the first one's grasp, hurling it towards the next nearest soldier to keep him off balance. Exposing her opponent's torso, she slashed at his throat before springing back to her feet.

As the pinned hájje struggled to get his dead ally off him, Luna retrieved the deceased's sword and stabbed it through them both. Shifting her focus to the next nearest enemy, who had already recovered, she led with a kick. With Bel' Mora's magic coursing through her veins, Luna felt unstoppable, the force of her kick enough to send this soldier reeling back. He knocked down two of his allies but remained on his feet.

Rushing in to keep the soldier on the defensive, Luna followed up by wrenching down on his shield. This left the soldier exposed, but he was quicker than most of the others, countering with a quick slash. Luna was faster.

She intercepted the swing, catching the blade in her claws and offering a toothy smile as she yanked it from the soldier's grasp. As the hájje stumbled towards her, she went for the throat, discarding him to square up against the next foe.

Keeping her eyes wide, she watched as the rows of soldiers began to wise up, circling around to entrap her in the center. Now would be the test for her allies. Scrambling to pick up two swords from the fallen soldiers, Luna held one in either hand and looked around at the more than dozen hájje that were encircling her.

Releasing a primal roar, she reached into that magic Bel' Mora was lending her and began spinning with arms outstretched. She spun around like a whirlwind, causing the enemies to fall back. Repelling sword and shield, she continued her rampage, her roar echoing throughout the battlefield. But she could already feel her stamina draining.

Seeing the opportune moment, she released the first sword. It soared through the air, skewering two of her enemies. As she slowed her spin, she threw the second sword, but this time her efforts weren't quite as successful. One of the enemies was quicker than she could have anticipated, swiping at the flying projectile with his sword and planting it harmlessly in the ground.

Shaking her head and blinking rapidly to help overcome the dizziness of her attack, she kept her hands up. While her maneuver kept the enemy at bay, she was disappointed to see how quickly they were recovering. These pale elves were hardier than she would have guessed.

Fortunately, the two lizock warriors took advantage of the situation. They slipped in behind some of the outer troops, all of whom had their attention on Luna. The troops didn't even turn around in time to see the lizock plant swords in their backs. Luna made a mental note to commit the lizocks' names to memory after this battle was over.

The cries of pain from these two hájje was enough to foment more chaos among the enemy ranks. One of the nearest hájje, who was moving in on Luna, paused and glanced back at the sound. Without thinking, Luna took advantage of his lapse, slipping in and clawing his throat.

Another hájje attempted to rush in with a wide overhead swing. Bobbing to her right, Luna avoided the attack and stepped inside the enemy's defenses to dispatch him. Not sure how to get out from the horde of enemies, she kept her hand clasped on this one's throat, grabbing his left arm, and spinning him around. His dead body served as the perfect weapon, knocking down three nearby hájje and creating an opening.

Not wasting the opportunity, Luna dashed through the gap, keeping her eyes wide. The enemy mage was in sight, her black robes cloaking much of her features. Despite the bedlam, Luna's felite hearing was enough for her to pick up murmurs of an arcane chant -that must have been how they were keeping up the barrier. But Luna had more pressing matters to tend to.

Spinning back around, Luna just narrowly caught the blade of another attack, twisting the sword away with her right hand and chopping down the foe's neck. The soldier fell with a thud to the ground, but as he did another took his place. He rushed in even quicker than any before, leading with his shield.

Luna didn't have time to respond, so she held up her hands, palms out. Squealing as the air was knocked from her lungs, she lost the battle to maintain her balance. Accepting the fall, she spread her arms and rolled over backwards, springing back to her feet.

As she gathered her breath, the large hájje continued his charge. Squatting down, Luna jumped with all her might, her magically enhanced muscles allowing her enough power to jump clear over the enemy as he charged harmlessly past. Without anything to stop his momentum, he stumbled.

Landing on all four, Luna lunged after him, jumping on his back. Again, this hájje surprised her, maintaining his balance despite her weight. But as he struggled to pull her off, she reached around for her signature target, tearing at his throat and leaving him to gurgle as he fell dead.

As Luna turned back to continue the fight, she could feel the magic draining from her muscles. The two lizock brothers were in the thick of it, fighting back-to-back as the remaining hájje soldiers closed around them. And Bel' Mora had been forced on the defensive, throwing up a barrier of green magic to keep a group of hájje at bay.

"Damn snow skins." Luna muttered. She hissed, looking for the fastest path through the remaining hájje.

Hesitating for only a moment, she reached down and picked up the shield from her most recent victim. Bracing it in her left, she charged with a primal roar, tearing through the enemy lines towards Bel' Mora. Confident the lizock brothers could hold out for a few moments, she spun around as she cleared the lines, chucking the shield towards one of the larger hájje.

The hunk of metal hit the hájje in the side, staggering him long enough for Luna to continue her momentum. With a growl, she darted in and snapped his neck. Getting a quick count, she moved towards the next nearest hájje, who was swinging wildly at the green bubble around Bel' Mora.

With his focus on the bubble, Luna again moved in without resistance. She tackled this one to the ground, hissing as she tore out his throat.

The four remaining hájje wised up, shifting their attention from the bubble, and turning back towards Luna.

"I've already lost count of how many of you insects I've squashed today. But I guess four more wouldn't hurt!" Luna held out her arms wide, claws out as she taunted the hájje.

She grinned at her own insult. They all looked the same to her, covered in their dark plate armor and holding matching sword and shield. Like little ants marching to war.

And as they approached, banging their swords against their shields, she felt a tingling in the back of her neck.

This was too fun.

CḨAꝐTEꝚ XXIV

Artimus Jr. took a deep breath in, closing his eyes as he exhaled. He could hear the melee in the distance, many of his allies already engaged with the enemy. The loud clang of the gate chains lifting the portcullis filled him with anticipation.

He expected to wake up at any moment, discovering this was all a dream. Sure, he was no stranger to combat, but this largescale siege was not just new; it was disturbing. How could anyone have such flagrant disregard for life?

The portcullis locked into place with a clack, startling Artimus Jr. into looking up.

"Let's all stick together," said his father. The experienced elf looked around at the group.

Mojo, Oogmut, Morn, Neman, and the two elves made for quite the ragtag crew. And as Artimus Jr. took in all their expressions, he couldn't help but feel he was alone in his trepidation. They all looked stoic.

"I'll lead the charge," offered Oogmut stepping through the gate. The massive troll popped his knuckles, reaching down and adjusting the pouches about his belt. His massive form was always a bit intimidating.

"And I'll take up the rear," added Mojo, grasping his gnarled staff, and stepping forward.

279

"May Evorath watch over us," Artimus Jr. muttered, his heart pounding in his chest.

"She always does," replied Oogmut eyes trained forward.

Without another word, the troll stormed towards the battlefield. Morn and Neman howled as they ran behind. And seeing his father take off, bow grasped in his right hand, Artimus Jr. sprinted after them.

As he ran, his mind raced through the possibilities. There was no way all his friends would come out of this alive. And this thought filled him with guilt as he began prioritizing which lives mattered most to him. What if his parents didn't make it? What about Luna Freya? Or, as much as they could annoy him at times, what if one of the barghest brothers didn't survive?

These thoughts were no good.

But as he charged through the open field, a memory from decades ago came to the top of his mind. And it was a useful memory, or so Artimus Jr. thought.

"If you do ever find yourself in that kind of battle," the words of his father echoed in his mind, "remember to focus on the immediate threat. In war, distractions will get you killed. Remember the purpose of all this training is so your body will know what to do should it ever need to. Don't let your mind interfere with that training."

Heeding his father's advice, the young elf focused on the battlefield ahead. He worked as much as he could to push out all these other doubts and fears. But as they grew near, the mayhem was even more overwhelming than he expected.

The sounds alone were horrifying. A profane chorus of breaking bones, rending flesh, and shrieks of pain filling the air. And as they drew near to the front-most row of soldiers, Artimus Jr. could once again feel his heart pounding away at his chest. As he reached back to pull an arrow from his quiver, he struggled to steady his shaking hand.

"Remember your training!" his father shouted, firing off the first arrow. His shot found its mark, landing square in the eye of a hájje in the first row.

The enemy was well-armored, clad from head to toe in dark plate armor and holding matching shields. This left only a few key areas where Artimus Jr. could aim. Largest of these targets was the enemy head, as their helmets offered only limited coverage on the top and sides of their head.

Artimus Jr. took a deep breath, steadying his hand and taking aim at one of the enemy's faces. He cursed under his breath, watching the arrow bounce harmlessly off the side of the hájje's helmet.

Taking another deep breath, he settled onto his back leg and steadied his aim again, notching another arrow. His father had already dispatched with three enemies, and Oogmut was moving into range.

Focus.

This time, his arrow flew true, skewering a hájje straight through his open mouth. Artimus Jr. winced at the sight but was determined not to slow. He reached back and readied another arrow, taking aim at the next soldier in line.

Oogmut arrived at the enemy line, his body glowing with green magic as he trampled through the small gap Artimus Jr. and his father had created. The massive troll flailed wildly, tossing aside the hájje infantry like stuffed dolls. Morn and Neman were not far behind, using their canine frames to tear into the enemy lines and further widen the gap.

Realizing his father had dispatched another couple of enemies, Artimus Jr. stomped his right foot and slapped his chest.

"Focus!"

Notching another arrow, the young elf exhaled and let his projectile fly. This arrow found its mark in a hájje's neck. And this time, Artimus Jr. kept up the momentum, immediately readying another shot and taking out another hájje. But while the front line was occupied with Oogmut and the barghest brothers, the next row of soldiers was fast approaching on horseback.

These were like the four guards that had accompanied the hájje commander, but they numbered in the dozens. Not allowing himself to be distracted, Artimus Jr. kept up his attack, firing arrow after arrow. Two hits, one miss, three more hits. Before he knew it, the young elf reached back and found himself grabbing for nothing but air.

Widening his gaze, he noticed his father had already joined the melee, fighting side-by-side with the barghest brothers. Oogmut had moved further ahead, stomping the ground and unleashing a quake. A half dozen horse riders were tossed from their steeds, thudding to the ground as the tremor continued.

Mojo had moved closer to the melee as well, spinning an invisible circle in the air, which formed into a mass of red/green arcane energy. He cast the projectile towards the enemy cavalry, reaching into one of his pouches as he ran after it. Watching his allies work, Artimus Jr. began to wonder if his concern was misplaced. Perhaps these hájje were not the threat they feared them to be.

Slinging his bow upon his back, the young elf drew his mythril sword and charged towards the melee. While half of his allies had moved on to address the enemy cavalry, his father and Mojo were still dealing with the remaining front-line infantry. His father danced around one of the remaining soldiers, parrying each of the enemy's strikes as he maneuvered to find an opening. Meanwhile, Mojo pranced up to another, blowing dust into the hájje's face. The enemy screamed in terror, throwing off his helmet and clutching his throat as he writhed around.

Not wanting to even guess what sort of magic was in that powder, Artimus Jr. narrowed his gaze. He charged into the action, running towards one of the few remaining infantry. Intercepting the enemy before he could interfere with his father's fight, the young elf made an aggressive start.

He leapt into the air, swinging his sword down with all his weight. The enemy hájje raised his shield just in time, the sword slamming into the metal plate and sending him reeling back. Keeping his grip tight, Artimus Jr. continued the momentum, replanting his feet and following up with a second and third swing. The crash of his mythril against the steel of his enemy's shield was deafening, but effective.

Each strike tested the metal of his enemy's shield. And with a fourth swing, the shield crumbled back. The hájje screamed in pain, the metal folding over his arm. Not wanting to prolong the moment, Artimus Jr. yelled, sidestepping, and stabbing his foe through the chest.

With eyes closed, the elf threw up his right foot for leverage, yanking the sword back out from his slain foe. Grimacing, he took only a moment before refocusing on the battlefield. Oogmut thundered forward, creating an opening in the row of cavalry, and revealing the target: a mage clothed in crimson robes with her hands stretched into the sky.

Equipped with a long spear, another horse rider attempted to flank the troll, charging towards him from behind. Mojo stepped in, tossing another projectile to knock the aggressor from his horse. The soldier stumbled to the ground, his horse trampling over him and leaving him limp.

Morn and Neman had engaged with another contingent of enemy soldiers, these hájje more lightly armed and wielding a variety of weapons. Artimus Jr. hesitated for a moment, wondering if he should join that battle or go after the mage. Seeing his father run to join the barghest brothers, he decided on the latter. But as he glanced at his sword, he hesitated.

The blue of the metal was stained in dark crimson, blood still dripping from the blade. It made his stomach churn, his mind again thinking of the grand implications of this battle. Death by the hundreds, or more likely the thousands when it was all said and done. What monsters would initiate such a battle?

Shaking his head, Artimus Jr. focused on the enemy mage. He narrowed his eyes, tightening his grip on his sword. Now was the time for action.

Sprinting for the gap, the young elf kept his gaze wide, witnessing Oogmut tear another enemy rider off horseback. Mojo was doing his part as well, casting an arcane mist that washed over another half-dozen riders. The horses appeared enraged by the mist, braying, and violently tossing their riders aside.

Running past an injured hájje, Artimus Jr. considered his trajectory, repositioning his sword for the imminent strike. His gaze narrowed on approach, focusing for a quick kill. But with this increased focus, he almost missed the arrival of another foe.

Arching his sword around, he just narrowly blocked the strike of his familiar new foe. Regaining his balance, Artimus Jr. took a few measured steps away from the hájje commander. His heart fluttered, looking at the well-fitted, black plate armor that covered her from the neck down. Of course, it was what was above the neck that drew his attention.

The black of her eyes drew him in, like staring down a deep well of mystery. Her long black hair and smooth, hauntingly pale skin created an intriguing contrast. And as he caught his breath, Artimus Jr. wondered if she felt the same magnetic attraction.

"You must be eager to die," the hájje commander spat.

"Eager to learn how someone so beautiful could ever resort to committing an act so ugly as warfare," Artimus Jr. quipped without considering his own words.

He felt embarrassed, but the subtle hint of color on his opponent's cheeks and the almost imperceptible shudder in her sword hand made him think that perhaps she did as well. This was his opportunity to make a difference.

"I mean it," continued Artimus Jr. with a flourish of his sword. "Why would you want such brutal, unforgiving violence against a people that you do not even know?"

The hájje stepped forward, maintaining her aggressive stance. She appeared uncertain, her mouth wavering before she regained her composure.

"These humans are dangerous. They fear our superiority so we must eradicate them before they seek to destroy us."

She recited these words like a well-practiced speech.

As she finished, she stabbed at Artimus Jr.'s heart. Anticipating the strike, the young elf dodged to his right and parried the blow. Sparks of green and blue complimented the crisp clang of their blades. Taking advantage of the momentum, Artimus Jr. followed up with a swing for his foe's leg. But he miscalculated his attack, the flat of his blade striking the foe in her rear end.

"Oh, I'm sorry," he blurted, immediately regretting the words. "I mean, you'll have to do better than that!"

Artimus Jr. parried a couple more half-hearted attacks, refraining from another counterattack.

Taking on a more balanced stance, the hájje commander extended her sword tip, circling around on her toes.

"Why do you protect these animals?" she asked, flourishing her adamantium blade.

"They are no more animals than you or me. Yes, they come from another world. But they have a divine creator, just as we do. They feel as we do, think as we do, and have souls like we do. We should seek to help them thrive here on Evorath."

The hájje commander paused, dropping her guard for just a moment. Though his training urged him to strike, Artimus Jr. felt a force tickling the back of his neck, commanding him to restrain.

"You are quite different than most elves, aren't you?" she asked, continuing to circle.

"I don't think so," Artimus Jr. mirrored her movements.

"I'm different enough I suppose. But my compassion is shared by many. I'd prefer not to fight, but to sit by your side and hear your story. My name is Artimus Atyrmirid Jr. What is yours?"

The hájje's eyes quivered as she lashed out with a wild swing. Again, Artimus Jr. deflected the attack, following with some fancy footwork and remaining on the defensive. Was she toying with him?

"My name is of no consequence," she spat. "And your stalling tactics will not earn you victory."

Artimus Jr. adjusted his stance, squaring his hips and taking his sword in both hands. His eyes were glued to the hájje.

But her movements were quicker.

With an almost imperceptible wave, she flung a bolt of arcane energy. Artimus Jr. was too slow to respond, a buzz filling his ears as his vision blurred. He was lightheaded, dizzy as the world tumbled around him.

He struggled to remain conscious, glancing back towards the city walls and witnessing the enemy behemoths closing in. The last thing he saw as his vision faded to black was the white of the hájje's teeth through her devious grin.

CHAPTER XXV

Paxvilla
20 Julla, 1149 MT

Zelag approached the enemy mage, his sword extended towards the ground.

"Drop the barrier and flee this battlefield. Paxvilla has no quarrel with your people and neither do I."

Zelag hadn't really expected this to work. But he figured it was right to at least offer. It certainly didn't warrant the response it got.

"We will fulfill my Father's vision!" the hájje exclaimed, his deep, deranged, decibels ringing throughout the battlefield.

With a shrill cry, the hájje gathered a mass of arcane energy, refocusing it into an eruption of dark magic.

The dark energy cascaded around Zelag, engulfing him for a moment in a torrent of death. But with all magical attacks, Zelag's unique physiology left him unaffected.

"I'm afraid that was a one-time offer." Zelag brushed off his right shoulder.

The hájje stared in disbelief, his mouth hanging open. As Zelag approached, the large enemy mage threw back his cloak and withdrew a sword of his own, a smile forming.

"You're the shapeshifter then," the hájje spat. "This victory will make my father proud."

Zelag squinted, looking closer at his enemy's dark aura. The erratic black pulsing caused him to miss it, but taking it in now, the shapeshifter realized. This was another one of Yezurkstal's children -a direct child by the looks of it. The energy was like that of the one back in Melora's Tavern, but much less powerful.

"I don't know how proud he'll be," replied Zelag whipping his sword around in a circular motion. "But I'll send you to oblivion to join him."

The hájje cackled, swinging his adamantium longsword in a figure eight. Zelag accepted the invitation, lunging in and feigning a slash. At the last moment, the shapeshifter spun around, dodging left, and swiping for his foe's leg.

It hadn't even occurred to Zelag that his foe would anticipate his maneuver. So as the green of his enemy's sword swung around and intercepted his attack, the young shapeshifter cursed. Wincing as his steel short sword cracked, crumbling under the force of his own attack, Zelag gasped.

A broken shard of steel ricocheted off his chest, his thick leather armor just barely surviving the impact. Allowing his momentum to carry him, Zelag opened his eyes. Before he knew what he was doing, he flung the rest of the sword, aiming for his enemy's thigh.

Again, his opponent presented lightning reflexes, deflecting the feeble attack with a grunt. Without pause, the hájje swung his blade down towards Zelag's right shoulder. Showing off his own reflexes, Zelag lunged towards his foe, swinging up and catching his enemy's wrists. This hájje was stronger than he looked.

Zelag groaned, the upward momentum from his lung only barely allowing him to hold his foe at bay. These hájje were much stronger than regular elves, and perhaps even than humans. But Zelag's human form had at least a few centimeters in height, and more than that in muscle mass. This allowed him to push back, but as he began to gain ground, the shapeshifter felt a feeling of dread overtake him.

The hájje channeled arcane energy, his aura stabilizing as the dark magic filled his body. Sinews bulged on his arms and Zelag could feel himself losing ground. Roaring to help motivate his muscles, Zelag tried in vain to fight back. He closed his eyes, pushing with all he had, but it was just a matter of moments until he'd fold under the pressure.

Snap.

Zelag opened his eyes, the sudden jerk of his upward momentum jarring him. He looked around, blinking a couple times to try and figure out what happened. Standing between him and his opponent was Ygabb, her hooves flaming with fierce magic. The hájje was a couple meters away, doubled over and clutching his side.

Ygabb stood at full height, which might not have been very high, but conveyed a distinct sense of confidence. Her mythril sword glowed with a white magic and her body pulsed with arcane energy. Even her horns were alight, green magic humming through the air.

The hájje coughed, leaning on his sword as he struggled to remain standing. Ygabb didn't give him the chance to recover. She rushed in almost too fast for Zelag to see, swiping her blade up across the hájje's throat. The hájje's aura faded, his body falling the floor.

"Are you OK?" Ygabb yelled, her rising tone revealing her concern for Zelag's safety.

"Surprised," Zelag admitted, "but in one piece. Thank you for the backup."

"Don't underestimate them again. I might not be around to save you. We wouldn't want that to happen!" Ygabb bleated, beaming with excitement as she bound off towards a contingent of heavily-armored enemies.

"How is she not considered a heavy?" Zelag muttered to himself while considering the battlefield. With his own sword useless, it seemed a shame to leave such a rare and finely crafted sword on the battlefield. Stepping over to the deceased mage, he bent over and retrieved the adamantium longsword.

The blade shined with the usual green glint from the metal and was alight with dark power. But looking closely, it didn't appear there were any enchantments on the weapon itself. With a smile, Zelag took a few swings, getting a feel for the balance.

It was a remarkably well-crafted weapon, the grooves on the handle feeling almost soft and comfortable in the hand. Its narrow blade was curved inward at an almost imperceptible angle, affording the blade a few extra centimeters in length without sacrificing any of the balance.

Refocusing on the rest of the battlefield, Zelag allowed himself another few moments of observation. He watched as Ygabb skipped from soldier to soldier, headbutting one and caving in his armor, stabbing another, spinning around and skewering a third. She moved so fluidly, her movement timed perfectly with small bursts of arcane energy, allowing her to zip from place to place in the blink of an eye.

He had never seen someone channel magic in such a way, and watching her move was mesmerizing. For a moment, he wished there was someone else who could witness the display and see it as he did. The bitterness of this sentiment was enhanced by the rest of the battlefield.

Savannah's golem was doing its job, taking out enemies by the pair as it thundered through ranks. Savannah was keeping herself at the perfect position between her golem, Ygabb, and Zelag. She was casting spells as needed, neutralizing any stray enemies that might slip through their formation. And that thought kicked Zelag back to action.

Giving the blade one final flourish, the young shapeshifter ran towards the next contingent of enemy soldiers. This group wore lighter armor, simple black studded leather. They were outfitted with a variety of weapons, and each had a red stamp across their armor, the rune of death.

As he covered the distance, a thundering crash from the north stopped him in his tracks. Turning towards the source, he watched in dread as the first of the enemy behemoths reached the walls, smashing into the stone with its massive horns, causing the ground to shake.

These demons were enormous, at least fifteen meters long from the back of their tails to the tips of their horns. Each had a large crest circling their heads with tiny little spikes, and two thick horns jutting symmetrically from either side of their skull. With dark purple fur, red stripes, and six hooved legs, they looked like a perverted cross between some sort of turtle, elephant, and horse. They were tall enough that they could almost reach the top of Paxvilla's walls.

And Zelag hadn't thought too much on that fact until he realized the large humps on their backs were not, in fact, shells. Instead, he stood with mouth agape, watching as one of the brown domes opened. Dozens of winged demons began pouring out from the dome, soaring over the walls towards the unsuspecting archers.

Zelag could hear the faint cries of the soldiers as they engaged the demons. His body felt hot, his mind racing as he considered the implications. There were only two of these massive juggernauts, but if the other had a similar payload, the odds of this battle were looking grim.

He felt heavy, like his feet were glued to the ground beneath. There had to be more than a hundred demons, and even from this distance Zelag could tell they were heavyweights. They weren't just outnumbered -they were outmatched.

"Regroup!" came faint shouts scattered throughout the battlefield. This sentiment echoed from every direction, snapping Zelag back into the moment. He looked back to the lightly armored group of hájje, witnessing Ygabb and Savannah's golem both tear through their ranks.

"Ygabb, Savannah!" he shouted while sheathing his sword. "What's the move? Main gate, or side entrance?"

Ygabb sliced through another hájje, her momentum carrying her towards Savannah's golem. Without a pause, she leapt towards the golem, kicking off its back and swinging her sword around to decapitate another hájje soldier. The golem continued uninterrupted, smashing another couple enemies.

The sound of crumbling stone pulled Zelag's attention back to the wall. The first behemoth had already torn a hole, opening a gap in the defenses. Across the other end, the second behemoth crashed into the gatehouse. Moments later, a horde of demons rushed out the dome on its back, swarming over the walls and rushing into Paxvilla.

"Maybe not the main gate!" shouted Savannah, her eyes wide as she looked back towards the destruction.

Zelag looked across the rest of the hájje army. The battlefield was already riddled with hundreds of corpses, mostly hájje, but a painful number of Marftaport warriors were also riddled about the field. And with an immeasurable number of hájje still marching towards the city, things were looker grimmer by the minute.

"Should we do cleanup duty?" Ygabb flung her sword overhead with both hands, letting it fly to impale the final hájje. Skipping to retrieve the blade, she continued.

"I mean, we're already at the rear of the enemy lines." She removed her sword, wiping it on the sleeve of her slain enemy. "Either that, or we slip back in the side entrance."

Savannah made her way towards Zelag, her golem standing in place like a statue. Ygabb sheathed her sword as she approached, her yellow aura betraying her otherwise cheerful demeanor. As the three fighters converged, Zelag considered their options.

"I think Ygabb may be right," offered Savannah shaking her head. "We can't stop until the fight is over, but our best bet will be picking off who we can before they arrive in the city. So fast, decisive action. But there's one thing I'd like to do first."

Savannah extended her hands to either side, reaching for both Zelag and Ygabb to take hold. Looking side-to-side, Zelag hesitated only a moment before taking her hand and extending his left hand to Ygabb. As the three joined hands, Savannah spoke.

"Evorath, please guide our hands in this battle. Keep our loved ones safe from harm and allow us your protection as we fight to keep this evil at bay. And if you will it, please send your Avatar to help us with this fight."

Zelag felt a subtle tingle in the back of his neck, closing his eyes as he listened. Now would be the time for the Avatar to show up. And when he opened his eyes, he half-expected to see some sign that the prayer would be answered.

Instead, he was greeted by a loud rumble and quake. Looking back north, he watched in terror.

The first behemoth had broken through the wall.

Luna Freya growled, wrenching the hájje over her shoulder and slamming him into the dirt. These insects were learning, another one grasping her left arm and two more moving in from the front. She stomped the grounded hájje's stomach, twisting around and punching the arm-grabber in the throat.

As the arm-grabber grasped at his throat, Luna wrenched herself around and grabbed hold of the grabber's ankles. With a feral roar, she swung back around, throwing the hájje like a rag doll. The two attackers were taken aback, unable to stop their forward momentum. While the trio tumbled to the ground, Luna turned to her right and held both her hands up, just barely catching the sword of yet another attacker.

Looking over this one's shoulders, she considered her objective. The crumbled gatehouse was still twenty meters away, the enemy behemoth trumpeting its victory as it trampled through the rubble. The screams from above were clear -those demons were tearing through the Paxvilla defenses. Luna needed to get back inside if she was going to help.

Yanking the sword from her enemy's grasp, she let the blade clatter to her right and twisted back around, elbowing the hájje in the chin and following up with a jab to the throat. There were dozens of enemies between her and the former gatehouse, but for the moment she was able to breathe and assess the situation. She needed allies.

Glancing back, she witnessed Irontail trample through an enemy phalanx. Tracing his gaze, it looked like he was headed for the nearby behemoth; best to leave him to it.

A couple more centaurs were rallying behind Irontail, along with the lizock brothers Luna had been fighting with earlier. She spotted Bel' Mora further to the east, working with a group of elvish hunters against a lightly armored contingent of hájje soldiers.

Gazing west, she spotted the allies she needed. Zelag, Savannah, and Ygabb were making their way towards the gatehouse. With a large golem leading the way, the trio marched forward with little resistance. Ygabb and Zelag were dispatching any foe that survived the golem's charge.

Narrowing her eyes, Luna considered the best path forward. She inhaled deeply, her nostrils flaring as she crouched. Blowing the air from her lungs, she took off in a sprint.

She jumped over a couple fallen enemies, holding out her left arm to clothesline an unsuspecting hájje. Without slowing down, she dashed between a couple enemy cavalry, ducked under a stray sword, and ran straight for Savannah's golem.

"Luna Freya!" Ygabb exclaimed. "Care to follow us into town?"

The small satyr leapt into the air, stomping down on a fallen hájje soldier, and stabbing him for good measure. Luna was always amazed at Ygabb's agility, but it was only now that she realized how brutal the energetic little mage could be.

"That's the plan," Luna replied running up alongside the group. "We need to get up on the wall -the humans don't stand a chance against those demons. Any chance you can transform into one of those behemoths Zelag? I spotted Irontail heading towards this one, but I don't know what he expects to do."

"I can't," replied Zelag hopping over a couple crushed enemies. "They are demons, and you know I can't imitate anything not of Evorath."

"Anything of comparable size?" Luna asked, keeping her eyes on the hoard of hájje ahead.

"Afraid the bulwark is the biggest thing in my repertoire."

Luna's whiskered twitched as she squinted towards Zelag.

"Right. Why aren't you using that form?"

Zelag rolled his eyes. "You think the enemy will stop the fight and give me time to shapeshift if I ask nicely?"

"Ah, you're too slow. Got it. Savannah!" Luna pointed ahead towards the formation of hájje soldiers. "Will your golem be able to get us through those lines?"

"Only one way to know for sure." The druid smirked.

With a toothy grin, Luna spread her arms wide, extending her claws. Falling into position directly behind the golem, she slowed her pace, syncing her movement with the automaton. She felt each step the golem took, the faint vibrations of its enormous weight as it trampled forth. Her breathing slowed as they made their way through the hájje formation.

The golem bulldozed forward, crashing through the enemy hájje.

The sickening crunch of metal as it trampled them. The shouts of surprise as it tossed them aside. The hard thuds of hájje bodies against the rubble of the gatehouse. Luna kept her focus through it all, claws at the ready in case the enemy tried to close in around them.

Veering to the east, the golem tossed aside another heavily armored hájje, stomping forth as the enemy fell back. Luna remained on her trajectory, running past the melee. A somewhat portly Paxvilla guard stood with his mouth hanging open, his head slowly turning to watch the golem at work. He and his allies seemed too enthralled to even acknowledge as Luna and the rest of her allies ran towards the tower steps.

With a quick glance back to confirm the others were still behind her, Luna bound up the steps. Ignoring the commotion around her, she kept her eyes wide as she ascended the wall and took in the scene.

It was a bedlam.

Soldiers lay slaughtered all along the stone wall. The remaining Paxvilla guards and allied Marftaport archers were scattered about, haplessly fighting against the horde of demons. From the near three-meter-tall demons to the cute little bat-like creatures that were even shorter than Ygabb, they were making short work of the defenses. For a fleeting moment, Luna found herself smiling.

This was her first time seeing actual demons, and they were not at all what she had expected. But as reality weighed on her, she grimaced.

These people were being massacred.

With that thought, Luna homed in on the nearest target. It was a pair of demons, who, by the looks of it, had just slain a handful of Paxvilla guards. Wielding only their clawed hands and covered in blood, these demons scowled as Luna approached.

They were near the inner edge of the wall, one of their victims laid out in a crenel. The demon on the left was all black with spikes jutting from its elbows and wings that seemed a bit too small for its body. In height and build, this first demon was only a few centimeters larger than Luna. To the right, the other demon had red stripes on his black, leathery skin and no spikes or extrusions of remark. This one was a bit taller and leaner than its counterpart.

Claws at the ready, Luna pounced on the leaner demon. Spreading his wings wide, the demon stood tall, its strong frame offering an unexpected resistance. These demons were stronger than they looked. But Luna was no pushover.

As she dug her claws into the demon's chest, she pulled it closer and bit its neck. She scowled as the foul taste of black ichor filled her mouth. The demon screeched, flapping its wings vigorously to escape. Pulling away, she slashed down the demon's chest and spat the foul blood at its spiked counterpart.

While the lean demon fled, hopefully to die soon after, the spiked one ignored her distraction, wiping the blood away without hesitation and ducking down to tackle Luna. Glancing to her side to account for the edge of the wall, the muscular felite grinned and grabbed hold of the demon.

She wouldn't admit it to another living soul, but this demon was even stronger than she was. It pushed her back, forcing her to the edge of the wall. As her tail brushed against the inner crenel, she dug her claws into the demon's back and twisted as only a felite could. The hard stone under her feet was just uneven enough that she could dig her heels in, and as she flung her body around she pushed the demon, its own momentum causing it to fall over the edge.

Disappointed to see its undersized wings were functional, she watched the demon spread its wings and land unharmed on the ground beneath. With a roar, the demon took off, soaring towards Luna. Dropping to all fours, Luna scrambled, grabbing a sword from one of the fallen humans. Just as the demon ascended back over the wall, she planted the sword in its chest.

She didn't waste a moment watching the demon's fall, instead turning back the melee. Ygabb, Zelag, and Savannah were all in the thick of the action, but there was something wrong. Luna felt a strange tingling run down her spine. Eyes wide, she spun around, looking for any sign of danger.

The ground shook, a crack spreading across the wall. Was it just the behemoth causing this sensation?

No, there was something else.

"Ygabb, look out!" Luna shouted across the wall.

The satyr headbutted one of the taller demons, running through its legs and causing it to topple over. Zelag was nearby, swinging around his sword for the finishing blow. But as Ygabb stood at full height, another demon swooped down.

The demon landed with wings wide, kicking Ygabb aside like a rag doll. Standing at least two and a half meters tall, it retracted its massive wings and stepped forward, smoke rolling from the corners of its mouth. It had two horns on the top of its head, a long tail spiked like a mace, and fingernails the size of daggers.

Zelag dove away, rolling towards Ygabb. Luna glanced to Savannah and the two exchanged a nod. Lifting her head and extending her claws, Luna emitted a feral roar before rushing the new enemy.

Opening its mouth wide, the demon released a torrent of fire. Red, orange, and yellow flames danced around Luna as she leapt towards the demon. A thin barrier of green formed on her fur, Savannah's magic counteracting the hellfire of this foe. The result was a strange tingling, an almost painful clash of cold and hot disorienting the felite warrior.

Barring her teeth to remain focused, she cut through the flames and crouched down. Keeping her right claws extended, she exploded into an uppercut. Her claws sunk into the bottom of the demon's jaw, the magically amplified attack forcing the demon's mouth shut and flames to diminish.

The demon's eyes went red as it reeled back groaning in pain. Luna bounced back as she landed, lunging for the demon's legs. With her full body weight committed to the tackle, she swept the demon's leg from under it, causing the great beast to topple over on top of some fallen humans.

Now on all fours, Luna scurried around. But as she moved in for the kill, the demon refused to yield. Flapping its wings, the demon sprang back up and kicked Luna in the side, causing her to double over and clutch her side. Just as she thought the demon had the upper hand, Zelag jumped into the fray.

But again, the demon proved quicker than its frame would suggest possible. With a backhanded slap, it knocked Zelag away. It turned towards the shapeshifter, chortling as it stalked its new target. Luna used the distraction to regain her composure, spitting as she considered her options.

Foolish Zelag, he should have transformed into a bulwark when he had the chance, or so Luna thought to herself before she charged the demon. She focused on his mid-section, wrapping her arms around and digging her claws in as she tackled the beast. As she hoped, her forward force was enough that she took the demon over the edge of the wall.

Squeezing the creature tight, she closed her eyes and said a silent prayer. Time seemed to stand, and then the rush of wind stopped suddenly. Hearing the demon scream out in pain, she cracked open her eyes to see a white light. And suddenly the demon was gone, her arms clutching to nothing but air.

As the light faded, she felt her feet touch down softly on the ground and opening her eyes she was greeted with the stoic face of a tan, bald man.

Only, it wasn't just any man. It was the Avatar.

With his plain brown tunic and pants, and unimpressive features, the muscular right arm of Evorath regarded the felite.

"That was reckless," he said, his voice deep and powerful.

"And you're late!" Luna exclaimed, her neck tingling with excitement.

The Avatar smiled and locked eyes with Luna.

"From where I'm standing, I arrived just in time."

Before she knew what was happening, Luna felt the ground shift beneath her. Vines shot out from all around, grabbing hold of her and the Avatar and jerking them up. As the vines set them gently down back on top of the wall, she looked towards Ygabb and her other allies.

Savannah and Zelag were both standing over the satyr. And for a moment, Luna expected the worst. She felt a knot form in her throat, fighting to hold back tears as she considered Ygabb. Sure, she was annoying at times, but she knew how to have a good time, something most of the mage's guild couldn't wrap their heads around. If the Avatar had just arrived a few moments sooner...

"I'm up!" Ygabb leapt to her feet, bleating as she shook her head and arms wildly.

Luna's heart skipped a beat as she let out a heavy breath.

"Avatar!" Savannah exclaimed, looking up towards Luna and the Avatar. Zelag turned, his face contorting from one of confusion to shock, mouth hanging open and eyes wide.

"Yes, Evorath heard your prayers."

Before anyone had a chance to say another word, a trio of impish demons flew towards the group.

The Avatar didn't hesitate, stepping towards the demons and holding his hand out, palm facing outward.

"You are not welcome in this realm!" he exclaimed.

A burst of light flashed throughout the wall. It was beautiful, a serene white energy branching out along the wall. Luna kept her eyes open until it got too bright, but as the light faded and her vision cleared, the aftermath left her in awe.

The demons were gone. Not just the three little imps, but all the demons on the wall, dead or alive, had vanished. As the ground shook, Luna refocused her attention back to the nearest behemoth, which was trampling further into the city.

"I think that's your next target," Savannah said pointing towards the juggernaut.

The Avatar nodded.

"Have your forces focus on driving the hájje back. I'll cleanse this land of these foul creatures."

Without another word, The Avatar leapt from the wall. And as he landed on the ground beneath, bound for the nearest behemoth, Luna felt a renewed sense of hope.

Perhaps she would come out of this alive after all.

CHAPTER XXVI

Paxvilla
20 Julla, 1149 MT

Darkness.

The muddled sounds of footsteps. Shouts, vibrations, a hint of light. His head hurt.

"Come on!"

Artimus Jr. opened his eyes, vision blurred. With a few blinks, the figures around him cleared up. Gasping as he sat up, the young elf looked around.

He was inside, the unpleasant smell of damp wood filling his nostrils. The canine features of Mojo came into focus first, the wizened old barghest staring him in the face.

"Thank Evorath. We must move!" Mojo exclaimed, jerking his head left and right.

Artimus Jr. took in the rest of his surroundings. They were in some sort of cellar by the looks of things. The stone behind him was crowded with wooden crates, the left and right walls lit with small torches. Thick wooden beams ran across the top of the room and a pair of wooden doors marked the exit, a small bit of light trickling through.

A raucous sound rang out from beyond the cellar doors, clanging of steel, cries of battle, and screams of pain. There was dust in the air, the ground trembling as Artimus Jr. came to his feet.

"What's the situation?" he asked, wiping himself off and checking that his sword was secure. Where was his bow?

"They've overrun the city. Those demonic behemoths of theirs were hiding a full contingent of demons. Your father is just outside with Oogmut, Morn, and Neman." The wizened barghest paused as the ground shook, looking towards the cellar doors while clutching his bone necklace.

"Any idea what happened to my bow?"

"No," Mojo shook his head. "We withdrew in a hurry. You'll have to thank Morn for carrying you back here."

Artimus nodded, closing his eyes, and rubbing his temples. There was pressure behind his eyes and his chest felt tight, but he was ready to get back into the melee, which felt odd. But he was grateful to be alive, and to hear that at least some of his family was as well.

"I'll thank him. And thank you for tending to me."

Mojo snorted, nodding his head as he reached down and inspected the pouches along his belt.

"You're welcome," his voice was laced with exhaustion. "I'll follow after you," he sighed, motioning towards the door.

Gripping his sword, Artimus Jr. charged the exit. He led with his left shoulder and shoved through the doors, busting out into the daylight, and drawing his sword in one, fluid motion. His eyes darted around the street, quickly taking in the lay of the land and positions of his allies.

A pile of hay rested just to his left, along with an assortment of crates and barrels. The stone walls behind these were thick, and for a moment the young elf mistook a pair of straw dummies for human combatants. This must have been an archery range, or some manner of martial training facility.

Morn and Neman were the nearest allied combatants, engaged with a large demon. They were taking the direct approach, grasping both the demon's sinewy arms. The demon screeched as they dug their claws in, spreading his wings wide and thrashing about. But as he wrenched towards Neman, Morn let go, allowing the demon to throw itself off balance.

Neman adjusted his grip, taking hold further up the demon's arm. Meanwhile, Morn dove from behind and grasped at the demon's throat. The wrestling match lasted only a few moments and after leaping up from their fallen enemy, the barghest brothers rushed towards another pair of demonic foes.

Widening his gaze, Artimus Jr. caught sight of Oogmut engaged with a massive demon across the courtyard. And further to the west his father was working with the Paxvilla soldiers, fighting back against some hájje infantry. Drawing his sword, the young elf rushed west.

His heart pounded in his chest as he ran across the grass, narrowing his eyes and focusing on one of the taller hájje soldiers. But he felt like he was being watched, the hair on the back of his neck standing on end. Still ten meters from the melee, he noticed a shadow cast over his shoulder and his ears twitched. There was an enemy above!

Artimus Jr. dove to his right, keeping his blade pointed away as he rolled over. Twisting as he sprang to his feet, he shuffled and sized up the winged demon. The black, leathery flesh of the demon was already stained with blood, its flagged mace a deep crimson. Wearing a malevolent grin, the winged creature stood nearly a meter taller than the elf.

The demon stomped towards him, letting out a low growl and lifting its mace menacingly. Artimus Jr. grinned, keeping his left hand held out to the side for balance as he stepped around, the tip of his sword pointed towards the enemy. At least he wouldn't feel bad about killing this one.

With a roar, the demon swung its mace towards Artimus Jr.'s head. Stepping to the right, the nimble elf retaliated with a thrust of his sword. With all the weight on his leading foot, he twisted around and leaned into the attack. With little resistance, his strike hit the mark, piercing through two ribs and skewering the larger foe.

Of course, an enemy like this wasn't going to die so easily and the young elf knew better than to stick around. So, he continued the momentum of his attack, releasing hold of his sword and diving to the right. Rolling back to his feet, he reached to the small of his back and pulled out his steel dagger, taking a defensive posture as he watched and waited.

The demon shrieked in pain, dropping its mace, and clutching the sword in its side. Twisting towards Artimus Jr., the

310

demon yanked the sword out and cursed. And for a moment, as the demon cast the sword to the side, it looked like the young elf had made a fatal mistake.

He could feel the heat from the demon's breath as the large creature lifted its head. Smoke billowed from its mouth as Artimus Jr. lowered his stance and prepared to dive away. The demon roared, spewing a turret of hellfire.

Closing his eyes, Artimus Jr. dove to the left and said a silent prayer to Evorath. He could feel the intense heat of the flames, his entire body protesting. He flattened his body and rolled to the side. But just as the heat was becoming too much, it vanished.

Opening his eyes, Artimus Jr. jumped up to his feet and looked back towards the enemy, who stood motionless. The elf's mythril sword was planted in the demon's skull, blade skewering through the top of its head, handle hanging out its jaw. Mojo stood a few meters away, his hands held up and clutching a small fetish in his right.

"Always assume they breathe fire!" the old barghest barked, dropping his arms. The ragged elder looked worn out, panting as his hands rested at his side.

"Thank you, Mojo," Artimus Jr. exclaimed, replacing his dagger in its sheath on his back.

As the elf went to retrieve his sword, he spotted enemy reinforcements entering the courtyard. They marched in from the western entrance, running through the archway. It was an eclectic group of hájje warriors, some in full plate armor and others wearing lighter mail and leather outfits. But at the front of their ranks was the most interesting target -the hájje commander.

"That's their commander," the elf pointed towards the enemy. "You still have enough juice for the fight?"

Mojo shook his head. "I'm running on fumes." He leaned on his gnarled staff, shaking a few of the pouches at his side.

"But I got a few tricks left. Morn, Neman!" He turned back towards the barghest brothers. "Enough horsing around. Come help Junior and I take out the enemy commander!"

Morn threw an axe, the projectile spinning over a few times before embedding itself in the skull of a small demon. It looked like this was the last of a trio of demons, all elvish in size and stature, despite their crimson-colored skin and goat-like horns. And after Morn retrieved his axe, he and Neman ran over to join Artimus Jr. and Mojo.

Artimus Jr. glanced back towards the approaching hájje contingent, which had fanned out to reinforce the ongoing battle. His father and the dozen armored humans had taken the number advantage against their enemies, but with a quick head count, it looked like the scales would soon turn. With Artimus Jr. and the three barghest factored in, the enemy now had a two-to-one advantage.

"They may have the numbers," said Mojo, "but we've got the brains. Do what you're good at and I'll make sure you all survive the day."

Feeling empowered by his elder's encouragement, Artimus Jr. charged the enemy. The hájje reinforcements joined

312

their allies, a handful of lightly armored enemies dashing in and disrupting the Paxvilla defenders. Artimus Jr. had his sights set on a lightly armored hájje wielding a polearm.

This enemy was a few centimeters taller than the elf, his lean physique barely covered by the black leather armor. The armor itself was unlike any Artimus Jr. had seen before, consisting primarily of a haltered top covering the hájje's chest and shoulders. With matching, studded leather shorts, most of his body was left exposed. The nimble way he moved, tripping one soldier, and skewering the next, was reminiscent of a felite warrior.

His weapon was peculiar as well. With a banded hardwood handle, the pole measured about 150 centimeters in length. The blade at the top was double-edged, with a curved part like a sickle sticking out front and an additional spearhead protruding from the top. He hacked and slashed his way through a trio of Paxvilla soldiers.

Artimus Jr. held his sword in both hands, swinging it overhead as he drew near. For a moment, he thought he'd take the hájje warrior by surprise. But the hájje glanced over his left shoulder blocking the strike with his polearm and pushing the young elf away.

With surprising dexterity, Artimus Jr. twisted his sword, flipping it under the polearm and embracing his backward momentum. Hooking the polearm with his sword, he swung down, forcing the hájje to swing his weapon harmlessly into the ground beneath. Continuing the momentum, Artimus Jr. rebounded his sword, slashing for the enemy's throat.

The hájje opened his right palm and Artimus Jr. gasped as an invisible arcane pulse struck his chest, knocking the air from his lungs. Barely holding onto his sword, he staggered back and shook his head.

"You fight better than these humans," the hájje grinned. "But you're no match for me miserable little elf. Fear not, Pollux, son of Yezurkstal, will end your misery." His words were caustic, their sardonic tone causing Artimus Jr. to cringe.

But worse than this was his arrogant posturing; spreading his arms wide as he spoke, shoulders pulled back and chin up towards the sky. Artimus Jr. was so irritated that he almost attacked in rage, but his training won out the day.

"Well, Pollux. Prepare to meet your end at Artimus, son of Artimus." He spoke slowly and confidently, a smile plastered on his face as he flourished his sword.

Pollux grunted, spinning his polearm in a figure eight before lunging forward with a wide, arching slash. Artimus Jr. dodged to the right, but as before Pollux demonstrated extraordinary speed, twisting back and swinging his blade for the elf's torso. With both hands grasping his sword, Artimus Jr. blocked the strike, his ears ringing to the loud clang of metal.

Sword scraping against polearm, Artimus Jr. took a step back. Shifting his weight to his front foot, he swung his sword straight down. Pollux dodged this time, stepping to his right and swinging his polearm around. Artimus Jr. couldn't react in time, the dull end of the polearm striking his shoulder and causing him to stumble away.

Just narrowly bringing his sword up to block, he locked eyes with Pollux as the hájje's polearm struck his blade again. His shoulders burned as he pushed back against the hájje's attack, the deep dark abyss of his enemy's eyes filling him with doubt as he struggled.

Artimus Jr. thought of the stakes, a surge of strength rushing through his body as he grunted. Thrusting his hands forward, he pushed Pollux away, giving him the chance to adjust his grip and take a few steps back. Just as he prepared to move in for a counterattack, he was joined by a welcome ally: his father.

The veteran elf charged Pollux with his sword held high. Without missing a beat, Pollux swung his polearm around to intercept the slash. But as he blocked the attack, Artimus Jr. used the opening to move in. Unfortunately, he wasn't the only one getting reinforcements it seems.

"Enough!" the assertive voice of the hájje commander rang in his ears. She swooped in at the last moment, deflecting Artimus Jr.'s stab and taking a position back-to-back with Pollux.

"I didn't ask for your help, sister!" Pollux objected, grunting as he used the dull end of his polearm to push Artimus away.

Meanwhile, Artimus Jr. stepped around his new foe.

"You didn't expect to see me again, did you?" the young elf asked with a grin. He took a couple measured steps back, his sword held defensively as he assessed his enemy. She didn't look any worse for wear, a few extra stains on her armor perhaps.

"If I didn't expect to see you, I would have killed you," the hájje smirked. She brushed her hair back, taking a step towards Artimus Jr. and flourishing her sword.

"Oh, was that not the intent?" Artimus Jr. asked. "And what about now? If you do plan to kill me, at least share your name with me."

The hájje lunged in, slashing towards Artimus Jr.'s face. The young elf easily blocked the attack, employing quick footwork to move further away from his father and Pollux.

"My name is Castora, daughter of Yezurkstal," she proclaimed without breaking her concentration.

She moved in again, this time leading with a stab. Again, Artimus Jr. stepped to the side, swiping his blade around to deflect her attack, and continuing to circle her. He had no intention of letting her beat him again.

"Castora," he said arching an eyebrow. "So pretty name, pretty face, healthy by the looks of it…what could possibly be your motivation to kill so many people?"

His comment worked even better than he hoped, a little color showing in Castora's cheek as she huffed, swinging wildly for Artimus Jr.'s head.

Artimus Jr. grinned as he parried the attack, arching his sword and swatting Castora's arm with the flat of his blade.

Castora cursed, her nostrils flaring as she stepped back and rubbed her sword arm.

"I had considered letting you live," she seethed, her face turning redder. "But now you leave me little choice."

Flipping her hair back, Castora clasped both hands on her sword and lunged in for another attack. She was quicker than before, her strike precise and deliberate. Artimus Jr. barely had time to dodge, parrying as he peddled back from his foe.

She was clearly more skilled with a blade.

A visible darkness exuded from Castora as she pressed her advance, like a mist of dark magic seeping from every pore. Artimus Jr. struggled to keep up, falling further back with each strike. His hands were growing weak, buzzing with each impact.

Gritting his teeth and scrambling to maintain sound footwork, he found his vision tunneling on Castora. But as he was pressed further away from the melee, he caught a glimpse of movement from the corner of his right eye.

With a grizzly growl, Mojo leapt into the fray. He barked, leading shoulder first and pushing Castora away from Artimus Jr. Catching his breath, the young elf took a moment to loosen his grip on his sword, his hands shaking -a combination of fear and exhaustion.

"Mangy cur!" Castora shrieked, dashing towards her new foe. Mojo held his staff up defensively and for a few moments, Artimus Jr. felt as if he had left his body, a helpless spectator.

Castora led with an overhead swing. Mojo's staff offered no resistance, the hájje's blade cutting through the wood like a sickle reaping a field. Mojo yelped as the blade cut across his

317

chest. He reached for one of the pouches at his side, but as his hand slipped in, Castora stabbed.

Her blade sunk into Mojo's flesh and the elderly barghest howled. Artimus Jr. felt dizzy, a bout of nausea creeping up as Mojo coughed up blood. But the old barghest wasn't done yet.

As Castora removed her sword, Mojo slashed her arm. Castora cried out as she dropped her sword. Artimus Jr. lunged in, leading with his sword.

He looked down, his hand still shaking, the tip of his sword piercing Castora's side.

"It didn't have to be this way," the words slipped from Artimus Jr. mouth. They almost felt like someone else's. His face was tight as he fell back and looked at the palms of his hands. The melee around him was silent as he was trapped in the moment. And then it all rushed back.

With tears in his eyes, Artimus Jr. regarded Castora. She clutched at the wound in her side, stumbling away from the scene. And then something else happened.

Vines shot up from the ground all around the field, grappling with hájje soldiers and neutralizing them.

"Could it be?" Artimus Jr. thought to himself, looking around the field. His heart skipped a beat as he caught sight of the muscular Avatar entering the courtyard. Would there be time?

Stepping over and kneeling alongside Mojo, Artimus Jr. inspected the wound. There was so much blood. And Mojo felt cold. The old druid coughed, his hand shaking as he reached out and touched Artimus Jr.'s shoulder.

Looking the elf in the eyes, he spoke his final words.

"Do not mourn, my friend. For today I dine with The Creator."

"My own death I do not fear, but to lose anymore whom I love is a burden I fear I cannot bear."

- Mojo's final journal entry

CHAPTER XXVII

Jaldor closed his eyes and took a deep breath. The fragrant aromas of the bakery filled his nostrils, offering him comfort. As he looked around and considered the size of the shop, he couldn't help but feel a sense of anticipation.

As he stepped up to the counter with George, Jaldor looked towards the baker, who was a few meters away kneading some dough. She was short and stout, at least eight centimeters shorter than George. She had a peculiar hat upon her head, tighter around the forehead and puffed out above, likely to keep her long hair out of the way. With a matching beige, long sleeve dress, she didn't acknowledge the visitors at first.

George cleared his throat. "Good morning Torrea," he said with a smile.

Torrea kept kneading, offering a subtle glance towards Jaldor and George.

"Ah, good morning Mr. Peterson," she replied adding a handful of flour to the dough and continuing to knead. Her voice was soft and gentle, perfectly matching her unassuming demeanor. She was the first elf Jaldor had seen with wrinkled skin, which made him wonder how old she must be.

"Give me just a few moments."

George nodded as she continued her work.

"Of course!" he exclaimed rapping his hands on the counter. "As promised, I brought you someone who can help with your predicament."

Torrea nodded, prodding at the dough a bit before dusting her hands and walking over to the counter. She looked towards Jaldor as she did so, tilting her head to the side and squinting.

"Human. You must be the new dairy farmer everyone is talking about."

Torrea grabbed a sackcloth as she reached the counter, wiping her hands on it and looking down in the cabinet underneath. After a few moments of rummaging, she pulled out a small pastry of some kind.

"I am indeed," replied Jaldor considering the pastry.

"Try this for me," Torrea slid the pastry across the countertop.

With a glance at George, Jaldor reached out and took the pastry. It was dome-shaped, golden brown in color with some dark waves running through the center. As he lifted it, the farmer could smell hints of cinnamon and nutmeg.

Chewing the small pastry, Jaldor was surprised by the sweet and creamy flavoring. The light, flaky texture was complimented by the chewy, dark cream and the surface cinnamon, creating a delightful cacophony of flavors. His delight must have shown because the baker nodded and smiled along as he chewed.

"You like it then?"

"Yes," replied Jaldor with a nod. "What is that sticky, creamy substance?"

"It's the reason George thinks you can help me."

"Oh?" Jaldor glanced at George, who nodded in response.

"It's called caramel," said Torrea. "And it requires quite a bit of milk to make. With the growth of the town recently, I can't even make enough of these to keep up with half the demand. I understand you raise bovine creatures for milk?"

"That's right," replied Jaldor finishing the pastry. "My parents started raising Erathal cows and I've been doing it my whole life. Have you not had cow's milk before?"

Torrea shook her head.

"Have you not introduced him to old Aristaios?" the baker asked George with an accusatory look.

"He's only just getting settled in!" George shrugged and looked at Jaldor. "He's the local sheep farmer. Really the only dairy farmer here other than you."

"I see," said Jaldor scratching the back of his neck. "Well, my cows produce at least three times as much milk as any sheep I've ever seen, but their milk isn't quite as rich."

"You let me worry about that," Torrea tilted her head back and flicked her hand as if swatting a fly. "I'll adjust the recipe as needed. But what do you think about trading some of that milk you get for fresh bread and pastries each day?"

"We use most of the milk to make cheese and butter. So, if you need whey for bread-making, I could provide quite a lot of that. Truth be told, I expected you to be inquiring about that. I used to sell most of our whey to the local baker in Paxvilla and the rest would just go to feed our garden or mixed in with water for the livestock."

"Whatever did the baker use whey for?" Torrea inquired, squinting at Jaldor, and puffing out her lips.

Jaldor nodded.

"For bread, mostly. He would use it instead of water. I'm afraid I don't know all the reasons why though."

Torrea widened her eyes looking up towards the ceiling as if in thought.

"I'll tell you what. Bring some of that whey by today or tomorrow when you can. If I like the results, maybe we'll add that to our trade. Do you have any milk to spare though?"

"How much would you like?" Jaldor asked crossing his arms.

"I'd just like to have a more reliable supply. Right now, Aristaios trades me anywhere from four to ten liters of milk a week. So, even a liter per day would be helpful. I can send a courier each morning to pick it up along with the whey, assuming I can use both."

Jaldor nodded.

"How about we start with a liter per day then? If you send your courier tomorrow morning after sunrise, I'll provide him with that first liter of milk and a few liters of whey. Perhaps a loaf of bread in exchange would be fair to start?"

Torrea smiled, her face scrunching.

"That sounds fair to me. Let's figure on that same exchange tomorrow and the next day. Then perhaps you can come back the third day and we can discuss whether I still want more whey and if we can increase the milk."

"Excellent!" George slapped the counter, grinning from ear-to-ear. "Thank you, Torrea."

"Yes, thank you," Jaldor added with a smile. "It's nice to know there's a need for me here."

"Oh, you just wait sweetheart," assured Torrea as she walked back over to the dough she had been kneading.

"I bet before you know it, you'll have supply issues too. It seems new people are joining the town every day now."

"I'll do my best to keep up then," replied Jaldor with a wave. George had already made his way towards the door, and Jaldor didn't want to belabor their departure.

"It was a pleasure to meet you."

"And you too, Jaldor. I'll see you in a couple of days!"

With a final nod, Jaldor followed George out the door. The cool morning air greeted them outside, a welcome change to the heat from inside the bakery.

"Alright," said George rubbing his palms together. "Your family should get a steady supply of baked goods at least. I know you said you prefer to barter wherever possible, but I still think our next stop should be the market square."

"I'll follow your lead," Jaldor looked around, wiping the sweat from his brow as he watched the windmill across the street.

"Very good! This way then."

Jaldor followed George south along the street, nodding to a couple of elves heading west past the windmill. Oinks from the south drew his gaze as they walked, a dozen or so pigs mucking around an enclosure by a nearby cottage. Following George east, they passed a few lizock and a couple elves drawing water from the well. And as they turned south again, the experienced farmer could already see the market square ahead in the distance.

Drawing near the tents, Jaldor started to consider how much different this was compared to Paxvilla's market area. Coming from a town of humans, the first thing he thought of was just how different everyone was. From barghest clothed in simple animal skins to lizock in formal court attire, no one here seemed to care about a rigid set of protocols or expectations. People came as they were, and the calm chatter and friendly faces created a relaxed, welcoming atmosphere.

Beyond the calming setting, there were no permanent structures in this market square -but at least it was an actual square. By his estimates, it looked to be comparable in area to the malformed square at Paxvilla. But with rich, green grass and wider walkways between booths, it made for a more inviting attraction. In fact, it looked like there were only eight vendors set up in the square.

"Is this a typical morning for the market?" Jaldor asked looking around.

George tipped his hat, smiling towards a passing family of elves. The father was carrying a crate, the mother cradling a baby while the small daughter hid behind her mother and giggled. Jaldor smiled at the family as they walked by, offering a slight nod of acknowledgement.

"More or less typical," offered George glancing back at Jaldor. "I won't bog you down with the details, but each day is a little different. There are few vendors who are out here every day, but most stick to a regular schedule."

"And who oversees scheduling to make sure there are no conflicts? I've always avoided setting up to sell in Paxvilla because the Merchant's Guild takes too much out of the profits. How much does it cost to setup here?"

George stopped and shook his head. He turned around, placing a hand on Jaldor's shoulder.

"No one oversees it," the wizard replied. "And no one is going to steal your profits from you. Though I know you'd prefer not to set up here anyways. So, let's introduce you to one vendor who is out here every day."

Turning around, George walked west along the road. As Jaldor followed, he did his best to smile at any who passed by, taking in all the new faces. A dwarf had set up a booth on the corner, his simple tent filled with an assortment of jewelry. Rounding the corner and heading south, he regarded another small cart with shelves full of wine bottles. A satyr stood behind the counter, but Jaldor couldn't make out the exchange he was having with a pair of felite.

327

Beyond these two smaller booths, Jaldor spotted a large tent on the southern end of the square. There was a crowd gathered in front of it, a couple distinct lines of people standing and waiting at the counters.

"That's our destination," said George pointing ahead. He stopped his advance, turning back towards Jaldor and tilting his head sideways.

"Do you want to stop at that cart?" he narrowed his eyes, motioning back towards the wine vendor.

"Oh, not now, no. I wouldn't mind meeting the owner at some point though and visiting his vineyard. I am curious how this all works so smoothly though without anyone overseeing the organization of it. Have there ever been problems between vendors over space?"

George shrugged as Jaldor approached him.

"Not that I recall," he gazed up and rubbed his chin. "Actually, I heard about a kerfuffle a few years back. But I think the rumors were worse than the reality of it. As for the vineyard, it's possible, but I'm afraid it's imported from the Satyr Island to the west. Napan, the satyr selling the wine, sails over and stays at Sissera's whenever he has excess to sell. Truth be told, wine, like cheese, is a commodity we could do with more of. So, if you know someone from Paxvilla who might want to start a vineyard here, let me know."

"I will keep that in mind," replied Jaldor.

"Wait. Sorry, do you hear that?" George asked, tilting his head up towards the sky.

Jaldor looked around. He heard the garbled amalgam of many conversations, the sound of footstones on the stone road, and as he listened, he heard a rooster crow from somewhere to the east. Looking up to trace George's gaze, he spotted a bird of prey high in the sky. With a screech, the bird dove at George.

Without a thought, Jaldor stepped in front of the wizard, holding his arm up to block the creature. He closed his eyes and shielded his face as it made its final approach.

George burst into laughter.

Head still tilted sideways, and arm held up, Jaldor opened his left eye to peek at the shorter man. The bird had landed on the wizard's shoulder. And as George composed himself, it almost looked like the creature was whispering in his ear.

It was a falcon by the looks of it, with a sharp beak curved downward, and grey and tan feathers covering its body. Its breast was solid white however, and by its petite size, Jaldor guessed it was not fully grown.

"It's a message from Savannah," George said with an amused grin. As Jaldor adjusted his posture and stretched his arms, a bit embarrassed by his confusion, he watched George's smile flatten out, transforming into a frown.

"I'm afraid I'll have to introduce you another time," said George reaching up with his left to move the falcon. "I need to get home to Sarah and give her the news."

George swept around, marching back north.

"Please feel free to follow," shouted George as he stomped away.

Jaldor hesitated a moment, glancing towards the larger tent set up just a bit to the south. There was a plethora of people lined up in front of this stall. And for a moment, the farmer considered joining the line and talking to the stall owner himself. But his curiosity got the better of him.

He needed to know what happened in Paxvilla.

CHAPTER XXVIII

Marftaport, Artimus Jr.'s Cottage
23 Julla, 1149 MT

Artimus Jr. stared at the palms of his hands. He couldn't say how long he'd been sitting there, his hands shaking as he relived the memories of the battle. But it felt like he could slip out of his body at any moment, a cold numbness overtaking him as he recalled it all.

The aftermath of the battle was still a blur. Yes, he helped stack up bodies and recount the dead. He was there for the somber conversations and the exchanges of tears. And when they finally returned home last night, he spent so much time scrubbing his hands that they still tingled. But staring at them now, he could see the phantom stains of dirt and blood. He could hear the screams of the battlefield.

That look on Mojo's face as he breathed his last breath was forever etched in the elf's memory. The barghest's final words still echoed in his head. But after seeing the carnage and mayhem in Paxvilla, he was faced with a fear unlike any before. What if the stories of the afterlife weren't real? What if that really had been the last time Artimus Jr. saw Mojo?

He should have done more. He should have fought harder. He could have saved Mojo if he hadn't been so distracted by the hájje commander's beauty. And this thought left him paralyzed, exhausted to the point that, even staring at his hands in despair, he couldn't muster a single tear.

His shoulders sagged as he considered the witch.

If Evorath had any sense of justice, the horrible murderess was dead, slain and being picked apart by vultures. It was a kinder death than she deserved. But that thought haunted him too -what if she had survived?

No matter.

In fact, as the thought crept into his mind, a devious grin formed on his face. He hoped she was still alive. If he had just one more chance to fight her, he would claim vengeance for Mojo and all the others who died.

But there was a faint voice in the back of his mind, almost too quiet to hear. He frowned, trying in vain to ignore it. Then he recalled the story Irontail always told about Slithero the Foolish.

"Be ever wary of revenge. It is more likely to consume you than it is to destroy your enemy."

"It's not fair!" He scoffed, shaking his head before jerking up from his chair.

Grasping the chair, he spun around and screamed. He chucked the chair at the wall and fell to his knees trembling. Hands spread wide, he looked to the ceiling and screamed.

Was anyone listening?

It all seemed so meaningless. So, he sunk to the floor, flattening himself to lay on his belly. And he wasn't sure how long he lay there before rolling onto his back. But even then, he didn't move. He didn't cry. He just stared at the ceiling, wondering how things would ever get better.

Was the peace and safety of Marftaport all just an illusion? For sixty years he'd lived such a carefree life. Enjoying fellowship with the community, hunting for food, studying philosophy and the arts. But what was the point of all that if monsters like these hájje existed? How could sentient creatures make the conscious decision to commit such acts of violence?

Artimus Jr. lay there for an uncertain amount of time. His thoughts kept drifting along the river of regret and despair, his entire body growing numb as he contemplated whether any of it was even worthwhile.

But after some time, as he lay staring at the ceiling, his thoughts were finally interrupted.

Knock. Knock. Knock.

He thought it was just his imagination at first. But the rapping on the door continued.

Knock. Knock. Knock.

"Artimus, are you in there?"

It was the voice of his mother. A voice that was usually comforting. But in this instance, it felt more like a nuisance.

"Go away," he whined.

With a click and a creak, the door swung open. Artimus Jr. heard his mother's footsteps. Scrambling to his feet, he scowled towards her.

"I told you to leave me alone!" he shouted.

Savannah sighed, stepping over to her son.

She had dark bags under her eyes and wore a frown as she stepped across the room. Artimus Jr. pulled away, refusing to meet his mother's gaze.

"Please Junior. You're not helping anything cooping yourself up in here," she spoke softly.

"And what use would I be out there? It's my fault Mojo is dead!" Artimus Jr. spun around and glared at his mother. He pointed towards the door and stomped his foot.

But as he looked, he saw she was not alone. His father stepped in, brushing back his dirty blonde hair.

"You can't carry that guilt," he spoke. "Trust me son. I was there too. There's nothing you could have done differently."

"Yes, please Artimus. The Avatar has called a debrief dinner for tonight. Everyone would like to see you there," his mother added.

"What do you need me there for?" Artimus Jr. shrugged.

His parents exchanged a look and stepped towards him. He recoiled instinctually, but that quiet voice inside told him not to resist. The two stepped along his side. His mother took his left hand, and his father placed his hand on his right shoulder.

"You're not the only one mourning the losses we suffered," his father said meeting his gaze.

And in that moment, seeing the turbulent blue ocean of his father's eyes, Artimus Jr. felt his heart break again. Clinging to his parents, he burst into tears.

CHAPTER XXIX

Marftaport, Vistoro's Manor
23 Julla, 1149 MT

Jaldor shifted uncomfortably in his chair, the wood creaking as he looked around the table. The air was heavy with the aftermath of the battle of Paxvilla. And from his vantage point in the center of this massive, oval table, he could see that some guests were taking it much harder than others.

The meal looked delicious, roasted lamb over asparagus. Presented artistically on a white plate with gilded etching and served on this elegant dining table, the whole gathering was much posher than the humble farmer was accustomed to. With strong notes of rosemary, garlic, and onion, the savory meal called to him. But looking at the downtrodden faces around him, he simply couldn't muster the appetite to start eating.

Sitting just across the table, Morn and Neman seemed the most distraught, their faces sagging low as they gazed listlessly down at their plates. Though Jaldor understood the comparison was offensive, he couldn't help but picture his livestock guardian dogs in their place. Samson had worn a similar expression in the aftermath of the attack on the farm, eyes heavy and labored at the loss of his companion Deliliah.

Thinking back to that night, Jaldor looked down at his own plate, stifling some tears. If that memory could bring such sadness for his lost Deliliah, he could only imagine the pain Morn and Neman felt for their lost mentor, Mojo.

335

The bald man sitting to the left of these brothers was perhaps the only one in the room who didn't have a dark cloud hanging over him. Jaldor wondered about this man. According to the others, he was some sort of Avatar for the goddess Evorath. It seemed unlikely such a being would deign to eat with the current company, but there he sat, his deep brown eyes projecting an air of confidence and strength.

The dwarf Keldor, seated on the left, past Artimus and Savannah cleared his throat. The exaggerated sound drew Jaldor's gaze. With his long, disheveled gray beard and unkept hair, it seemed he was even more out of place than Jaldor.

"Someone might as well have the first word," remarked the dwarf as he held up his mug. He had a deep rumbling voice, a bit of gravel sprinkled about his words. "So, I'll say the only thing I can think of to say. Here's a toast to our fallen neighbors of Marftaport. Their selfless sacrifice will be forever remembered."

Most of those gathered raised their glasses to various levels of enthusiasm. Jaldor offered a nod as he lifted his glass of wine, taking a sip before placing it back down. The dry red wine had a subtle hint of sweetness behind its full-bodied flavor. Morn and Neman continued staring aimlessly at their plates.

"I fear there is more loss yet to come," added Tel' Shira from the right side of the table. The white-furred felite placed her glass down gently, grabbing for her knife and fork and beginning to work on the meal.

"You are correct, of course," said the Avatar. Whether he was truly what he claimed or not, the man spoke with such authority and strength, the low timbre of his voice echoing through the large dining room.

"I assume the Paxvilla officials are treating the battle as a victory though?" Vistoro asked. The former lizock nobleman sat on the right end of the table past Artimus Jr., George, and Sarah, and immediately to the left of Tel' Shira.

"Of course," interjected Oogmut slapping his hand on the table. The table lifted a centimeter off the ground, falling back into place as he raised his hand.

"Sorry," he added. "It's just." The lumbering troll looked down and gulped. "I told you we shouldn't just leave the hájje be! We should have known they would follow the example of their creator. We could have ended them before this happened!"

His voice rose in tone as he spoke, ending as he stood up abruptly, pushing his over-sized chair back and stomping on the floor. Keldor, who was seated just to his right, scooted his chair back a few centimeters. Irontail placed his hand on Oogmut's back between his shoulder blades.

"Please my friend. We all mourn the loss of Mojo and the others," the centaur said softly.

Oogmut shook his head, shrugging the centaur off. "But you should have known," he shouted, pointing towards the Avatar. "Why couldn't you at least imprison them in their little fortress like you did Yezurkstal?"

"He makes a good point," interjected Zelag.

The mysterious man sat just a couple seats from Irontail, between the Avatar and a satyr whom Jaldor hadn't yet met. He twiddled his fork around his plate, as if picking at the lamb, but disinterested in eating it.

"We should have stormed in there and ended them while we had the chance," Zelag continued.

"And what sort of legacy would we be leaving this world?" Savannah asked. Her voice was shaky, her usual serene tone replaced with anxiety.

"Maybe you don't remember," she continued, "but Yezurkstal's 'wives' were all victims themselves. We left them be because we couldn't rightly murder them and their children. They did nothing wrong."

"Well, they have now!" shouted Oogmut, his voice cracking. He brought his hands up, shielding his face. Irontail stepped back in. The centaur's eyes were heavy, his simian face downcast as he patted the troll's back.

"Wasn't there an option other than murdering them all?" interrupted Luna Freya rising from her chair. She glanced at the Avatar before turning to Tel' Shira.

"Couldn't you have foreseen what would happen?" she asked before turning back to the Avatar. "And couldn't you have gone in and worked with the hájje to ensure they didn't go down this path?"

"No!" shouted Morn, his chair scratching the floor as he pushed away from the table. "They all deserve to die. Every. Last. One."

"Come now Morn," pleaded Artimus. The elf leaned forward and Jaldor scooted away. "You were there sixty years ago. Mojo wanted to give the hájje a chance. For all we know, this hájje commander was an outlier. With their defeat, we may not have any more aggression to worry about."

"If you and your wife love the hájje so much, why not go live with them!" yelled Neman, pounding his fists on the table, rattling the food and drink.

"Come now," Vistoro raised his voice. "We can't let this attack break us apart. We need each other now, more than ever."

The satyr burst into tears, pushing back from the table and sobbing into her hands.

"Enough!" The Avatar's voice boomed as he stood up.

Jaldor startled, eyes wide as he clutched the leather armrests on his chair. The room was quiet enough to hear a mouse's footsteps.

"If you want to blame anyone for the hájje, blame Yezurkstal." The Avatar continued. "And if you insist on blaming anyone here, I'm the one responsible for keeping them alive."

He turned towards Oogmut. The troll wiped away some tears, sniffling as he rubbed his eyes. Everyone else remained silent for a few moments, until Oogmut looked up and met the Avatar's gaze.

"Oogmut, my dear friend. You knew Mojo longer than anyone here. He was a faithful servant of Evorath. We should be celebrating the next step in his journey as he ventures to the afterlife. Let's not waste breath with what could have been and focus on what is."

"And that's pretty grim," Zelag quipped.

The Avatar glared at Zelag, the color leaving the man's face as he looked back down at his food.

Sarah stood up from her seat. She walked over to the crying satyr, leaning down and embracing her. The young mage looked to be offering words of encouragement, but Jaldor couldn't make out more than a whisper.

Morn and Neman both exchanged glances. Jaldor could almost feel their anger, but recent events made him aware the rage was only a cover for their deeper pain. They were in great anguish, and seeing them sit across the table, their hands shaking and eyes burning with rage, the farmer felt his heart break.

"The Avatar is right," said Irontail. "No one here is to blame for this. And even if we were, the time to act has passed. Our job now is to look forward, not back."

"There will be goodness from the hájje," interrupted Tel' Shira. It felt like the air was sucked out of the room as everyone turned towards the elder felite. Morn grasped the table, as if anchoring himself to avoid an outburst.

"I had only shared it with Vistoro, but I had a vision last night. I'm afraid this conflict is only just beginning, but before it's over, there will be hájje who play an instrumental role for the forces of Evorath. Like every one of our species, hájje have the capacity for great good."

340

"Yes, these hájje did a bad thing, but let's not fall into old prejudices." Added Vistoro, adjusting his tunic and retrieving his fork and knife.

"Exactly!" exclaimed Savannah, her voice still a bit shrill and excited. "Wars are fought by armies, not individuals. We can't condemn an entire species because a group of them gave into evil."

Neman stood up, sniffling as he looked around the table.

"I'm not hungry," he muttered, his shoulders slumped over. "I'll be at the memorial for Mojo."

Without another word, the barghest skulked to the door, leaving the dining room. Morn huffed, following his brother's lead, and stomping out of the room without a word.

Jaldor looked around at the others. The air was thick enough to cut with a knife. And though a part of him was glad he had accepted the invitation, he longed for a quiet dinner at home with his family. And then the reality of events really sunk in.

"How many people were killed do you think?" he asked sheepishly, looking down at his plate.

"Too many," replied Oogmut with a sniffle. He pulled back his oversized chair, plopping back down and poking at his tray of food.

"I'm going there tomorrow with some volunteers." George leaned forward, looking at Jaldor. "You'd be more than welcome to join us if you're able to."

"I would like to," replied Jaldor. "So long as I have time to finish the morning milking first." His voice trailed off as he looked around.

"I'll tell you what," said George. "After I send the others off to Paxvilla, I'll head up to your farm and we can go together when you're ready."

"Thank you," Jaldor considered the somber faces around the room. He had felt so sorry for the losses they had endured, but it wasn't until this moment that reality sunk in about his own losses. How many of his own people had suffered and died?

The room fell into silence again. And this time, Jaldor wasn't sure how long it lasted -it felt like an eternity. But like waking up from a dream, Irontail interrupted the silence.

"George, I'd like to ask a favor. Silkhair will undoubtedly be eager for an update. So, by everyone's leave, I could use portal home when you're ready."

"Urgo. I get the feeling we're at a closing point here?" George looked around with raised eyebrows, a spark of hope glistening in his eyes.

"Yes, I think we are," exclaimed Vistoro standing from his seat. "Please, everyone remember that I am available to you all. I wish I had something more to say, something more to contribute. But for now, I raise one final glass. To our fallen family, and to victory of Life over Death."

With just one thought on his mind, Jaldor raised his glass.

"No matter what, my family will survive."

CHAPTER XXX

Somewhere in the Runeturk Mountains
21 Julla, 1149 MT

Castora stumbled, clutching her side, and wincing at the warm touch of blood. She felt dizzy, weak, every muscle in her body crying out for her to give up and collapse.

Had she been misled?

That was Evorath's Avatar who showed up. It had to be. But her father had destroyed him.

Or was that a lie?

And where had those others come from? Yes, her cousin had reported some outside interference when he had attacked that farm, but this was organized. Moreover, this was far too motley a party to be from one nation.

What force could lead a barghest to work alongside a felite? Or lizock and elves to cooperate when their nations were at such odds with one another? The whole puzzle had her mind racing. But since her defeat yesterday, she was unable to think about anything else. And she kept coming back to two thoughts.

First, Evorath was much more powerful than she was taught. Perhaps that was it. Maybe her father was so powerful that he hadn't given Evorath's servants enough credit for their strength. If this was so, then it meant she was the failure.

After all, it was her forces that had met defeat. No, her forces had been humiliated. But it was more than that.

Yes, there was a second force at play here. If these foul blooded creatures were all so savage and disorganized, why would they defend humans at all?

None of it made sense.

And as she dragged herself into a dusty cave, limping over scattered rocks and ashy debris, she found herself thinking more blasphemous thoughts.

What if hájje weren't superior after all? What if their destiny of conquest was a lie? What if the world was better off without the iron fist of control her father promised?

She moaned, stepping over to the cave wall and looking down at her side.

"This one is my own fault," she muttered, inspecting the damage to the armor. The sword had pierced through the steel, her armor bent inward around the impact. Looking at it more closely, she realized her armor was still cutting into her side. At least she had shaken her pursuers.

With a deep breath, she closed her eyes and focused on the latent magic in the cave around her. She held her hand up to the wound, willing the metal to bend away from it. Despite it already being malformed from the attack, she could feel the strength in the metal, resisting her will.

"Feklar!" She felt dizzy, but finally the metal creaked, bending outward.

Castora doubled over, crying out in exertion. She needed to lose all this extra weight.

Beginning with her gauntlets, she started to remove her armor one piece at a time, huffing and wincing with each painful maneuver. But even through the pain, she continued to question her purpose.

She thought of the elf who'd stabbed her, stirring conflicted feelings of rage and intrigue. How could such an inferior creature dare speak of her beauty? As if he knew anything of beauty. He was a foul blooded elf, primitive and impure. And the audacity for him to act as if she was in the wrong when his very existence was an afront to order.

But even as she thought these things, she couldn't deny what she felt. He was handsome. She wanted to feel his lush brown hair, to again see his smooth, tan skin. And his eyes, the way the blue/green sparkled as he fought. He was full of passion and strength.

"No!" she cried, bending over, and unlatching her greaves. How could she be attracted to such a vile, disgusting creature? Elves weren't even capable of true intelligence.

That one did seem articulate enough though. And he moved with such grace and confidence.

She shook her head, groaning as she stood back up. With all her armor removed, she inspected the rest of her body. There was the gash on her arm and the puncture in her side, but otherwise her black leather under armor appeared undisturbed.

Sighing as she leaned against the cave wall, she looked more closely at the wound. With her lighter armor, the cold, moist wall offered some relief to her pain.

345

"I should have taken healing magic more seriously," she mumbled, closing her eyes, and focusing on the energy all around her. These mountain caves were filled with a plethora of rocks, minerals, and stones. But she was searching for something different. Fungus, water, plants -anything that would offer healing properties.

The pain from her wounds diminished as she cast her spirit outward, seeking out any source of magic that might assist. And to her surprise, she found the magic deeper within the cave, a powerful energy calling for her. Gasping as she returned her attention to the moment, she stood up straight.

Forgetting about her doubts and fears, she took a deep breath and pushed herself forward. With the cave wall for support, she limped further into the tunnel, the air growing humid as she descended. Dragging herself along, the wound at her side continued to throb, screaming for her attention.

Even with her superior night vision, she found as she descended that it was growing difficult to see. So, she paused, seeking out the source of magic again. It felt so close, and yet her efforts to summon the energy to her failed, as if the magic was resisting her call.

Determined to solve this mystery, she pressed forward. And in an instant, she regretted her curiosity.

The ground shifted beneath her feet. She screamed, sliding on the slick cave floor, and tumbling forward. Loose stones pelted her hands, reopening the wound on her arm and preventing her from stopping her forward momentum.

Frantically pulling in any magic she could, she tried to slow her descent in vain. It felt like she was being raked over a washboard. Her mind raced, thinking again of the elf who stabbed her.

It felt like she was falling for an eternity, each moment bringing a new torment as she bumped her head, scrapped her knuckles, smashed her elbow. And through it all, she could only wonder one thing.

"Do I deserve this?"

She landed on her backside with a thud, screaming as the pain shot up her spine. But as she opened her eyes, she could see flicking candlelight ahead.

Moaning as she crawled forward, she felt ahead for the source of magic. These candles. It was close.

Crawling into a small tunnel, she squeezed her way through, grinding her teeth to try and ignore the pressure against her sides. The light grew brighter as she reached the opening at the end.

Just at the edge of the cave, she beheld a large cavern. It appeared natural, no signs of mason work along the floor or walls. And yet candles were spread all about the area, an assortment of different sconces and candelabras holding candles of all shapes and sizes.

Scanning the area, she spotted some more points of interest. A shelf with books, a table with food, and glancing to left, a pot with a small elf standing before it. No, it was smaller than an elf.

The brown-skinned creature couldn't be more than a meter tall, wearing a simple green tunic, brown pants, and pointy-toed boots. Atop its head, it wore a green brimless, triangle hat and on its face was a well-shaped, gray beard.

Castora wasn't sure whether it was the battle wounds, the fall, or something else. But as she pushed herself through into the cavern, the room spun around her.

She collapsed, falling flat on her stomach.

And everything faded to black.

Castora's story has only just begun. Stay tuned for Book 2 of the Legends of Evorath, *The Dark Elf and the Gnome,* releasing February 2025.

Enjoy this story? Leave a review and help others discover the world of Evorath.

The Shadows of Erathal is the first book in the Legends of Evorath trilogy. Visit us online for free access to additional stories, and to sign up for notifications about future releases.

If you enjoyed this book, please help other readers find that same enjoyment by returning to where you purchased it and leaving a positive review. Your voice matters.

www.evorath.com

Explore the Legacy of Evorath

The Evorath Trilogy

Over sixty years before the events of this story, see how Artimus, Savannah, Irontail, Tel' Shira, and the other heroes of Evorath formed unbreakable bonds of friendship. As they all find their world shaken, they must set aside their own ambitions and focus on a way to defeat this terrifying new evil.

Read Book 1 of the Evorath Trilogy Now

Appendices I

The Evorath Calendar

A small planet with five distinct continents, Evorath has a total of 356 days spread over 12 months. The Evorath calendar begins in Spring, with the New Year commencing on 1 Pertga.

Appendices II

Glossary of Selected Terms

◆ Barghest - A broad-shouldered and wide-chested species of bipedal canines. Nearly all living barghest in Erathal make their home in the town of Marftaport.

◆ Bulwark - A rare creature native to the Runeturk Mountains. Believed to have developed in volcanic activity and is known to have skin as hard as diamonds. They have two pairs of arms, one large and muscular, the other smaller.

◆ Centaur - Half-horse and half-man, the centaurs of Evorath make their home in the village of Dumner.

◆ Dryad - Guardians of the forest, there is one dryad for each type of tree on Evorath. They have untold powers over the forest and work to maintain balance.

◆ Dwarf - A short and hardy species that is known for having thick, full beards. Though primarily living in the Runeturk Mountains, there is a growing dwarven population among the forest of Erathal, specifically within the town of Marftaport.

◆ Elf - Similar in stature to the humans of Earth, Elves are the most abundant sentient species in Evorath. They have pointy ears and almost exclusively have light features.

◆ Erathal - Name of the continent this story is set in. Also, the name of the major Elvish City.

◆ Ergolicious - A contemporary slang term to express happiness or satisfaction with a choice.

352

- Ether - The space between different worlds. Reaching through the ether requires great magical abilities and allows a mage to summon creatures from one of these other worlds.

- Feklar - An expletive often used to express anger, fear, or similar unpleasant responses.

- Felite - One of the most populous species on the continent of Erathal, felite are a bipedal feline species that resemble their four-legged cousins.

- Hájje - Elvish word for a dark elf. It comes from the elvish word Haijja, which means 'dark', or 'evil'.

- Imp About - A common colloquialism that indicates one is fooling around or otherwise being reckless in their behavior.

- Lamia - A sentient race with the lower half resembling a snake and their upper half is that of an elf. With dwindling numbers, many fear the once powerful and noble species is nearing extinction.

- Lizock - One of the most populous sentient species on the continent of Erathal, lizock are a bipedal reptilian race that resembles the common lizard. Though they can vary in size, shape, and color, the race is most well-known for its warriors and merchants.

- Marftaport - A free society without any formal rulers or authorities. Established by Vistoro and a group of Lizock who grew disgruntled with their government, it serves as the first truly free community in Erathal.

- Rocpiss - A profanity that suggests something is untrue or otherwise fabricated.

- Runeturk Mountains - Major mountain range bordering Erathal forest to the north. This range is populated by thousands of dwarves, some gnomes, and less civilized creatures like ogres, orcs, goblins, and wild animals.

- Sandy foundation - A common colloquialism used when someone is behaving erratically, or irrationally. Often meant to imply the person in question is mentally unstable.

- Satyr - A sentient species of Evorath once known for great works of art and music, they are now known more for their proclivity towards alcoholism. These bipedal creatures are half-elf, half-goat, with their upper half being the former and their lower half resembling the latter.

- The scales fit the dragon - A saying that indicates something fits as expected. In contemporary earth terms, "par for the course." roc

- Troll - A sentient species of Evorath. Nomadic in nature, trolls are both tall and menacing in their physical features.

- Urgo - An elvish word of affirmation. Essentially equivalent to saying "yes, sir" or "understood."

- Xyvor - A compilation of stories written by the ancient prophets of Evorath. Details stories of the world's creation, its early history, commands from Evorath herself.

Appendices III

Assorted City Maps

The human city of Paxvilla

Marftaport, Town Proper

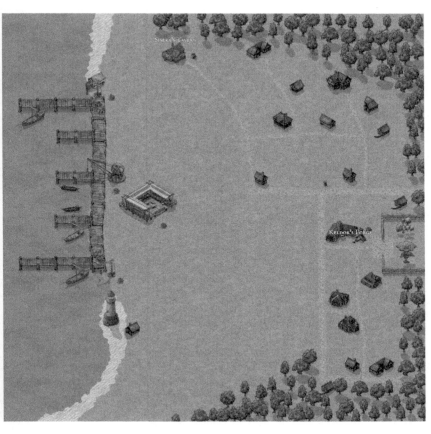

Marftaport, Docks

Printed in Great Britain
by Amazon

56526577R00209